BROOKE J LOSEE

Published by Golden Camel Press

Content Warning:

This book contains mild romance (kissing only), reference to suicide, and mild violence.

ISBN: 978-1-954136-29-8

DEDICATION

To my critique partner and best friend, Justena, who helps me through dreadful edits, procrastination (and by help I mean enables), and bouts of self doubt. I would not be the writer I am without you.

Suffolk, 1815

Nicholas

The bright-colored feathers adorning Lady Garrick's hair made glaring at her rather difficult for Nicholas Betham, but determination to hold his icy stare won out over his amusement. He had, after all, good reason to retain contempt for the viscountess, and despite the impoliteness of offering such a bold expression within the walls of her home, guilt eluded him.

He squared his shoulders, coaxing the tightness in his face to soften. It was unlikely to help his cause, but it would not hurt it, either. "I must appeal to your better senses again, my lady. Surely a request to court—"

"My answer is no, *Lord Keswick*." She spat his name as though it were poison on her tongue. For that, he could not blame her. He despised the title as much as she did; however, as his father's only heir, he had no choice but to claim it following the late marquess's recent passing. Inheritance often proved a double-edged sword, bringing wealth to those fortunate first sons like himself, but his title carried a great deal of weight, too—a name tainted with the ill reputation of the man who had borne it for three decades.

And years of misdeeds were difficult for members of the *ton* to ignore.

"For what reason am I denied?" he asked, tempering his irritation as best he could.

Lady Garrick scoffed. "You very well know the reason as it has not changed since last month. I will not have my daughter's name bandied about with *yours*. It is a matter of our family's honor."

He caught the weary look of the butler, who stood with his hand wrapped around the door handle, ready to excuse the unwanted guest. Lady Garrick had met Nicholas in the foyer, and the absence of an invitation into the drawing room indicated his visit would be a short one.

As they always were.

Every few months for the last two years he had come to Rusgrove Hall with but one intention—courting Katherine Garrick. But the request had been denied each time, often by Lady Garrick and occasionally by her husband, when they agreed to see him at all. The viscount deferred to his wife's judgment on matters regarding their daughter's courtship, it seemed.

Or perhaps Lord Garrick simply feared facing his wife's wrath.

Nicholas could not entirely blame the man for that, but such catering to the woman's erroneous judgment kept him from the thing he wanted most.

"As I have often reminded you, my lady, the rumors surrounding my name are rarely true. I do my best to avoid unscrupulous activity, despite what the gossips would have you believe."

Defending his character came at the expense of wasted breath, he well knew, but it did not stop him from trying all the same. If he could rein in the constant badgering of his reputation, perhaps he might have a chance to repair it, but with each rumor he doused, several new ones rose to take its place in a vicious, unending cycle.

Lady Garrick turned away, her pointed nose lifted in a haughty expression that proved he would not succeed in convincing her. The reaction was of no surprise, for he had long suspected the rumors doing the most damage to his name originated from the very woman standing before him.

Of course, making the accusation aloud would only further wound his chances of courting Katherine; therefore, questioning Lady Garrick's responsibility on the matter was unwise. The knowledge did incite his ire, however, and typically resulted in a complete lack of patience with the viscountess, leading to quarrels that did nothing to aid his cause.

The muffled sound of hoofbeats announced the arrival of a carriage, and Lady Garrick's eyes widened. "You may take your leave now, Lord Keswick. Do consider abandoning this foolish inquiry. I shall not change my mind."

He replaced his beaver hat and gave her a curt nod. The butler opened the door, and Nicholas stepped into the frigid December air. His lungs protested each inhale, every one an icy dagger to his chest, but all thought of the weather faded the moment the carriage door opened and Miss Katherine Garrick's face appeared from within.

He halted in his tracks. The mere sight of her sent his heart into a gallop. Her lovely golden curls were half hidden beneath a bonnet, her cheeks a rosy color from fighting the cold. Her pale blue morning gown complimented her in ways he should not notice.

He chided himself for staring so unabashedly while a gentleman, whom he recognized as Lord Emerson, the Earl of Getsby, handed her and her lady's maid from the carriage.

The man offered Katherine his arm, and Nicholas fought a wave of jealousy. The two of them came forward in quiet conversation but stopped several feet shy of the door upon noticing him.

Nicholas bent into a bow. "Good afternoon, Lord Emerson. Miss Garrick."

"A cold one, I am afraid," Emerson replied after they had exchanged pleasantries. "I escorted Miss Garrick to the village, and we are both frozen solid."

"Not a difficult feat, I'd imagine," said Nicholas, "but with such pleasant company, a worthwhile endeavor, nonetheless."

Emerson looked down at the woman on his arm and smiled. "Indeed."

Katherine's expression presented no response to either of their flattery, her face softly stoic. He could not be offended, however, for he knew the lady well. Her lack of reaction was not a result of an arrogant demeanor, but ignorance. After years of observation, he had come to realize Katherine simply did not understand the intricacies of subtle flirtation.

"Will you join us inside, Lord Keswick?" she asked.

He would have liked nothing more than to accept the offer, but Lady Garrick might glare holes through him. Besides, he had no desire to watch Lord Emerson interact with Katherine. It had been difficult enough observing her from afar this last Season, unable to claim any of her attention for himself beyond a few stolen moments out of her mother's watchful eye.

"I appreciate the invitation, but perhaps another time. Good day to you both."

Katherine curtsied, and Nicholas stepped around them, taking the stone stairs with haste to the dirt drive where his horse awaited. He had once again failed to accomplish his goal, and the sting of defeat already ate at his soul.

NICHOLAS STARED DOWN AT HIS DESK WITH FURROWED BROWS. Gently, he scooped up the letter resting there and held it up to catch the light entering the nearby window. The edges were worn from the number of times he had removed the folded foolscap from inside, and his eyes traced his name where it appeared on the front, written in an elegant hand. Luke Halford, his dearest friend, had always possessed the better handwriting between the two of them.

A heavy pressure constricted his chest as though someone had placed an anvil there. Five weeks ago, Luke had agreed to join him for a round of fencing. Nicholas had believed that if he could convince the man to leave his study—to leave his estate—then he might help Luke recover from his heartache. The letter was proof of Nicholas's failure. Proof he should have done more.

Three taps on the door with a long pause between the first and second informed Nicholas that his mother stood outside the study. The long-established habit had been a form of communication between them for years—an indication that whoever sought an audience bore no ill will as other inhabitants of the household might.

"Enter!"

He returned the letter to the desk before the door slowly opened and his mother peeked through the narrow crack. Her lips lifted into a soft smile when she spotted him, and Nicholas mirrored the expression. He rose and gestured for her to come inside, an invitation she obliged before she closed the door and crossed the room without a word. He had always found his mother's quiet demeanor elegant. Though she often withheld her words, she made up for her reserved nature with intent observation. She had a way of deciphering people that would make the greatest spies in the British Army jealous.

She settled in the seat across from him, and Nicholas reclaimed his chair. They sat in silence for several minutes, but what most would consider awkward came as no surprise or concern to him. He could see his mother's mind working in the way her features pinched. She needed time to sort through her thoughts, which meant whatever she had to say would bear a great deal of weight.

He used the opportunity to look her over. Her hair, like golden straw, was pinned in place atop her head, the shade a sharp contrast to her black dress. He hated that she would be forced to wear such a dreadful color for the next year. Someone so lovely should never be required to don clothing that mimicked a gloomy storm, especially to mourn a man who had given her no reason to express sorrow for his passing. The event should have her outfitted in a bright yellow.

Her gaze flitted to his shoulder. "You have decided to wear a band?"

Nicholas shifted his focus to the black crepe armband wrapped around his bicep and nodded. "I have, but not for Father."

"For His Grace," said his mother with a nod of understanding. "His passing has been difficult for you."

He could not deny it, and part of the reason was because he felt more than mere sorrow. "I should have done something. If I had, perhaps he—"

"You cannot blame yourself. No one could have known the duke would take his own life."

Nicholas winced. He had seen how depressed Luke became after losing Miss McCarthy, the young lady who had completely captivated his friend and then shattered his heart when she disappeared. Even so, Nicholas had not believed the man would go to such extremes to cure himself of the pain.

His mother placed her hands over his and tilted her head. "I'm sorry, my sweet boy. You have lost much the last few weeks."

"I lost my friend. I care not about my other so-called loss."

"Nicholas—"

"Please do not defend him. Father does not deserve your loyalty." He rubbed his fingers over the long scar on his mother's wrist, and she grimaced. He could remember that night vividly—the last time he had allowed the despicable man whose name he shared to harm her.

"You deserved so much better," he whispered.

She averted her gaze and said nothing. She never said a bad thing about anyone, even the most deserving. If only he could be more like her and forgive so easily, but having watched her suffer through the years, he simply could not. The physical abuse, the mistresses, the verbal lashings— he could never forget.

"Was there something you wished to discuss with me?" he asked.

Her green eyes—not unlike his own—glanced up, and Nicholas saw the hesitation in them. Whatever she had come to tell him likely would not improve his mood.

"I heard a rumor today," she said quietly.

He scoffed. "A rumor? Who paid us a call and thought to offer prattle hearsay instead of condolences?"

"Lady Aldridge called this afternoon."

"That explains it then, does it not? The woman knows everyone's business before even they themselves do. How many people have been ruined by her gossip?"

His mother's lips twitched, but she made no indication otherwise that she agreed with his assessment. He had learned her expressions at a young age and could read the slight changes in her features well, a useful skill when living with a woman who spoke so rarely.

"Let us have it, then. What did Lady Aldridge say this time?"

"It is rumored that Miss Garrick is soon to be engaged."

His heart lurched. "What?"

"Miss Garrick...she is soon to be engaged."

Images of Katherine and Lord Emerson filled his mind, giving evidence he wished to ignore. His jaw clenched, and he commanded his thoughts into silence. "And pray tell, why am I in need of this information?"

His mother's face contorted to reflect her annoyance. "I am not blind."

"Indeed, but—"

"I know you have a *tendre* for her. Do not bother to deny it."

He scrubbed a hand over his chin and shook his head. "Fine, but my feelings hardly matter if she is soon to be engaged."

"You still have a chance. A handsome and kind gentleman of title has no reason not to be a suitable match for a lovely young lady."

Perhaps his mother should tell Lady Garrick that. "Handsome and kind? I appreciate the flattery, but I believe you may have a prejudice for me as your only child."

A lightness entered her features, a spark Nicholas had rarely seen the last few years, and her eyes shimmered with the smile she hid. "I cannot refute such a claim, but that does not mean my compliments are without substance."

Nicholas raked a hand through his hair—less golden and more like his father's, muddied with hints of brown. "I am at a loss as to what more I could do, and it seems time is no longer on my side."

His mother pulled a folded letter from the pocket of her gown and handed it to him. "Lady Aldridge is to hold a ball in a fortnight. Seems the perfect opportunity for you to discover the validity of her claims about Miss Garrick and perhaps put in a bid of interest."

He held back a laugh. He had attended many balls in which Katherine Garrick was present. Not once had he dared ask her to dance since the young woman's mother declared him unsuitable.

"I suppose you will refrain from joining me?" asked Nicholas.

"Expectations must be met, Nicholas. The *ton* is not forgiving of failure to meet them. I will join you in social excursions in a few months or so, but for now, I shall remain here. I have lost my husband."

Irritation coursed through him. "But you did not love him, nor did he love you."

She flinched, and he immediately regretted the words. The last thing his mother needed was to be reminded. He took her hands and enfolded them in his own. "Forgive me. I merely hate seeing you trapped. You have lived in his shadow long enough, and I want nothing more than for you to be free of it."

"Free," she said quietly. "I am afraid freedom for me might be nothing more than an illusion. Regardless, I loved your father once, and however brief that may have been, I will always mourn those moments, even if they were not real."

The pain in her voice pierced his heart. She had never told him the precise circumstances that bound her to his father, but Nicholas had always suspected foul play. The man had been no stranger to ruining reputations. Nicholas had acquired some details over the years from conversations in the ballroom, but not all. His mother had eloped to Gretna Green with his father, which he could only assume had occurred by means of deception on the late marquess's part. She never would have married the man otherwise.

Nicholas stood when his mother rose from the chair, and she squeezed his hands before releasing them. "I know you resent your father, but now is the time for you to focus on *your* future. Do not let the judgment of others shape it for you."

He swallowed, unable to respond with more than a nod as she departed, leaving him alone with his thoughts. He had spent years contesting the rumors about himself to no avail. The effort exhausted him, and he felt certain his reputation claimed responsibility for Lady Garrick's sheer disapproval.

Regardless, he would speak to Katherine at the ball—would discover whether an understanding existed between her and Lord Emerson—and hope he was not too late.

Chapter 2

Suffolk, 1815

Katherine

*O*ne. *Two. Three.* Katherine Garrick slid each strand of ribbon between her thumb and forefinger, counting the variety on display until she reached thirty. For such a small shop, there was certainly a plethora of options in regards to ribbons and bobbins.

Her mother stood several feet away, speaking with the modiste about commissioning a gown, and while Katherine did not particularly mind having a new one, she also saw nothing wrong with the dozens of dresses already hanging in her wardrobe. Had she not acquired enough months ago for her second Season?

No. Mama insisted those would soon be out of style, and she was inclined to believe the woman. There were a number of subjects in which Katherine happened to be less than knowledgeable, and fashion trends ranked near the top. Styles and colors came and went with such frequency that she could hardly keep up, though her lack of interest had more to do with that than anything.

Thirty-one. Thirty-two. She continued along the display, taking the time to appreciate the different colors and fabrics. She may not have much sense of current trends, but she enjoyed perusing the shop all the same. What were the fashion trends of the future like? If her endeavors to discover the hiding place of a certain set of pearls had been successful, she might know. Since they had not, studying the trends of her own era would have to do. Regardless, she would much rather count the ribbons than stand idly by her mother while the two women discussed the newest laces and trimmings.

A soft jingle announced the arrival of another customer, but she spared no glance to the door as she already knew their identity. Her dearest friend, Eleanor, was meant to meet them this morning, and being that she was far past due, it could only be her. The frightful weather kept most indoors at the early hour, but Mama preferred to shop when fewer people were around.

Forty-eight. Forty-nine. Katherine smiled. There were precisely fifty different ribbons on this row. Why the even display satisfied her so greatly, she did not know. Something about numbers and the order they could create soothed her. They were firm. Reassuring. And above all, never held secrets.

She could not say the same for Society and its intricate rules. Compared to formulas, people were simply beyond comprehension. Complex and often irrational. Mama had the skill to decipher and maneuver through the social maze and its hazards; Katherine did not. She needed to be more like Mama, but how did one learn such things when it went against their very nature?

"I believe you should purchase that one," a deep voice whispered next to her ear.

Startled, she jerked her hand away from the last ribbon spool, and the movement knocked it from the display. It tumbled to the floor, and she quickly crouched to retrieve it. A gloved hand met the satin fabric at the same moment hers did, and she glanced up to find a pair of warm green eyes on her.

"Lord Keswick."

"Good morning, Miss Garrick." He dipped his head, for they could do little more by way of greetings in such a position. "Forgive me for startling you...and the ribbon, it seems."

"It is not so difficult to be startled when one is deep in thought. Of course the ribbon was not so deep in thought. Either way, I am certain you did nothing wrong, and therefore have no need to apologize."

His lips twitched as if to smile, but it never quite appeared. He scooped up the ribbon, and they both stood before he offered it to her. "It matches your eyes and suits you."

She turned her attention to the ribbon. Yes, she supposed it did match her color to perfection, the same chocolate brown. "Perhaps I should adorn a hat with it."

"It matters little what you adorn your headwear with. You could look no less lovely."

She hummed, glancing over the shop and taking note of a pale green bonnet before her gaze dropped to the burnt orange ribbon in front of her on the display. That would certainly be a horrendous match. "I cannot agree. There are always colors that would not go well together. They would look no more pleasing to the eye on me than anyone else."

Lord Keswick's smile appeared, mirth clear in his sparkling eyes, but she could think of no reason her response would amuse him so. What was he doing in the shop anyway?

"Perhaps you are right," he said. "Some things simply do not match, but I believe we can never truly know until they are given a chance to be together. Matches can be surprising." He bent closer, and his shoulder brushed against hers. With the air so frigid, the warmth he exuded was enticing, and she leaned into his conspiratorial whisper. "Take Mrs. Fletcher, for example. Not many would think to combine her choices of color, but she pulls them off marvelously."

Katherine studied the modiste. Lord Keswick was correct. Pairing the soft pink dress with the yellow pelisse, which happened to be an unpleasant hue that reminded her far too much of the last time her stomach was ill, worked well in some unusual way. She would have never thought to put the two together.

"You have clear cause for argument," she said. "But that does not mean I would be capable of pulling off such colors. In fact, Mrs. Fletcher may be the only one."

Lord Keswick opened his mouth, undoubtedly to disagree with her, but snapped it closed when her mother turned to face them. Mama's eyes fell on Lord Keswick and ignited with fury.

"Oh, dear," Katherine muttered. Mama had a firm disdain for the marquess, though why, Katherine had never comprehended. The man seemed jovial and respectful. Not once had he given her any reason to think him anything but a gentleman.

Unless, of course, one considered the rumors. She should, as Mama certainly did, and Katherine needed to be more like Mama.

Lord Keswick shifted his attention to her. "It is likely best I take my leave of you, Miss Garrick. Before your mother threatens me, I wonder if I might request a set with you at Lady Aldridge's upcoming ball?"

The ball? That was still a fortnight away. Had he come in here simply to ask her that? "Of course."

He gave her a curt nod, but there was no mistaking his delight. It crinkled the corners of his eyes in an endearing sort of way that added to his handsome features. For Lord Keswick was a handsome man, certainly. *No one* could deny that.

"I look forward to it. Good day, Miss Garrick." He quickly skirted around the ribbon display before Mama arrived at Katherine's side, and had it not been for the lopsided grin he wore, she might have thought he feared for his life given the haste.

"What did that man want?" Mama demanded, watching Lord Keswick exit the shop with her menacing scowl.

Katherine hesitated, uncertain whether to tell her mother of the marquess's request to dance. It would not improve her mood. "He suggested I purchase this ribbon." She held up the satin brown strip. "It matches my eyes."

Mama ripped the spool from her hand and returned it to the display. "You are not in need of new ribbons. Or *suggestions*."

No, but she was not in need of new dresses, either.

KATHERINE PERUSED THE FULL SHELVES OF THE LIBRARY AT RUSGROVE Hall, her fingers sliding along the edge of the mahogany as she read the spines. She would not find a new book on her favorite topic, she knew, but her restless mind enjoyed reading the titles nearly as much as counting. Mama would chide her should she discover her daughter so much as touching a text about mathematics during the day. Those sorts of pursuits were only to be indulged late into the evenings and sometimes early mornings when there were no guests to entertain or chance of visitors.

"Indecisive today, are we not?"

Her brother George's deep voice brought a smile to her lips, and she turned to face him. He stood near the entry, his wide grin bringing out the dimple on his right cheek. His light brown hair had been tousled during his afternoon ride, but the disarray somehow matched his teasing persona.

"I am merely admiring at present," said Katherine. "Since I have not convinced you to purchase a new one on my behalf, I am left to study these. I fear they have been read cover to cover more times than mother would wish me to admit."

George chuckled, coming away from the doorway to stand next to her. "We both know our mother would prefer you to not have read them at all."

She could not argue that point.

Ladies do not spend time studying numbers to forgo the practice of talents that will attract a husband.

Mama was right, of course, but that did not stop Katherine from wishing for new books. Papa had once been quick to indulge her, but Mama had corrected the error, leaving Katherine to beg for others to acquire new books for her. George, close friends—several people had been willing to assist her in the past. Things had changed, though, as she had grown older. Perhaps they had all expected her to grow out of the strange interest in numbers in favor of more ladylike pursuits.

And she had tried. Sitting in a parlor embroidering or playing the pianoforte did not elicit the same spark of curiosity, and therefore did not maintain her attention for long.

Katherine turned back to the bookcase and sighed, running her fingers on the spine of the first book. If only she lived in a time where women were permitted to pursue whatever interests they wanted. She had been given a glimpse, in a sense, of what the future might be like. Her friend, Magdalena McCarthy, had described a world where women could be anything they wanted, a time when they were permitted to attend university and manage businesses. Miss McCarthy had claimed to be from that future, brought back in time by her heirloom pearls, and for weeks Katherine had wondered whether the woman spoke the truth.

Her analytical mind had come to the conclusion that too much about Miss McCarthy provided evidence of the declaration. And then there was the woman's disappearance to consider. Miss McCarthy had vanished after revealing the truth, and subsequently, the duke who's heart she'd claimed had disappeared as well.

The entire situation had been the center of gossip for months.

"Mother seemed in a mood upon your return from town this morning." George leaned against the bookshelf and crossed his arms. He was a year her junior but had always carried himself with more maturity than his age gave him credit for. "What have you done this time to agitate her."

"It was not me," she defended. "I merely perused the ribbons while Mama spoke to Mrs. Fletcher about a new gown for me."

"What color gown have you commissioned—or, I should say, what color gown has our mother commissioned for you? I know you had no say in the matter." George's eyes still held amusement, but there was a hint of agitation there as well. Katherine suspected their mother's tight grip extended beyond her wardrobe.

"A lovely ivory with a dark red sash, or perhaps it was blue? I am not entirely certain what was settled on because I entertained myself with the ribbons, as I said."

George's brows drew together. "Have you not counted them several times before?"

"Well, yes, but counting is preferable to standing still while two women speak of me as though I am not there. And Lord Keswick—"

"Lord Keswick was there?" George pushed away from the wall, his brows furrowing even more.

"Yes," she answered slowly. Why did he wear such a sharp expression? "I know the rumors about the man. You needn't stare at me that way. Nothing untoward happened. We were in the middle of the modiste's shop, for heaven's sake."

George shook his head. "That was not my concern. Is the man unharmed? Did mother spear him with her dragon glare?"

"You read far too many novels. Mama is particular, but she is no dragon."

George scoffed. "There are many gentlemen and ladies alike who would disagree with you, I think. Mother is the most formidable woman of my acquaintance, and you give her an indecent amount of control over your life."

Katherine turned away and pinched her lips to keep a rebuttal from passing over them. It would do no good to defend Mama. George simply did not understand. Mama was the epitome of what society expected from a lady born to title. She needed to be more like her.

"Perhaps," said Katherine, "but I trust Mama's judgment. I certainly would not navigate society well on my own."

This much she knew, for any number of house calls, dinner parties, and balls could attest to her lack of social eloquence. She had no trouble interacting with others, but according to Mama, she did not interact *well*. Being made aware that she had given offense to several conversation partners with her impertinent comments did not, however, provide her with understanding of how to avoid it.

George swatted the air. "You would do fine. Mother's constant intervention will do more harm than good, in my opinion. How are you to find a love match if she never allows you to be yourself?"

He was teasing, of course. George could not possibly be a romantic. Gentlemen simply were not such things. Katherine was not, either. "That is easy to answer. I am not looking for a love match."

Faux horror filled her brother's expression, though his eyes betrayed his curiosity too. "Not looking for a love match? Why not?"

She would not tell George her doubts that any man would so much as blink at her if she unleashed the full force of her personality. No gentleman wanted a lady who spent her days learning equations or studying Newton. Music and needlework, sophistication and grace—that was what Society expected of her. That was what husbands wanted in their wives.

"I see no point in fantasizing about it," said Katherine. "*You* may lose yourself in novels, but I would prefer to approach the notion of matrimony with a more sensible viewpoint. So long as I have stability for myself and my family, what more can I ask for?"

George's expression sobered. "A great deal more if you would only allow yourself the chance."

Katherine tilted her head, confused by the lack of jest in his tone. Few people could claim their marriages were based in love, not even their parents, and she would not allow herself even a speck of hope for it. What use were cradled dreams that would never come to fruition?

If only she could be herself around men and find someone who did not mind her odd interests. If only women were permitted to openly study mathematics—were treated as equals like those in the future.

Miss McCarthy had painted a glorious picture of a different time, and Katherine desperately wanted to see it for herself. In 1815, she was considered abnormal. She did not fit in nor did she necessarily want to be like everyone else. Conforming was the only way to secure her future, but just once she wished to feel accepted as herself. Spending even a single day in a time like the one Miss McCarthy boasted of would reassure her, would validate her love of numbers as something to be celebrated and embraced, not hidden away and frowned upon. That validation would fill the hole she felt.

One day in the future was all she needed. Then she could carry that acceptance through her dull life as a lady who entertained and embroidered cushions. Become more like Mama.

But the task of finding the pearls capable of fulfilling her dream was another thing entirely. Thus far, her efforts had yielded nothing. She suspected they remained at Windgate Estate, but where...

"Katherine?" Mama peeked inside the library, and her expression immediately pinched with annoyance. "Lord Emerson has requested a private audience with you in the drawing room."

"A private audience?" She glanced at George, who simply shrugged.

"Do make haste," Mama chided. "You can stare at books later."

Perhaps not if this meeting with Lord Emerson meant what she thought it might.

Chapter 3

Suffolk, 1815

Nicholas

The longer Nicholas and his mother stood near the entrance of the church, the more agitated he became. Why Mother did not simply excuse them from the conversation, he could not fathom. She was far too kind, ignoring their slights with more grace than humanly possible. He had half a mind to make their excuses himself, but his mother always chided him after such interventions.

"And my eldest is recently engaged, if you had not heard," said Mrs. Pinkerton, a stout woman incapable of avoiding the topic for more than ten seconds. Had they not had this very discussion Sunday last? Surely all of England knew of the nuptials by now.

"I did hear the banns last week," his mother politely responded.

"They will make a lovely couple."

"They are quite in love. It has been difficult for them to wait, but what are a few months when they shall have a lifetime together?"

"Indeed." Mrs. Felding, who could always be counted upon to be seen at Mrs. Pinkerton's side, huffed, releasing a cloud of smoke into the cold air. "As I often say, it is important to begin a marriage on sure ground, and there is nothing as uneven as running off to Gretna because one cannot exert a bit of patience. If a woman can throw herself into matrimony so quickly, what is to stop her from throwing herself into the arms of another? Waiting is proof of character."

The woman's accusatory eyes settled briefly on his mother before she looked away, raising her chin, her wrinkly nose scrunched. Fury boiled inside him. For years, his mother had dealt with the cruel contempt of the *ton*. Either they snubbed her completely or they invited her into their inner circles long enough to make an example of her to impressionable misses.

The rumors infiltrated every social gathering his mother attended, and despite the constant attack on her character, she accepted the blows with dignity and grace. He had not inherited her temperament.

A squeeze to his arm stopped the rebuke from leaving his lips. He glanced into his mother's eyes, and the subtle shake of her head deflated his determination, though the desire to put the two women in their place remained. With clenched fists, he put on a smile and bowed. "I believe we shall take our seats. I hope you enjoy the service."

And he quite hoped the vicar would preach about casting judgment, but it hardly mattered. The message would unlikely change anything.

Nicholas entered the church with his mother on his arm and navigated toward their family bench, passing between those chatting in the aisle.

"Keswick. My lady."

Nicholas nodded curtly to a man not much his senior, and his mother curtsied, but Lord Doxly likely hadn't noticed given that he looked away before the gesture could be delivered, his attention stolen by the group of young ladies who had entered the chapel.

"I trust you are well, Doxly." Not that Nicholas cared much. The man was a nuisance. A scoundrel. The rumors floating about ballrooms that included Doxly's name were true, unlike the ones surrounding his own.

"Well enough. A shame there is one less miss on the market, but fortunately there is hope yet. Excuse me." The man slipped past them and straight for the young women.

One less miss on the market? Nicholas grimaced. A man in Doxly's financial situation could only be after a fine dowry.

He guided his mother to their family pew, and they took their seats. She leaned closer to whisper in his ear. "You still have a few minutes. Perhaps you ought to make use of your time by visiting with the Garricks."

Nicholas winced. He would like nothing more than to walk up to Katherine and offer her a Sabbath greeting, but that would not be received well by her mother. The last thing he wished to do was cause a scene, and in the church, no less.

"I hardly think that is a good idea," he whispered back.

"No? A smile and a little flirtation would go a long way to securing her heart."

"You would have me flirt with her *in the church?* What quicker way to ruin her reputation than to have a known rake flirt with her directly in front of the vicar." Not that Katherine would recognize such attempts even if he were inclined.

"Then it is a good thing you are not a rake, isn't it?" His mother leaned back against the pew, indignation written over her expression. "You are not your father, Nicholas, whatever people may say. Whatever rumors they spread."

His heart might have leapt at her defense of him had he believed the words. True, he did not engage in activity that would paint him as a rake, but the blood that flowed through his veins had come from a man who took no issue with the whole of society knowing his many misdeeds. Did he inherit that title the same way he had become a marquess? Did being his father's son make him susceptible to succumbing to the same flaws?

"Besides," his mother continued, lowering her voice further, "there are certainly quicker ways to ruin a lady's reputation than flirting with them."

"Mother," Nicholas chided as loud as he dared.

Her eyes crinkled, clearly amused. "Do you intend to call on her soon?"

"I cannot."

"Whyever not?"

Nicholas heaved a sigh. He did not wish to speak of his many failed attempts, especially where prying ears might overhear. He had never mentioned them to his mother, or to anyone but Luke, for that matter, and would keep it that way.

His mother took his silence as a sign of hesitation, or perhaps fear. "You must gather your courage, darling. How shall Miss Garrick ever know of your interest if you do not put forth the effort to show her? I know she will not turn you away."

He chuckled. If only she knew how hard he *had* tried. "It is not Miss

Garrick that I must convince to give me a chance. She and I get on well enough. Impressing her mother is another challenge entirely."

"It helps little that she was determined to dislike you since birth."

He started to question the statement, but her sharp inhale gave him pause. He followed her line of sight to the front of the church where Katherine had stood to take Lord Emerson's arm, her face half-hidden beneath the brim of a white hat accented with flowers and ribbon. A few stray pieces of her golden hair hung near her shoulders, like strands of sunlight on a dress the color of the sky.

Lord Emerson shook the vicar's hand, and Nicholas's breath hitched when the word 'congratulations' flitted to his ears. He had imagined it, surely?

But the pure bliss in Emerson's countenance suggested otherwise. Nicholas watched the two of them approach the Garricks' pew and take a seat. The vicar began his sermon, Katherine Garrick and Samuel Emerson were announced as engaged, and Nicholas closed his eyes to avoid the spinning of the room. He might very well lose his breakfast onto his boots.

When his mother told him of the rumor, he'd thought there was still time to win Katherine's hand—still time to convince Lady Garrick he was not the man society believed. Evidently, he'd thought wrong.

Warmth seeped through his coat sleeve, his mother's voice a soft whisper. "Nicholas, are you well?"

No. He wanted to run from the room, but that would certainly cause a scene. The church had shifted from his weekly chance to see Katherine to a torture chamber with no escape.

"I will manage," he muttered.

His mother relented as the vicar began his sermon. Nicholas's mind wandered, and he heard little of what the man said. Did Katherine love

Lord Emerson? The two of them had seemed content with one another, but he would not have called what he witnessed love. Then again, not every match was formed under such pretenses. Emerson could easily provide a comfortable life for a wife, and no other suitor had stepped up to court her.

At least to Katherine's awareness.

He was quite certain she knew nothing of his requests. Lady Garrick would have ensured that.

Nicholas leaned back against the pew and released a slow breath. The best thing to do was forget Katherine—forget any notions of courting her. There were plenty of women who would jump at the opportunity to marry for his title.

The thought twisted his stomach into a tight knot. Marrying for convenience had never been his intention, but the idea held merit. Things would be less painful if his heart were not involved. Regardless, he would not continue his pursuit. He would not put Katherine's reputation on the line with his attention now that she was engaged. It would not be easy to persuade his heart, but it must be done.

What he needed, most decidedly, was advice. Someone who could tell him how to remove Katherine—Miss Garrick, for that was how he must now think of her. Or as Lady Emerson—from his mind.

Nicholas's gaze shifted to the pew in front of him where Edwin Halford sat with his daughter, Juliana. A visit to Windgate Estate would provide what he needed. Luke could no longer offer him advice, but the man's brother had been in love once. Perhaps he could help Nicholas gain control of his heart.

Katherine

LORD KESWICK LOOKED RATHER UNWELL.

Katherine watched him from her place at Lord Emerson's side while her intended spoke to the vicar. She hardly heard the words exchanged between them, focused as she was on the marquess who was presently attempting to escape the church with haste, a task prevented by the chatting matrons blocking his path. He maneuvered between them with whispered apologies, and she worried he might cast up his accounts before he reached the door given the paleness of his face.

Someone should ensure a doctor was not required.

She gave her excuses and curtsied to her betrothed and the vicar. Lord Emerson offered her a nod and a stiff smile, the same one he had given after his proposal days ago. The offer hadn't been entirely surprising, considering his active courtship over the last month, and she had given her answer without hesitation. Lord Emerson was a good match, one that pleased her parents and promised a stable future, and she should be grateful a man of his station and wealth had chosen her. She *was* grateful. Only his timing put a constraint on her dream of seeing the future. She would need to find the pearls soon, before they wed and she lost the opportunity completely.

But that was a matter for later.

She weaved through the lingering crowd, responding to any well wishes with a quick smile. It took several minutes for her to reach the chapel doors leading to fresh air and freedom. The cold filled her lungs, and she glanced around the churchyard for any sign of the marquess. She spotted him rounding the corner of the building and, gripping her skirts to hold them off the damp ground, followed his course.

She rushed around the church into a grove of the silver birch trees that flanked the gray stone walls and nearly collided with the person hiding in the shadows. With his head leaning back against the rough stone and his eyes closed, Lord Keswick remained unaware he'd been followed. He still appeared pale, his skin a ghastly color even with the church shrouding his face from the sunlight.

"Are you well, Lord Keswick?" she asked softly.

The man started, and his eyes flew open. Even in the darkness she could see their deep green color, a welcome sight among the bare branches of birch trees who had been stripped of their own color when the cold settled in.

His gaze settled on her, and he dipped into a bow. "Good morning, Miss Garrick. I am well. Thank you for asking."

Katherine folded her arms. "You do not look as though you are well. What have I done to cause you to question your confidence in me? Have I offended you?"

It would not surprise her if she had. Mama complained Katherine often spoke her mind too freely. But then, Lord Keswick had approached her in the modiste's shop. Surely he would not have claimed her first dance at Lady Aldridge's upcoming ball if he were repulsed by her lack of etiquette?

Lord Keswick's expression relaxed. "You've done nothing of the sort, Miss Garrick. I am simply unaccustomed to anyone besides my mother taking such careful note of my distress. You surprised me."

Was that a good thing? She hardly knew. "I am glad to have not caused you offense. Awareness of my discourtesies often eludes me, but they are not intentional."

"Never?" His lips lifted slightly on one side as he stepped farther from the wall and into the sunlight, chasing what remained of the shadows from his face. "You must intentionally offer slights on occasion. Surely they cannot *all* be unintentional."

She considered the accusation a moment. No, she could not claim to never give her words a bit of bite. "Eight percent."

"Eight percent?"

"Yes, that is how often I estimate I offer slights intentionally."

His laughter broke free, and she was amazed at how much humor changed his features. At least the color had returned to his face. Besides, the man was far more handsome wearing a smile.

Lord Keswick shook his head. "That is far lower than the score I would give myself were I to analyze my offenses."

"What score *would* you assign to them?"

He hummed for a moment, his light brows furrowing slightly. "I am embarrassed to say that eighty eight percent of my slights are likely intentional."

Katherine gaped. "That is terrible, Lord Keswick. You mustn't let the vicar hear."

"It matters not." He shrugged. "My egregious faults ensure I am clearly beyond saving."

"With a little effort, I am certain you could lower the score to fifty percent. Perhaps more. No one is beyond saving so long as they are willing to do better."

"You have too much faith in me, I think." His expression grew somber as he glanced around. Realization of some kind washed over his features. He cleared his throat and retreated several steps, positioning himself back in the shadows as if the yards between them hadn't been enough. "You should return to your family, Miss Garrick."

Oh dear. He did not wish to be caught alone with her. Perhaps she should have considered that before following him, but as Mama often complained, Katherine had a habit of disregarding propriety, especially when her determined mind was focused on something.

Like ensuring the marquess's well being.

Katherine bobbed a curtsy. "If you are certain you are well, then I will go. Good day, Lord Keswick."

She managed only a few steps before he called out to her. "Miss Garrick?"

Katherine turned to face him. Lord Keswick opened and closed his mouth several times before he finally spoke again. "Lord Emerson...do you love him?"

Heat flooded her cheeks. Apparently she was not the only one who disregarded propriety. What an impertinent question! She ought to rebuke him for it, but any irritation she might have felt was drowned by curiosity. Why would the marquess ask her such a thing?

"I beg your pardon, Lord Keswick, but I must ask why you have an interest in my engagement."

"I suppose I...." He averted his gaze and shifted, discomfort written in his pinched brows. "You needn't answer. I simply wished to know."

That did not explain *why* he wished to know. Should she pursue the issue further? The lack of a clear response pestered her, but for whatever reason, she felt inclined to grant him an answer.

"No," she said. "I do not love him."

He winced, a reaction she had not expected nor one she could make sense of. When he said nothing more, she bid him farewell again and returned to the churchyard where much of the congregation stood chatting in the late morning sun. She joined her mother, vaguely aware of the gossip being exchanged between Mama and several other matrons.

Katherine did not love Lord Emerson, and she had never *needed* to love him.

Why then, did the answer she'd given the marquess niggle at her?

Suffolk, 1815

Nicholas

Monday brought with it a cloudless sky. Nicholas stared out the carriage window at the passing barren trees. He had spent much of his morning walking the gardens of his estate despite the frigid air, which had served to numb only his extremities rather than the ache in his chest as he'd hoped.

Katherine was engaged.

But she also did not love Lord Emerson.

That knowledge brewed a mixture of emotion within him. He felt relieved that another man had not stolen her heart, but it was squandered by regret and sorrow. Katherine would marry for convenience, not love. She deserved the latter.

The carriage jostled Nicholas as it wheeled over a bumpy patch in the road, and he pushed thoughts of Katherine to the back of his mind. Fifteen minutes was all it took to reach Windgate Estate, the home of his late friend, Luke Halford. Fifteen minutes of silence to contemplate how he had failed miserably to keep the man from succumbing to his depression.

A few months ago, Luke had rescued a young woman from highwaymen just outside his estate. Once she had recovered, the two of them had fallen madly in love. Nicholas could tell the moment he saw them together. The way the duke's eyes lit up every time the young woman spoke said it all, and Miss McCarthy had returned Luke's sentiments.

Or so Nicholas had thought.

The night of her disappearance played across his mind. Lady Garrick had thrown a ball, and after much pleading on Nicholas's part, she had granted him permission to attend. Luke had been completely giddy when Nicholas first spotted him. He had half-expected an announcement of engagement that night.

Instead, there were only rumors of foul play. A pearl necklace, a scheme to trap Luke into marriage, and a conspiracy involving Lord Doxly—Lady Garrick had the entire county in an uproar by the end of the week, but how much of her accusations were true, Nicholas could not say. Miss McCarthy had not given him any inclination that she was so deceitful, but then, those desperate for a title often went to great lengths to attach themselves to the nobility.

The carriage turned as the horses clopped up the long drive through rows of shrubs and garden beds. Nicholas pulled the letter from the pocket of his greatcoat and unfolded it. The edges were worn due to how many times he had read the message it contained, and the ink was smudged in spots where his own tears had fallen.

Nicholas,

As I write this letter, my heart aches. You know well my pain and the cause of it. I fear the unbearableness of such emotion weighs heavily on me, and I have reached the limit of my endurance in the matter. For this reason I wish to extend my final goodbye to you.

My friend, you cannot know what your friendship has meant to me. I am grateful to have been given so many years of good humor and frivolity, and I thank you for providing me entertainment from my boring life, as you so often professed. It is my wish that you will find the happiness you deserve. And you do deserve it, Nicholas. Do not give up hope on Miss Garrick. Fight for her. Confess your affection before you can no longer do so.

I have left my estate in order so Edwin may take over the title and properties. I offer you this letter, I hope, as a comfort. I am at peace. Happy. Know that you could have done nothing more to assist me. I also request that you present it to the constable as proof of my intentions. I wish for Edwin to be granted my title as soon as possible. Look after him and Juliana for me. And, Nicholas, do not forget my advice regarding Miss Garrick.

Always your humble servant,
L. H.

It had taken two months for the courts to make their ruling. The Crown had nearly claimed Luke's estates and rescinded the family's titles. Nicholas had offered evidence to Luke's melancholic state, in addition to the servants at Windgate and Edwin, which convinced those making the decision that the late duke had succumbed to depression and madness.

It was not an untruth nor was it completely correct. Luke had clearly been in his right mind when he wrote the letter, but Nicholas was well aware of the man's state before his passing. Luke had locked himself in his estate, receiving few visitors and rarely leaving, his responsibilities to his political ambitions and tenants abandoned. He had become a shell of the man he once was. Certainly one could consider that madness.

Nicholas's throat and eyes burned. No matter how many times he read the letter, his emotions rose to the surface. He had failed to help Luke, and now he had failed to heed his friend's final words of advice, too.

The carriage came to a stop, and Nicholas tucked the letter back into his pocket. His boots met the ground with a thud, and he stared up at the estate he had spent so much time at during his youth. He and Luke were always getting into trouble—well, *Nicholas* had gotten into trouble. Luke had simply shook his head and watched with a grin. That had never stopped the housekeeper, Mrs. Bielle, from chiding them both, though.

Nicholas rapped on the door, and a man with wispy gray hair answered. His lips twitched, a twinkle in his brown eyes as they roamed over him. Mr. Tolley had worked for the ducal family for years, and he knew Nicholas well.

The man bowed, and strands of his silver hair brushed over his forehead. "Good afternoon, my lord. We received your card. His Grace is expecting you."

"Thank you," said Nicholas as Mr. Tolley took his hat. "Shall I wait in the drawing room?"

"Yes, my lord." Mr. Tolley escorted him down the hall and gestured to the open doorway. "His Grace shall be with you momentarily."

Nicholas offered him a firm nod and entered the room. Nothing had changed since Luke's death. Nearly everything donned forest green, deep gold, and white. Paintings lined the western wall, and a dark mahogany pianoforte rested in the back corner, its ivory keys catching the sunlight pouring through the window.

The room held memories, and if standing here was painful for him, he could only imagine what it must be like for Edwin.

"Branbury—er—Keswick, I mean."

Nicholas turned toward the door, and a sheepish smile stole over Edwin's lips. The man looked similar to his brother—shorter in stature and his hair a lighter brown, but the resemblance remained unmistakable. Edwin entered, and the light from the windows settled on his fine-tailored gray waistcoat and black pantaloons. "Forgive me. I may never grow accustomed to the change."

"That would make two of us. I take no offense to the error." Indeed, he would have preferred to remain Lord Branbury if Society had allowed it. "I would much rather you call me Nicholas, as you always have."

"So long as you continue with my given name." Edwin clasped Nicholas's shoulder. "How are you holding up?"

"I should be asking you that. In fact, it is one purpose of my visit."

"Ah, well you needn't worry about me. I am weathering just fine."

Nicholas studied Edwin's face. The man truly *looked* well, all things considered. "And Juliana? How is she?"

Edwin's brows furrowed. "She is having a far more difficult time. She misses Luke dearly."

"Juliana and I share that in common."

"You were always his closest friend," said Edwin. "I daresay one of the few he had. You meant a great deal to him."

Nicholas nodded, swallowing against the lump forming in his throat. "Not a good enough friend, I am ashamed to say. I should have seen...done more."

"Do not put that on your shoulders. Luke would not have wished you to mope about. Besides"—Edwin scuffed at the rug with his boot—"he is happy now; you should find your own happiness."

"Happy? Edwin, he is dead. He's gone, and I should have done something to help him. You should be angry with me. I spent more time with Luke than anyone, save the servants."

Edwin shrugged and shifted his weight. "It cannot be helped. I do not blame you even a little. He made his choice to go—*do* what he did."

Nicholas hadn't known what to expect upon visiting Edwin, but this...was not it. The man appeared anxious, but nothing like the grieving brother Nicholas had presumed to see. Perhaps Edwin had come to terms with what happened. He did have a great deal of new responsibilities now that he stood in his brother's shoes. Still, something seemed off.

Mr. Tolley appeared at the door, drawing their attention. He bent into a bow, his silver strands falling over his forehead once again. "Lady Garrick and Miss Garrick have paid a call. Shall I see them in, Your Grace?"

Edwin sighed. "It seems I am to entertain all of Suffolk today. Please, see them in. Thank you, Mr. Tolley."

Nicholas's heart skipped several beats. He had come to Windgate to check on Edwin and his daughter, Juliana, to fulfill at least one of Luke's requests, but he'd also hoped to ask for advice. How was he to do so now when the subject of his heartache would soon walk through the door?

It seemed fate wished to see him suffer today, but no matter what his heart wanted, he would let Katherine go.

And he would start right now.

Suffolk, 1815

Katherine

Windgate Estate was of the most elegant design. Katherine enjoyed studying its Greek columns and intricate carvings any time she paid a visit. She and Mama had ventured here less frequently since the late duke's passing, and now that she had secured an offer from Lord Emerson, the occasion to enter the estate's walls would be rare.

She had tried, during her last few visits, to seek out the pearls, but the task was impossible. Without the ability to explore corridors and rooms on her own, she would never locate them.

At least she had believed as much until she overheard a conversation between the housekeeper and one of the maids. The mention of a glass full of loose pearls had been enough to demand her attention. With only a few moments to eavesdrop before Mama led them out the door, ready to visit another one of their neighbors, Katherine had been thrilled to learn the little beads were kept in the duke's study.

All she needed to do now was convey an excuse to get her out of the drawing room. Alone. Then she could make her way to the study. Surely it would not be difficult to find.

In three week's time, she would marry Lord Emerson, but not until she had the opportunity to see the future. Not until she filled the empty space in her chest caused by the need to be understood and accepted. The earl's offer, poor timing that it had been, constrained that opportunity.

But that was not the only reason regret and unease about her impending nuptials niggled at her. Perhaps it was ingracious of her to feel a little disappointed at the pronouncement of her engagement, but the feeling had only intensified after she left the churchyard yesterday.

Do you love him?

Lord Keswick's question had been impertinent, of course, but she had not managed to forget it. Her mind saw fit to repeat the words, each pass more difficult to ignore than the last. She had given her answer without hesitation. Love had never been essential for matrimony, a notion she'd accepted since her come out. So long as her husband provided security and was a decent man, she would find happiness.

Would she not?

Her mother and father certainly never had, but she had also never seen them put much effort into the cause. Would her marriage become nothing more than two people living as though they merely suffered through one another's existence?

Do you love him?

No, she honestly did not love Lord Emerson. Neither did he love her. He had made it quite clear that his heart was not involved in their arrangement, and that had suited her just fine until Lord Keswick's voice filled her mind, leaving confusion in its wake.

Curse the blasted man for making her more unsure of herself than ever! Why did he take interest in her affairs, anyway? He hadn't provided a suitable answer to *her* question, but it mattered not. She had accepted Lord Emerson's proposal. He would acquire a special license within a sennight. And they would wed once the banns had been read.

But first, she had one more thing to accomplish.

She should not know the first thing about the future. She should not wish to see it for herself, to possibly risk her life for but a glimpse. But Miss McCarthy's words pulled at her much in the way Lord Keswick's did. Katherine found she could not ignore them, no matter how hard she tried. They kept her awake at night. They stole her attention during tea and dinner.

The only cure for her curiosity was to simply see for herself. She could let it go then. Move on with her life and live as a titled woman should—throwing parties and playing hostess, a perfect example of what any countess should be.

Katherine grimaced. She would be perfect when others were around to see, but she would never give up her studies. It would be the death of her. Perhaps Lord Emerson would indulge her with a new book on occasion.

"Do not scowl so," her mother whispered from across the foyer. "You must be presentable, especially in the home of a duke."

The butler returned, and Katherine pasted on a soft smile as he led them into the drawing room. She nearly gasped when not only His Grace stood upon their entry, but Lord Keswick as well. She expected anger to fill her chest, for the man had plagued her, but her body reacted with a wave of warmth, and her lips lifted despite her annoyance. Something about Lord Keswick put her at ease, no matter the turbulence within.

Mama could not claim the same reaction, for it was she who now bore a scowl.

Pleasantries were exchanged, and Mama replaced her disdain with feigned content. Unless Lord Keswick excused himself, their visit would be awkward, indeed.

The whole of the *ton* had dubbed him a rake, and Katherine supposed he might very well be one. It was impossible for her to say when rumors followed wherever he went. *She* had never seen the man drink to excess or display financial instability due to time spent at the card tables, but Mama insisted this was the case, and her mother was never wrong about these things.

At least, Katherine had thought not, but her mother *had* been wrong about Miss McCarthy and spread rumors that simply were not true.

The duke gestured to the sitting area, a gracious smile on his lips. His features were quite similar to his brother's but his presence was far less commanding, gentler in a way that betrayed his unpreparedness for the role he now filled. She sympathized with the man, for anyone paying notice could see he had yet to grow comfortable in the late duke's position.

Previous duke, she corrected. Katherine did not believe Luke Halford had taken his own life. No, she suspected his disappearance was the result of something else—something few would believe. Today she would find out for certain whether the outstanding claims Miss McCarthy had made about time travel were true.

Mama took a seat in the vacant armchair next to the settee where the duke sat. No doubt her mother wished her to assume the empty space next to the man. She may be engaged, but Mama firmly believed in social connection. That was what had ultimately convinced her to pay the new duke a visit today.

Katherine did not, however, wish to be seated next to His Grace, instead choosing the vacancy next to Lord Keswick. He stiffened and sucked in a breath, a reaction to her presence she found odd. He had seemed nervous at the end of their discussion beneath the trees, but she could think of no reason for him to be so now. They were not alone in the drawing room.

Katherine glanced at the duke, ready to ask a favor of him Mama was sure to dislike, but she paused upon seeing his face. His Grace stared at Lord Keswick, one of his brows raised and a slight smirk on his lips. The expression seemed to unsettle the marquess further, and he shifted next to her.

"Shall I call for tea?" The duke directed his question to Mama, and she responded with pleasant agreement. Her lips immediately flattened when her gaze shifted back to Katherine, however. Oh, she was most certainly displeased with the seating arrangement, but it would not matter much longer.

"I thank you all for visiting," said the duke after asking a servant to bring them refreshment. "These last few weeks have been difficult. I know you were all well-acquainted with my brother."

"Such a terrible shame," said Mama. "He was a wonderful man. Honorable. Kind. It pains me to think how things could have been different had Miss McCarthy not appeared in his life."

The duke cleared his throat. "We mustn't put blame on anyone. My brother would not wish us to do so."

An awkward silence settled around them. Lord Keswick's discomfort and fidgeting she somewhat understood given the way Mama continued to glare at him, but it was the duke's unease that perplexed her most. He seemed rather uncomfortable speaking of his brother. Perhaps it was only grief. After all, it often affected people in unusual ways, but what if that was not the reason for his squirming? Did he believe his brother to be alive? The man's body had never been found, after all.

Such a thing would certainly have ramifications and easily cause the duke distress. Well, she would not let the silence go to waste. Now seemed as good a time as any.

"I hope you will forgive me, Your Grace," Katherine began, "but I have a request to ask of you."

The duke looked relieved by her words. "Of course, Miss Garrick. What can I do for you?"

"Your brother once told me of a book he obtained. He thought it might be of interest and offered to lend it to me. I hope it is not too thoughtless, but I wondered if I might search your library for it?"

"No, no. It is not thoughtless at all. I would be happy to oblige you." He gestured to the door and smiled. "By all accounts, help yourself."

How very accommodating of him.

Katherine stood and bobbed a curtsy. That had been far easier than she imagined. Her heart raced with excitement, and she did her best to temper the feeling. "Thank you, Your Grace."

"And of course, you are likely unaware of the library's location," the duke continued. "I must insist you be escorted."

Her heart sputtered. "I am certain a servant could show me."

Ignoring her, the duke turned, his eyes settling on the marquess with a mischievous glint. "Lord Keswick, would it be a terrible inconvenience for you to accompany Miss Garrick?"

The man's face went pale. "Me? No, not an inconvenience, but—"

"Oh, we shan't bother you, my lord. I can go with her." Mama started to rise, but the duke held up his hand. She froze for a moment before sinking back against the cushions.

"I must insist," said the duke. "Besides, I should assume you are also unaware of the library's location, my lady?"

"Well, I..." Mama's eyes darted between the two men. "I am certain I could find it. And without a chaperone—"

"Nonsense. Lord Keswick is quite familiar with the estate. His assistance will make quick work of the matter. If they are gone more than a few minutes, we can see to their rescue."

Where the duke had not seemed commanding before, his tone now took on a tone of finality. Mama had no choice but to feign a smile. "Very well, Your Grace. I suppose I can see the logic."

Drat. How was she to search for the pearls with Lord Keswick as her escort? And why did the duke insist on it? Mama was right on one aspect; without a chaperone, it was hardly proper.

The marquess stood and came to her side with his arm proffered. Katherine accepted it with a bit of reluctance, and his brows furrowed in response. Not wishing to cause him offense, she offered him a smile that seemed to set him more at ease, and together they crossed the room and left Mama and the duke to their tea.

How was she to get rid of the gentleman? He would not approve of her plan any more than Mama, nor was he likely to believe her should she give him the reason for her impertinent behavior.

Lord Keswick leaned toward her, his breath rustling the fine hair at her neck. "So, what book are we looking for?"

She stopped, released her hold of his arm, and glanced around him to ensure there were no servants who would overhear. "I am not looking for any book."

"But you said—"

"I know what I said. I...lied."

To her surprise, Lord Keswick seemed more amused by the confession than perturbed, his lips twitching as if they wished to smile. "You lied? Pray tell, where are we going then?"

She did not like the idea of *we*, but there was little choice now that the man had been assigned to accompany her. Besides, she had clearly sparked his curiosity, and Lord Keswick did not seem the sort of man to abandon a lady when his intrigue had been thoroughly engaged.

She shoved her gloved finger into his chest. "You must not tell anyone. Promise me."

His gaze dropped briefly to her finger. "How am I to make such a promise without knowing to what I am committing? You could be planning any number of atrocious crimes."

The mirth in his green eyes betrayed the serious tone with which he had spoken, and she could not help the rise of her lips. "You must agree, or I shall take you down with me. You have now become my accomplice."

"I rather hope I am to be rewarded for taking on such a dangerous role."

She crossed her arms. "I should think us both escaping my mother is reward enough."

Lord Keswick laughed, and she found that should she be required to have an accomplice, he was not so bad a choice. At least she did not feel the need to impress him or maintain perfect propriety. The man had an easy way about him that made her feel comfortable in her own shoes, so to speak, and that made him a good ally.

"Very well," said Lord Keswick. "I will swear to you my allegiance and confidence. Now, where are we going if not to the library?"

"His Grace's study. You know where it is, do you not?"

All amusement faded from his countenance. "I do, but—"

"Please, Lord Keswick," she rushed to say. She could not lose him now. It would ruin her only chance. "It is most important."

His jaw clenched, his eyes searching her face. This, of course, was not the best of ideas, but she simply could not let it go. She needed to see the future. Just once.

Lord Keswick studied her for what felt like a long time, his hesitation evident. When he finally sighed, there was something more hidden in his features, as though he had come to some silent decision. "Follow me."

He led her up the stairs and down the hall. They reached the study, but before Lord Keswick could grab the knob, the door swung open. A woman with gray and white hair appeared in front of them, grinning from ear to ear.

"Mrs. Bielle," said Lord Keswick, shock lining his voice. They were caught, and Katherine could think of nothing to say that would offer a plausible explanation. What would the duke think of them roaming his home? She shuddered at the image of Mama's deep scowl. There would be consequences.

"Good, you have come!" The woman's heavy French accent filled the corridor with a mixture of excitement and annoyance. "I wondered if the two of you would ever make an appearance."

Lord Keswick tilted his head. "You say this as though you were expecting us?"

"Indeed, my lord, and you should never keep a lady waiting, even one who spends her days cleaning dust from the furniture. Now"—she darted around them much faster than Katherine anticipated and gave them both a gentle shove, guiding them into the room—"you'll find what you are looking for on the desk."

"What we are looking for? Mrs. Bielle, I do not understand." Lord Keswick dug his boots into the floor which only made Mrs. Bielle increase the pressure on their backs.

"Katherine will explain. Good luck, dears!" The woman leaned in close to Lord Keswick's ear and whispered something Katherine couldn't hear. Whatever the message was, it brought a slight red hue to the man's face, and he looked as though he were utterly panic stricken.

Mrs. Bielle scurried out the door and pulled it closed behind her. Lord Keswick went rigid. Katherine had never seen the gentleman look so uncomfortable, but despite how unacceptable their present situation, she had no time to fuss about it. She wandered toward the desk, taking in the vase full of iridescent pearls with renewed excitement. "How did she know?"

Her mumbled words pulled the marquess from his frozen position, and he came to her side. "Know what? You must tell me what is going on."

"Maggie's pearls," she whispered. "I wanted to see them and hoped His Grace had not taken them all with him."

"Maggie? You mean Miss McCarthy?" Lord Keswick shook his head, sending strands of his light brown hair swaying against his forehead. "I do not understand. Why would Edwin—His Grace—take the pearls anywhere?"

Katherine sighed. Lord Keswick would think her mad, but there was nothing for it but to tell him the truth. "These belonged to Maggie. They are how she traveled through time."

Silence settled around them, and she dared not meet his gaze. He certainly thought her mad.

Finally, he said, "Through time? Is that how she disappeared, also?"

She could hear the amusement in his voice again, but this was no laughing matter. The beads held her greatest hopes and dreams, and she wanted to see the reality for herself. Katherine turned to face him, her brows slightly furrowed. "Precisely."

Lord Keswick studied her for several seconds, seeming to realize she did not mean her words as a jest. Gently, he took her hands, and the contact sent chills racing up her arms and through her shoulders.

"Perhaps you should lie down," he said.

She ripped her hands away. "I know how it sounds. Did Luke not tell you the truth? I thought the two of you were close."

The accusation seemed to irritate him, and his concerned features shifted into a scowl. "To what truth do you refer?"

"The truth about Maggie. She was from the future."

His mouth opened and closed several times, but she could not waste more time. Someone was bound to come looking for them if they did not soon return.

Katherine grabbed the vase and carefully dumped the pearls onto the desk. She countered silently, pointing to each one as she went. "Seventeen. I knew it."

"Knew what?" asked Lord Keswick with an air of unveiled frustration.

"That His Grace went after Maggie."

"Miss Garrick..." His head tilted, and sympathy shone in his eyes. She could see the pain there. Lord Keswick had been close to the duke. She knew that. This would be difficult for anyone to accept, but for a man who had likely spent weeks mourning the loss of his friend, it would be salt in an open wound.

It did not, however, change the truth. "There were twenty pearls. I know there were; I counted them before I gave the necklace back to Maggie."

Admittedly, there was a chance she could be wrong. Maggie might have taken all three of the missing pearls, which meant the duke had not gone after her, but Katherine refused to believe it. Why wallow in sorrow when she could linger on hope that the two of them had found happiness together in another time? She did not consider herself a romantic, but that did not mean she could not wish joy and love for someone else. Maggie had made the duke happy; that much had always been clear.

She picked up one of the pearls and rubbed it between her fingers. "I wonder how they work?"

"I imagine they work best still strung and around one's neck." Lord Keswick grabbed a single bead from the desk and rolled it across his palm.

"You are making fun of me," Katherine accused.

"Of course not. It is only that..."

He thought her ridiculous, and his glance toward the door suggested he did not care to be in a room alone with her. She supposed she could not blame him for either thing, but that did not make her any less frustrated.

"We should return to the drawing room," he said.

"Not yet. I want to see the future. I want to witness everything Maggie told me about."

Lord Keswick ran a hand through his hair, his sarcastic tone evidence he had lost patience with her. "And I want to see the future with you, but this is silly. You cannot believe such notions are true?"

"I do, and..." Warmth spread over her as if someone had suddenly lit a fire in the hearth on the opposite wall. Her knees wobbled, and the room tilted, throwing off her balance.

"Katherine?" Lord Keswick placed a hand on her shoulder, stabilizing her.

The concern in his voice was enough to scare her if the sudden dizziness did not, never mind that he had used her Christian name without permission. She had felt perfectly well a moment before, but something had certainly changed. Her fist clenched around the pearl, and she closed her eyes. "I do not feel well."

"We should—" Lord Keswick lifted a hand to his mouth, and his words came out muffled behind it. "I do not feel so well myself."

She had no chance to question him. Darkness ate away at her vision, and the remaining strength in her legs evaporated. Her knees bent, and her vision went black before her body ever met the floor.

Oxford, 1811
Four years previous...

Nicholas

Nicholas stumbled, nearly losing the book tucked under his arm, and laughter filled his ears. The world had taken on a lopsided angle, and the path before him moved like shifting sand. Perhaps he had drunk a bit too much after their university classes ended for the day. A walk through the nearby gardens had seemed the ideal thing, but now he questioned the notion.

His knees wobbled, and he reached out to catch himself on the wall, gripping the edges of the rough stone.

Yes, certainly too much drink.

A hand slapped his shoulder, and Nicholas turned toward his dark-haired friend, Luke Halford. The man's expression was half objurgation, half amusement. Luke always chided him for his mischievousness, forever taking on the role of the responsible one in their games and adventures. "I told you to slow down, did I not? You should have listened."

Nicholas swatted at the air, and the movement nearly threw him off balance. "Yes, yes. Always the voice of reason. This time I may have to agree, however."

Luke wrapped Nicholas's arm over his shoulder. "Allow me to assist you home. You shall never make it in this state, and it will be hours before you can walk without tipping."

They started forward, Nicholas's steps clumsy and slow. "I have no wish to go home. That bench ahead will do fine."

"Branbury, you are in no shape to remain here, and I cannot stay—"

"Then go home. You are under no obligation to stand at my side. Once the effects wear off, I will return home." Perhaps not even then. Nicholas had little desire to be in the same city as his father, let alone the same house. Why had the man come to visit?

Business, Nicholas reminded himself, for the marquess would never take time out of his busy schedule to visit his son out of sentimentality.

Luke guided him onto the stone bench and used both hands to steady Nicholas's shoulders. "Are you certain? You may come with me if you prefer. Someone needs to look after you."

"I wish to think. And be alone."

Luke heaved a frustrated sigh. "Very well, but do not stay out here all night. I shan't be held responsible should you get yourself into trouble."

"I am never trouble." Nicholas tilted his head back and rested it on the bench, listening to the sound of Luke's boots tapping against the pathway as he left the gardens. The sun presently warmed his skin, but the air would cool once night settled in.

He would not go home. Not yet. Entering the house foxed with his father present would be unwise, especially given their last interaction. The man would take advantage of Nicholas's inebriation, and he was not in the mood to be beaten.

His mind wandered until he drifted to sleep. The sun rested just above the horizon when his eyes blinked open again, his head pounding to the symphony of crickets welcoming dusk. He sat up. The world was less fuzzy now, but his stomach coiled. He would wait here a little longer before daring his return.

He pulled a letter from his pocket and unfolded it. Squinting to bring his eyes into focus, he read over the words his mother had sent him. She wrote of afternoon tea with Lady Aldridge and an upcoming ball. She told him how much she missed having him home, and how empty Ravenhall Manor was with him gone off to Oxford. But it was the last line that claimed his attention.

My injury is nearly healed. Do not worry yourself over it.

Nicholas folded the foolscap and stuffed it back into his pocket. Anger swelled inside him all over again. He had knocked his father out cold a fortnight ago after the man had given his mother a severe burn along her left arm with a hot iron poker.

He had inquired after the wound in his last letter, and although the doctor insisted his mother's arm would heal without problem, Nicholas still worried. The letter had both comforted him and reignited his rage. The rage had led to drinking, and now, he regretted it deeply. The last thing he wanted was to be anything like the man who had sired him.

He shifted the book resting on his leg to the bench. How could he go home? His temper would get the best of him. Perhaps he should have gone with Luke.

Rising, Nicholas drew in a deep breath. He grabbed the book and headed deeper into the gardens. A walk would do his mind some good, surely, and any delay to seeing his father would prove beneficial. He wove through beds of roses and medicinal herbs. At least the world had settled and he could think straight.

Somewhat.

Mumbled voices brought his feet to a halt. As they grew louder, he could make out two distinct female tones. One sounded almost frantic—pleading—and the other annoyed, which peaked his interest further.

"We should go back the way we came, miss."

"And do you know which way that is? How many circles have we gone in? I daresay retreating will do us no good."

"But continuin' will make us more lost, won't it?"

Ah. They were lost. Perhaps he could be of assistance. He knew the botanical gardens well enough, having spent years strolling their paths. He waited for the two misses to appear around the hedges, watching the very tops of their heads glide forward, the rest of them concealed from his view.

The ladies turned the corner, and the dark-haired one gasped when she spotted him. The second, a young woman with golden hair and chocolate brown eyes, patted her companion's arm. "Look, Cecily. We have found a gentleman. He is sure to help us on our way."

She marched up to him with a determined expression, the other lady trailing behind several steps, whisper shouting. "Miss, we should not approach him!"

No, they should not approach a man they did not know without protection, but Nicholas trusted himself. He strived to be an honorable gentleman, unlike the man who's name he shared.

They stopped in front of him and curtsied. This close, he could see the lighter flakes of brown in the braver of the two's eyes. She smiled as he bowed. "Forgive us, sir. We know it is untoward, but we seem to have lost our way."

"I would be honored to offer my assistance."

"See, Cecily. He is a gentleman. You have worried for nothing."

Cecily did not appear convinced.

Nicholas took in the outspoken lady's appearance. She seemed familiar to him, but he did not recognize the woman as one he had seen out in society.

"I will escort you to the garden entry," said Nicholas. Perhaps it was too forward of him, but he offered the woman with golden hair his arm. He told himself it was his duty to protect her with the skies darkening as they were, but the desire to have her next to him stemmed from more than that. Something he couldn't quite pinpoint.

It must be the brandy.

She accepted his offer, and Nicholas turned his eyes to Cecily. He did have another arm, but where would he put his book? Based on the glare Cecily was giving him, she likely would not accept the gesture, anyway.

"Do not mind, Cecily," said the woman on his arm. "She is quick to remain proper, even when a gentleman offers her assistance."

"I'm a lady's maid, miss. Not a lady."

Ah. That clarified things.

The blonde woman scoffed. "I do not see why that should matter in this instance, but do as you like."

"Of course ye don't," Cecily muttered.

Nicholas chuckled and started forward. "I hope you will forgive my impertinence, but being that there is no one here to introduce us, might I ask your name? I feel as though we have met."

"Miss Katherine Garrick."

Nicholas's brows lifted. "A relation of Lord Garrick? The viscount?"

She nodded. "He is my father."

That explained it. Nicholas had grown up not far from the Garricks. He knew the viscount had two children, but both of them were younger than him. He likely recognized Miss Garrick from Sunday services, hence the familiarity he couldn't place.

"And your name?" asked Miss Garrick.

Cecily muttered something again, but Nicholas did not catch it with his back facing her. "My name is Nicholas Betham, Earl of Branbury."

Miss Garrick gasped, her hold on his arm tightening. "Oh! Forgive me, my lord. It has been an age since I have seen you."

Nicholas smiled. He could say the same. He remembered Miss Garrick being much younger, the last image of her his mind could draw one with braids and youthful cheeks. "I take no offense." They walked in silence, passing several beds of purple flowers before he spoke again. "May I ask how you came to be lost in the gardens?"

"I did not believe I would get lost. I simply wanted to take a walk. My parents are visiting my uncle, you see, and the man has tongue enough for two sets of teeth. The gardens were my only escape. I shan't ever wish to know another thing about hunting."

Her words drew a laugh from him. "Tell me, Miss Garrick, what would your preferred topic of conversation be?"

"Well, I—"

Cecily cleared her throat, and Miss Garrick bit her lip. "I suppose I enjoy music."

"You suppose?"

"I think I should."

Nicholas stopped and turned to face her fully. "You think you should? Does music not interest you?"

"Not particularly."

"Then why would you say you enjoy it?"

Miss Garrick settled her gaze on the path, a light blush tinting her lovely face. Nicholas nudged her chin with his knuckle, bringing her eyes to him. The thin layer of fabric of his glove did nothing to curb the odd tingle he felt fire through his fingers. He would never drink brandy again if it caused such strange sensations.

He dropped his hand, attempting to keep his confusion from showing. "Tell me what truly interests you."

"Mathematics, sir."

Her hesitation made sense. Young ladies were not encouraged to educate themselves in such subjects, a notion Nicholas fully disagreed with. "You enjoy numbers. A happy coincidence."

He held the book he carried out to her, and Miss Garrick's eyes rounded. "*A Treatise on Plane and Spherical Trigonometry.*"

"Have you read this publication?"

"No, but I wish to."

"You may have a look at my copy if you like."

Behind them, Cecily heaved a sigh, but Miss Garrick paid her no heed. Letting go of his arm, she took the book and began thumbing through its pages with a ravenous look in her eyes. The way the light settled on the intensity there stirred something deep inside his chest. Miss

Garrick's face illuminated, but not from the dimming sunlight, and there was something all too captivating in her features.

"This is brilliant," whispered Miss Garrick, continuing down the path without regard to where her feet landed. Nicholas kept pace beside her, thoroughly enjoying the way her brows moved in response to what she was reading. Sometimes they drew tight and other times they lifted nearly to the top of her head.

"Has your father not acquired this book for his personal library?" he asked.

"My father does not take an interest in mathematics, nor reading in general."

"I see. Perhaps you might convince him to purchase *you* a copy."

Miss Garrick laughed humorlessly. "My father would take no issue with the request. My mother is not so quick to indulge me."

Nicholas fought the scowl working its way onto his face. "A woman should not need to hide her interests."

"Mama says gentlemen have no desire for a wife whose interest lies in numbers." She glanced up at him and tilted her head. "You are a gentleman. Would *you* want a wife with such interests?"

The lady's maid gasped, but the young woman at his side gave no indication that she realized how impertinent her question was. Her youthfulness must be to blame. Many a gentleman might have been horrified, but the earnest look in her eyes encouraged him to answer.

He cleared his throat. He had never given much thought to that particular part of his future. At one and twenty, he had plenty of time to figure out what he wanted in a marriage. He knew he desired one nothing like what his parents shared, and he had every intention of being in love with his companion, but his thoughts had never roamed beyond that.

"I would not be opposed to a match with someone who enjoyed mathematics, though I admit I may be lacking for conversation and expertise on the subject. Perhaps my wife would find my unintelligence appalling."

A wide smile lifted Miss Garrick's lips, and strange flutters twisted his insides.

"I cannot imagine that," she said. "You seem intelligent to me even if mathematics does not suit you."

A compliment had never created a whirlpool inside his stomach before. Heat crept up the back of his neck, and his entire body grew warm. Miss Garrick returned her attention to the book while Nicholas stared at her. What was it about her that made him both uncomfortable and comfortable at the same time?

Cecily's shriek snapped him out of his musings. Miss Garrick stumbled when her feet met a rock, her arms flailing to maintain her balance and severing her hold on his book. Instinct took hold, and Nicholas wrapped his arms about her waist. He pulled her tight against him, bringing her hands to rest on his chest as he stepped away from a shallow pond. His book landed in the water with a heavy splash that sent droplets raining down on them, and Miss Garrick buried her face in the crook of his neck.

"Are you well?" he asked, his breathing far heavier than it should have been.

Miss Garrick looked up at him, but her fingers remained clenched, gripping handfuls of his waistcoat. "Yes, thanks to you."

She was close...*too* close for propriety's sake. The proper thing would be to release his hold. The young woman was safe now, after all. But his muscles ignored the instruction. He could see the small dusting of freckles on her nose and the different shades of brown in her eyes, and he wanted to study them. Memorize them.

The hues of the setting sun basked Miss Garrick's face in a warm glow. A few strands of her hair had come unpinned, and he fought a desire to sweep them away from her face. What had come over him?

She smiled, lifting her soft-looking lips and drawing his attention to them. How inviting they appeared as dusk settled over her. He had never wanted to kiss a woman so desperately, but he could not—would not—kiss Miss Garrick. She was far too young, and they had only been reacquainted minutes ago. The desire was absurd beyond reason. But, oh, how he wanted to touch his lips to hers.

Blasted brandy.

"I am sorry about your book," said Miss Garrick, her tone light. She released her hold on him, but his arms remained frozen in place. Was she not affected the same way he was by their proximity?

"My book?"

Her brows furrowed. "Yes. Your mathematics book landed in the pond."

Yes. It had. "I can purchase a new one."

"Very well, sir," Miss Garrick whispered.

She must be wondering why he had not yet released her. *He* was wondering the same, and heaven knew what thoughts the maid must be entertaining. This woman affected him differently, and he knew a strong desire to find out precisely why. Perhaps it was the alcohol or, perhaps, something else entirely.

Footsteps pounded against the stone path behind them. "Over here! We've found them!"

Nicholas dropped his arms just as several people stormed into view.

Chapter 7

California, 2023

Nicholas

Nicholas's ears rang, but he could still make out the muffled chirp of birds somewhere nearby. He moaned. His body felt stiff, and something heavy pressed on his chest. Forcing his eyes open, he squinted until the sky came into focus.

Where the devil had he fallen asleep? Had he drank too much brandy?

No. He refused to believe that. He hadn't allowed himself to dive so deep into his cups since the night he met Katherine.

Katherine. Memories blurred across his mind. He had been with her right before—

A quiet whimper cut off his thoughts. Nicholas glanced at his chest. Indeed, there was a weight there. One with golden hair and that smelled of flowers. His arms were draped around Katherine, and part of him feared to release her. Was this all a dream?

If it were, he could imagine few better.

Katherine stirred, and every muscle in his body tensed. She lifted her head, and her brown eyes settled on him. For several long moments, they simply stared at each other.

"What happened?" she asked, tilting her head.

"I am not certain."

She glanced around, and all he could focus on was the way her palms pressed into his chest. He became keenly aware of every place their bodies touched and just how inappropriate the situation was. He should encourage the removal of her person from him, but the pleasure of holding her kept the words stuck in his throat. Katherine seemed oblivious to his plight at present, taking in their surroundings with a mixture of curiosity and concern.

He drew a deep breath. Blast. Why must she smell so good?

"Katherine." His voice croaked, deep and strained. "It would be in our best interests to remedy ourselves of our current position."

Her gaze dropped, and after several blinks, her eyes rounded to the size of luncheon plates. "Oh!"

She threw herself off of him so hastily she landed in the grass with a grunt. He sat up and assisted her into a sitting position. She straightened out her skirts to cover her exposed stockings, and Nicholas forced himself to keep his focus on her face. A blush crept into her cheeks, an endearing color he was growing quite fond of. "Forgive me. I do not know how we ended up in such a way."

"No harm done." Except to his heart, perhaps. The new memory of holding her like that would surely haunt him forever.

Nicholas turned to his right, hoping he might gain a clue as to their whereabouts. Trees and brush surrounded them. A forest? They sat in what appeared to be a small clearing, an opening in the canopy overhead allowing rays of sunlight to find their way to them. He shook his head and pinched his eyes closed for a moment, but upon opening them again, the same sparse greenery filled his view.

"Do you have any idea where we are?" he asked, still pursuing the area. He could make out nothing familiar, and that concerned him more than anything.

"Not *where*."

His gaze snapped back to her. Katherine stared at the ground, more red creeping into her cheeks as she nibbled her lip. When she finally looked up at him from beneath her lashes, he noted the worry in her expression had grown.

"What do you mean, not where?" he asked, ignoring the way he wished to pull her back against him, to protect her from whatever troubling thoughts she was having.

"I suppose I cannot say precisely *when* we are, either."

When? What did she mean?

Memories flooded back to him, their conversation in Luke's—Edwin's—study coming to the forefront of his mind. Katherine had spoken of time travel, an outrageous notion. Surely she did not believe it were possible?

"Katherine," he began slowly. He had no desire to scare her but also could not deny his concerns for her mental state. "Time travel...well, it..."

How could he put his words so as to not offend her?

"I know how it sounds," she interjected before he could decide on a course. "But Maggie told me she came from the future, and I believe her. His Grace knew, too. The pearls brought her to the past—into our lives. She told me such wonderful things about the future, and I have wanted to see it for myself ever since. Does this not prove it all?"

She gestured to their surroundings.

No, a forest did not prove much of anything. Though, admittedly, it was rather sparse compared to the woods surrounding Windgate. And the trees were...different.

Nicholas rubbed his gloved hand over his chin. "I did not know Miss McCarthy well before she disappeared, and neither did you. You cannot take such claims to heart. The woman must have been mad to tell you she came from the future."

However, Miss McCarthy had seemed perfectly normal during both of his interactions with her. In fact, he had enjoyed their verbal sparring in the drawing room of Windgate Estate. Had his heart not been otherwise engaged and his friend not clearly smitten, he might have considered courting the intriguing woman himself.

"Maggie was not mad." Katherine folded her arms, and her brows drew together. "How do you explain our present circumstances, then?"

Admittedly, he had no answer for how they had traveled from the study to the forest, but time travel was not an option he would consider. It was utterly preposterous.

He pushed himself off the ground and extended a hand to help Katherine. "I haven't the slightest idea, but we shan't discover the answer sitting in the dirt."

Katherine heaved a long sigh, and with obvious annoyance, placed her gloved hand in his. He panned the surrounding woods once more.

They needed to return to the estate before anyone took note of their absence. How long had they been gone?

His gaze flicked to Katherine, who stood with her arms crossed and an expectant look on her face. Did she realize the consequences of the situation? Being alone with him in the study had been disastrous enough; if anyone found out they had left the estate together...

Nicholas shook the thought from his mind. He would not be responsible for ruining a young lady's reputation, especially the one standing next to him. Returning Katherine to her mother was his priority, and he would do so with the greatest haste.

He offered her his arm. "Come. We need to return straight away."

"We cannot *simply* return. Windgate may not even exist now."

Nicholas bit his tongue to keep his retort from escaping. "Then let us find out if you are correct."

"Why is it so difficult to believe? Has waking up in the forest not piqued your curiosity at all?"

"Of course it has. But I will not waste consideration on ridiculous answers." He lifted his hand to tug at his cravat. The fabric clung to him too tightly. "Pearls do not allow one to travel through time."

Katherine gasped, and the sound made him jump. She crouched, her skirts cascading over the ground while her eyes darted over the clearing. "I've lost it! We cannot leave until I have found the pearl."

His fingers twitched when he realized he no longer held a tiny bead, either. He cared not for such an insignificant item, but if finding them would convince Katherine to return to Windgate, he would humor her. Kneeling, he ran his fingers over the dirt.

After several minutes without success, Nicholas heaved a heavy breath. "We must return. Pearls can be replaced. I am sure His Grace will not—"

"These pearls cannot be replaced. Don't you understand? They are special."

Nicholas ran a hand through his hair. He was getting nowhere with her. What if the pearls were still in the study? They could search all day and never find anything. The longer the two of them were alone together, the more damage would be done.

"Katherine, please. We must return before any rumors can begin."

She continued her search, shifting close to the shrubbery surrounding them. "If you are so worried about my reputation, then why do you keep calling me by my Christian name?"

His mouth dropped, but he had no refute. He *had* been calling her Katherine, unintentional as it was. Waking up with her atop him had befuddled his thoughts—thoughts that never referred to the woman as Miss Garrick. "Forgive me."

She ignored him, thrusting her hands into a nearby bush. The leaves rustled as the shrubbery swallowed her arm up to her shoulder. "They could not have gone far. Surely they—" Katherine's sharp inhale stilled him. Smiling, she pulled her hand from the greenery. His gaze fell to her open palm where two iridescent beads rested.

"Found them." She lifted her chin in triumph, and Nicholas lost his battle against the lift of his lips.

"Very good. Might we return now?"

"I am not ready to go back. I have yet to see anything I came to see."

Stubborn woman. Thus far, his words had done little by way of convincing her, so he did the only thing a gentleman could in such situations.

He offered her his arm. "If you insist, then at least allow me to escort you."

That earned him another smile, and guilt pricked at his gut. He would escort her...right back to Windgate. Katherine needed to rest, perhaps even required a doctor.

She took his hand and tucked the pearls into the pocket of her dress. Carefully, Nicholas led her through the thick overgrowth. How far had they traveled from the estate? And how?

Despite his façade, he desperately wanted to know how the two of them came to be alone in the woods. He remembered feeling odd and then blacking out in the study. What had followed remained a mystery. Someone had moved them.

Had they not?

Images of Katherine resting on top of him, her floral scent filling his nose, flooded his thoughts. What purpose would anyone have to leave them in such a position?

None. Which begged the question of how accurate his assumptions were. What if they had been transported—

No. He mustn't allow himself to consider the notion of time travel. At least one of them needed to remain sane.

"Thank you for listening to me," said Katherine, her tone cheerful. "I know the idea is not easy to accept."

Nicholas cleared his throat. He hadn't accepted it but dared not say as much. She might refuse to accompany him, and he could not leave her alone in the woods.

The abrupt halt of Katherine's feet tugged him to a stop. He turned to face her, and she stared back at him with furrowed brows. "You still do not believe me, do you?"

Blast. His heart squeezed at the hurt that washed across her face, but what more could he do? "Katherine, I think it best we get you inside."

She yanked her hand from the crook of his elbow. "I am not mad."

"I never accused you of being so."

"You needn't say it. I can read your expression well enough."

Frustration filled him, but whether it was the result of her stubbornness or his inability to hide his thoughts from her, he did not know. "What do you expect? How can I respond to your declarations any other way? Believe what you wish, but we must return to Windgate before our time together is questioned for something more than...whatever this is."

He gestured between them, and Katherine's expression softened. "You think people will assume that we have an understanding?"

Something like that, but he was not about to explain to her what conclusions the *ton* would make. "People *always* assume the worst. Always. The gossip will be the highlight of the Season if we are not careful, and I have no wish to be the center of it. Our names cannot be associated in that way."

Because he would never forgive himself if they were.

Nicholas spun around and pushed through the bushes blocking his path. He made it all of three steps before regret constricted his lungs. His feet kept moving, but he glanced over his shoulder to see if Katherine was following him. Flashes of her golden hair seeped between the dark green foliage, and he sighed with relief.

Pressing on, he kept an eye on her trailing form as he pushed leaves and branches aside without heed to where they were going. The sky changed from blue to shades of bright orange and pink. Little sunlight reached them beneath the thick canopy now, making the forest harder to navigate. They needed to find shelter before night completely descended upon them.

Nicholas's hands met air when he entered a clearing, and he paused to wait for Katherine to catch up with him. Once she had exited the overgrowth, he faced forward and stepped out of the shadowed woodland. His foot met something hard, a strange black surface with a white line.

What the devil was this?

A loud screech startled him. Nicholas looked up, a bright light filling his view and rendering him blind. Something solid smacked into his thighs, and Katherine's scream pierced his ears. He toppled to the ground, and his head hit the strange surface with a heavy thud.

The world went dark.

California, 2023

Katherine

Katherine crouched at Lord Keswick's side and kneeled on the strange black surface. It made her knees ache, but she had no time to think on the discomfort. She pressed her hands over the marquess's chest and watched as they rose and fell with his steady breaths.

Good. He was alive.

She touched her fingertips to his strands of light brown locks. He had hit his head when the odd carriage toppled him, but there was no blood to suggest a wound. The low hum emanating from the conveyance continued to pierce the silence, and an impossibly bright light shone over them, dispersing the darkness.

This carriage was nothing like she had ever seen, possessing strange wheels and no horses to propel it forward. When Lord Keswick awoke, surely this would prove to him once and for all that they had, indeed, traveled to the future.

She glanced up at the sound of a heavy thud. With the relentless bright light, she could only decipher the outline of a person approaching. Her stomach knotted, though whether it was from hope that they would receive assistance or fear, she did not know. What were the people of the future like? Would they be willing to help strangers?

Maggie had been pleasant company, but Katherine could hardly hold everyone of the future to the same standard. After all, even among the *ton* there were all sorts of people, some kind and generous while others sought only to fill their cups and coffers.

Katherine squinted as the figure darted around the carriage and rushed toward them.

"Kill the high beams!" the person shouted, slowing as they drew closer. They crouched, and Katherine blinked, attempting to discern the features framed by strands of dark brown curls.

The lights dimmed to a bearable degree, and Katherine gasped. The person across from her was none other than Miss McCarthy.

"Katherine, are you hurt?" the woman asked.

"No," Katherine sputtered. "Maggie?"

A hint of a smile graced Maggie's lips, and she nodded. The expression quickly faded into something more serious as she leaned over Lord Keswick and pressed a finger to his neck. Another thud drew Katherine's attention, and her mouth dropped when the late—or perhaps not late—Duke of Avendesh fell to his knees next to Maggie.

"Next time, instruct me to turn the lights off, not *kill* them," he said.

"I was rather confused for a moment."

"Sorry." Maggie glared at him, but it was a playful sort of glare. "I was too concerned about Nicholas to think about my wording." She leaned back and sighed. "His pulse is strong and his breathing normal. I don't think he's hurt too badly, but we should take him to see a doctor anyway."

"I believe he has only hit his head on this strange surface," said Katherine. "There is a bump just here"—she pointed to Lord Keswick's head—"but it does not appear to be bleeding."

"That's good." Relief swept over Maggie's face, and the duke scooted closer to Lord Keswick. He seemed to want to make his own observations about the man's condition, and Katherine took the silence as an opportunity to study the two people before her. They were familiar, of course, but their clothing was nothing like the current fashion of her time. What shocked her more than anything was Maggie's pantaloons. Did women no longer wear dresses in the future?

She had far too many questions, but a low groan doused any chance of obtaining answers. Lord Keswick stirred, and the pain lacing his moan struck her heart. Perhaps he was not well. Oh, dear. What would she do if he suffered a lasting injury because of her curiosity about the future? She could not bear the thought of it.

She placed her hand on his arm and leaned close to his ear. "Lord Keswick? Can you hear me?"

"Do not worry yourself," said the duke. "We shall get him to a doctor, and all will be well."

Katherine nibbled at her lip. She hoped he was right because she would never forgive herself if not.

Nicholas

A DEEP, MUFFLED VOICE RESOUNDED IN NICHOLAS'S EARS. HE attempted to make out the words, but the effort only increased the throb at the back of his head. A groan escaped his lips, and the voice responded with excitement, their pitch lifting a few notes. It sounded familiar but most certainly did not belong to Katherine.

Where was she? He'd passed out—or was knocked out, judging by the pain currently shooting through his skull—for the second time today. Had she succumbed to the same fate? What if she were hurt?

His eyes blinked open to search for his companion only to catch the blurred outline of a broad figure with black hair hovering over him.

Not Katherine.

"He appears to be coming to," said the figure, who was slowly becoming more detailed as Nicholas's vision cleared.

"Don't you dare give me that look." The second voice was higher—feminine—but still did not belong to Katherine. "It isn't my fault he wandered onto the road. He's lucky I wasn't driving very fast and saw him in time."

"Not quite in time." There was amusement in the deeper voice's tone. "You did hit him."

"You aren't going to let me forget this, are you?"

"Have *you* forgotten the mailbox?"

The woman scoffed. "*Agatha* isn't a person. She didn't just wander onto the road out of nowhere."

"I fail to see the difference."

Nicholas lifted his hand and rubbed his eyes. Who was Agatha? A horse? Dog, perhaps? He cleared his throat, but it did nothing to stop the raspy way his words came out. "Where am I? Where is Katherine?"

He pushed himself upright, and the throbbing in his head worsened. Touching a hand to the wound, he winced. A rather large bump had formed there, but best he could tell, there was no blood.

Arms flew around his neck, startling him, but the faint smell of flowers eased his surprise. He wrapped one arm around Katherine, and his view filled with her blonde curls.

Safe. She was safe, and that relieved the tension in his shoulders, nevermind the way his heart reacted to the way she had thrown her arms around him. She released him far sooner than he wanted, pulling away but remaining close enough that he could see every detail in her eyes. Terror lined her expression, and her fingers clenched the sleeve of his coat.

"You scared me," she whispered.

His heart gave a happy flop. "My apologies. Are you hurt?"

She shook her head, sending the strands of hair that had broken free of their pinned confinement tossing against her cheek. Relief flooded over him. He would gladly take the brunt of things to keep her safe.

What exactly had he taken the brunt of, though?

With his vision restored, Nicholas turned his attention to the two other people kneeling next to him. His mouth dropped. Had Katherine not kept a firm grip on his arm, he might have believed himself dead, for peering at him with the smugest of expressions was his best friend. His *dead* best friend.

"Luke?

The man's lips twitched. "Nicholas."

Impossible. Luke had taken his own life to escape his broken heart months ago. That he sat beside him now, the embodiment of perfect health, left Nicholas's mind completely befuddled. And who should be next to his friend but the woman who had caused Luke's tragic death in the first place.

"Miss McCarthy? I do not understand. How...?"

Luke stood and extended his hand. Nicholas accepted it, and the man tugged him to his feet with a grin, also providing a bit of stability until Nicholas could recapture his balance. "I can sympathize with your confusion. Perhaps blunt honesty would be best. Welcome to the future, my friend."

The future? Nicholas's gaze darted to Katherine. She offered him a soft smile and a nod.

He shook his head. "No...this is ridiculous."

Miss McCarthy folded her arms. "Why are men so reluctant to believe in the idea of time travel? Katherine believed me when I told her."

"Perhaps if you run him over again, he shall see reason," suggested Luke.

"I didn't run him over." Miss McCarthy whacked him on the shoulder. Luke flinched, but his laughter betrayed the reaction. The man's eyes danced with mirth, and Nicholas did not miss the deeper emotions swirling there. Admiration, happiness, love—it was all crystal clear in the way Luke looked at her, just as it had been the day he first met Miss McCarthy in the drawing room of Windgate Estate.

"You are not dead, then," muttered Nicholas, rubbing a hand over his face.

"Technically, no." Luke shrugged. "Only according to England, or at least that had been the intention of my letters."

The letter. The one currently tucked away in Nicholas's pocket. He wanted to withdraw the piece and rip it to shreds. The confusion brought on by the situation irritated Nicholas, but the heat filling his chest had little to do with the questions swarming his mind. Luke had staged his death. He had allowed him to believe the act. For over a month, Nicholas had mourned the loss of his friend, and now anger replaced his grief.

He swept forward and shoved Luke backwards. His friend stumbled several steps before falling to the ground in the grassy area next to the strange black surface, and Nicholas hovered over him with clenched fists. "How could you do that? I thought you were dead! Do you have any idea how your façade affected those you left behind?" Nicholas reached for the black band adorning his arm, ripped it free, and tossed it onto the grass.

Luke held up a placating hand that did nothing to douse Nicholas's anger. "I needed to make sure Edwin would have no trouble taking over the duchy. I saw no other option." His friend's expression twisted with evident guilt. "I thought to tell you the truth but, knowing you as I do, realized you would not believe me."

Well, he was not wrong to make that assumption. After all, Nicholas had spent the greater part of the last hour telling Katherine he did not believe in notions of time travel. The admission served to ground him, and hurt once again filled him instead of ire. "I mourned you. Wore a band. Everyone assumed it was for my father, but I..."

Luke's shoulders slumped. "You have lost your father as well?"

"Do not bombard me with pity. You know that man's death is of no consequence to me. The world is a better place without him in it." He glanced at Katherine, curious to know her reaction to his harsh words. Her gaze remained fixed on the ground, her lips pinched. Nicholas's father had not been discreet about the nature of his character. She likely knew of the rumors, confirmed or otherwise. Indeed, the whole of the *ton* was aware.

"Perhaps," said Luke slowly, "but having the burden of an inheritance thrust upon a person is no easy weight to carry. I am sorry I was not there to help you ease into the transition as you did for me."

Claiming his birthright had felt like a burden at first, but not because he could not handle the weight of it. The greatest burden lay in carrying a title once owned by his father, and that was not the sort of thing Luke could help him *ease into.*

"I managed well enough," said Nicholas, hoping Luke would drop the matter. With his anger subdued, he offered Luke his hand. As he pulled him from the ground, Nicholas took note of his friend's strange attire. Luke wore a shirt the color of dark leather with a short coat that stopped at his waist, and his pantaloons were made of an odd blue fabric.

He found the style in no way appealing, but now wasn't the time to taunt Luke for his choice in clothing.

Miss McCarthy came to Luke's side and brushed the dirt from his right thigh with her ungloved hands. The intimate gesture lifted Nicholas's brows. He should have looked away but found himself incapable, too shocked by the woman's attire to do so. She wore a pair of tight, black pantaloons that accentuated every curve from her hips down to her shoes and a shirt that draped just past her waist.

A *female* wearing pantaloons? He had never seen such a thing, nor should he have. His eyes had gone dry with his lack of blinking.

Luke snapped his fingers in front of Nicholas's nose. "I realize this must all be rather alarming, but if you could refrain from staring at my intended in such a manner, I would greatly appreciate it."

Katherine gasped from where she stood at Nicholas's side and darted forward to pull Miss McCarthy into an embrace. "Oh! Such wonderful news. Congratulations to you both."

"Intended?" muttered Nicholas. The overwhelming amount of information was doing nothing to ease the ache in his head.

"Indeed," said Luke. "Surely that does not surprise you?"

"That revelation may be the only thing not to evoke surprise from me today." Nicholas shuffled closer to Luke while the ladies carried on in happy chatter. He lowered his voice to a whisper. "The future...are you in earnest?"

Luke gripped Nicholas's shoulder. "I am. It is a shock, I know. Maggie came to the past by way of her family heirloom. After the Garricks' ball, she told me the truth of the situation. I did not believe her at first, but the longer I thought on it, the more sense it made."

"And you came after her?"

"Yes. I made the decision not long after your last visit. It seems Miss Garrick was also aware of the circumstances that had brought Maggie into my life." His grin turned smug. "It appears the two of you have come to know one another quite well since my departure. I presume you have taken my advice?"

Nicholas turned away. He had not taken Luke's advice, and because of his lack of action, Katherine was engaged to someone else. "Not so, I'm afraid."

Luke's expression pinched with confusion, but he allowed the conversation to rest. The lady in question was present, after all. His friend would demand more answers from him later, undoubtedly.

Nicholas ran a hand through his hair and winced when his fingers found the bump. "The future? How long did it take you to fully grasp the idea? I confess my mind struggles to do so."

Luke hummed for a moment before grabbing Nicholas's shoulders and turning him to face the opposite direction. "Having visual proof is useful. It helped me, at least."

For not the first time, nor likely the last, Nicholas's jaw dropped. Before him sat a strange-looking carriage. The metal, bright red frame glinted in what remained of the sunlight, and through the glass windows, he could see two rows of seats. It had four wheels like his own conveyances, but these were constructed of a black material and were several times thicker than wooden wheels. What confused him most, however, was the lack of horses. How did the thing move without animals to pull it?

"It is called a car," said Luke. "Fascinating, is it not?"

Fascinating hardly covered it. Nicholas had many questions, but finding the right one to begin with was akin to choosing a flavored ice from Gunter's; he simply had too many options, none less appealing than the others.

"It runs on gasoline," Luke continued. "A type of fuel. Cars are much faster than horse-drawn carriages—even faster than locomotives." He squared his shoulders. "It made me sick the first time, but I did not cast up my accounts."

Nicholas stared at his friend with a raised brow. "Proud of that, are you?"

"I would like to see you do as well. It was not easy, I assure you."

Nicholas shook his head. "So, no horses?"

"No horses. Maggie and I are driving to Los Angeles to make preparations for the wedding. Her mother is expecting us."

"She is." Miss McCarthy bounded to Luke's side. "And we should get going. We need to take Nicholas to see a doctor, and we still have a long drive tomorrow. Besides, I don't like sitting out here...exposed."

Exposed? What did she mean by that? "I do not need a doctor. I am fine."

Miss McCarthy speared him with a look. "And we will make sure of that by seeing a doctor."

"Best not to argue with her," said Luke. "She is right. You should have a doctor look you over before you attempt to go back."

"Go back?" asked Katherine. "I wish to see more of what the future is like first."

Miss McCarthy and Luke exchanged concerned glances that did nothing to ease Nicholas's own worries. They clearly could not stay here on the—road? Yes, it must be a road. Regardless, they needed to go home. The longer they were away, the more likely Edwin and Lady Garrick were to panic. It had been midday when they went to the study, and now the sun had set. "If the pearls brought Miss McCarthy to and from the past, then they can return us home, can they not?"

Miss McCarthy nodded, watching Katherine pull the two tiny beads from her pocket and display them in her open palm. "Yes. They can take you back, but you will return at the same time. The pearls can't hop days or minutes. Only years. They have a mind of their own, but that is a tested rule, according to my father."

That would certainly present a problem.

"No," Katherine pleaded. "I cannot return yet! I must see the future. Why travel all this way only to turn around?"

Nicholas bit his tongue. He would not remind her that they had not technically traveled a great distance. Their journey through time was more like a nap. They simply hadn't woken in the same place they fell asleep.

"As good as it is to see you," said Luke, "I do not think it wise for you to stay. It is not...safe."

Not safe? Nicholas did not care for the sound of that, either.

He snatched Katherine's hand, and she started. How could he make her understand? She had been desperate enough to wander an unmarried man's home without a chaperone just to find those wretched pearls. Her determination would not be swayed easily.

He swallowed. "Nor is it ideal for maintaining your reputation. The longer we are gone—"

"I know." Katherine huffed with irritation. "My reputation is in jeopardy. It always seems to be, or so people are continually telling me. You sound like Mama."

Nicholas did everything he could not to be compared to his father; however, being compared to Lady Garrick might be the only thing that was worse. "I am only being logical."

Katherine glared at him a moment before heaving a sigh. "We have already been gone for some time. Can we not stay a little longer? A few days? Please, Lord Keswick."

She tilted her head, and those brown eyes began working on him. Gads. They were like the perfect key for the lock on his resolve. His desire to say yes did not help matters. If they were truly in the future, then no one could stop him from spending time with Katherine. Lady Garrick could not forbid him from speaking to her. Touching her. Was this opportunity, as ludicrous as it was, not giving him precisely what he had always wanted?

It was wrong to even contemplate remaining in the future with her. He knew that with certainty. But was it wrong to take advantage of time when he would never be presented with the chance again? Could he live with the regret that would surely come if he said no and returned home this instance?

The devil take it. She was nothing if not persuasive. He should remain firm, but between the *look* she was giving him and his own desire to have more time with her—an opportunity that might well be his last—he found the endeavor impossible. "Very well. Two days, and we shall need a story to tell your mother upon our return. I refuse to allow the *ton* to make us the talk of the Season."

Her brows drew tight, and her gaze dropped to the ground as she pulled her hand from his and nodded. "Of course, my lord. We would not want that."

She sounded almost contrite. Surely Katherine did not wish to be the subject of ridicule? Either way, her downcast expression twisted his stomach into knots. He would give her the two days. Admittedly, he had his own curiosities about the future. After that, they *must* return. He would not put her in the line of fire. He would not soil her name as his father had done to so many ladies. Two days would not damage her reputation beyond repair.

He hoped.

"Well, now that we have that sorted." Miss McCarthy darted past him to the carriage—*car*. She opened the back door and gestured inside. "Let's hit the road."

His head had already done that, assuming he was correct in his assumption that the black surface was, indeed, a road, but Miss McCarthy likely hadn't meant her phrasing to be taken literally. Katherine rushed past him with airy steps of excitement.

"I'm not certain this is a good idea," Luke whispered to Nicholas.

"Nor am I."

Luke chuckled. "I would ask why you yielded to the lady's pleas, but I already know the answer." He gave Nicholas a pointed, amused look and then followed the women before Nicholas could deny the unspoken accusation.

Not that Luke would have believed any excuse Nicholas came up with.

"Sit in the middle," said Miss McCarthy to Katherine as his time traveling companion took a place on the fabric-covered seat in the back of the car. "You'll be less likely to get sick."

Luke cocked his head, and one of his dark brows lifted high onto his forehead. He also wore a smile that suggested the woman's words were not to be trusted.

Odd. Why would Miss McCarthy lie about such a thing?

"In you go, Nicholas." Miss McCarthy beamed at him, but he did not miss the mischievous glint in her eyes. Nor did he miss the use of his Christian name. How was he to feel about that? He had told her to use his given name when they met, but that permission had been a jest merely to gauge Luke's reaction.

Nicholas glanced at his friend, who seemed to have taken no surprise by the informal address. So very odd.

Nicholas sat down on the seat. Apparently only Katherine would be granted the *less-likely-to-make-you-sick* spot, assuming there was any truth to Miss McCarthy's words. At least he would have a nice view being next to the window.

"Be sure to buckle," said Miss McCarthy, pointing to a strap near his shoulder.

They both followed Miss McCarthy's instructions, and Katherine's arm brushed against him as she maneuvered the belt over her lap and into the small clasp next to his leg, sending tendrils of heat through him. Luke took the seat in front of Nicholas, and Miss McCarthy rounded the car to the other side.

"Take it slow," said Luke, his tone chiding but his deuced grin betraying any hope Nicholas had of the woman taking the order seriously.

There was a jingle, and then the entire carriage grumbled to life. Nicholas's heart rate spiked, and his gut clenched. This contraption was safe, was it not? It had technically already injured him, but surely the inside would keep them in good health?

The car jolted into motion, its roll over the road surprisingly smooth. Nicholas had been expecting much worse based on Luke's earlier declarations and found himself wishing carriage rides back home were as quick and even as this.

At least he did until they rounded the first turn. The sharp force sent Katherine pummeling into his side. Nicholas steadied her before assisting her upright again. Miss McCarthy certainly had not taken that portion of road slowly. In fact, he felt certain she had increased their pace.

No sooner than Katherine had regained a more proper position did the car speed around another turn. She slammed against him, her hands landing on his legs to brace herself.

His heart sputtered, uncertain whether to be happy or terrified by his current predicament. Was he imagining things, or did Miss McCarthy keep glancing at them through the small looking glass near her head?

"Maggie." Luke's deep voice held a faux warning mixed with a chuckle.

"What?"

"You are quite aware of *what*."

"No idea what you're talking about, *darling*."

Good heaven, Miss McCarthy was driving recklessly on purpose. How long was this trip to last? He hadn't asked, a regret made more prominent by the second.

Gads. What had he gotten himself into?

California, 2023

Nicholas

I dentification. Nicholas stared blankly at the woman behind the counter. He hadn't any idea to what she referred. How did one prove who they were? He was a marquess. No one had ever questioned his title.

He gestured to Miss McCarthy. "This woman can assure you that I am Nicholas Betham, Marques of Keswick."

The woman's brows raised high on her forehead as she dragged out her response. "Okay."

Miss McCarthy bit her lip. "She wants to see your license, Nicholas." She shifted her attention to the woman at the desk. "He doesn't have one. He's visiting. From England."

"What about a passport then?" the woman asked, her eyes trailing up and down Nicholas's body, making him squirm. "Do they still dress like that for real?"

He scoffed. Maybe his waistcoat had gathered a bit of dirt, but he had always ensured his clothing was in line with the height of fashion.

Before he could say as much, Miss McCarthy cut him off. "Lost his passport. Dropped it in the street gutter when he hit his head. We figured the rats have probably eaten it by now so we started the process of getting a new one, but they said it would take a few weeks." She rolled her eyes dramatically. "You know how it is with the government."

Rats? And they ate his passport? This was positively ridiculous. Miss McCarthy had insisted he went along with her story that he'd tripped like some clumsy drunk, and that had been annoying, but *rats?*

Miss McCarthy's last words seemed to distract the woman from questioning Nicholas's fashion sense, however. "Oh, I certainly do. The less I have to deal with them the better." Her fingers flew across a board with raised letters, and Nicholas watched her intently. Words appeared on the illuminated square in front of her, and he gaped.

Impossible.

He leaned forward to get a better view. "Psych eval needed? What does that mean?"

"Psychological evaluation," answered Maggie.

"What? I am not mad." He hadn't felt good about visiting the hospital before, but this put his feet into motion of their own accord. Miss McCarthy grabbed his sleeve and tugged him back beside her.

The woman glanced between them, her eyes rounded. "It's normal procedure, sir."

"Would you calm down," Miss McCarthy chided in a whisper Nicholas was certain the other woman could still hear. "You're only making this harder."

Could she truly blame him for being leery? He'd experienced too much in the last hour, and having his mind overwhelmed did nothing to help. The ache in his head and lingering nausea from being trampled by modern transportation didn't, either.

"Any insurance?" the woman asked.

Ensurance of what? Had she rounded back to his identity again? How many times would she ask his name?

"No," answered Miss McCarthy. "He doesn't have any."

"Okay. Billing address?"

"You can use mine. I'll be taking care of everything." Miss McCarthy sputtered off her address, and the woman gave her a confused look.

"We're on our way to visit my mother," she explained, placing her arm around his shoulder. "Nicholas has been dying to see LA. So he's tagging along."

The woman nodded, but there was no doubt she thought this entire thing suspicious. She placed a thin, rectangular box on the counter and looked at him. "Okay, if you'll just sign this form stating you agree to be treated and to pay all bills incurred by the visit." She tapped the box and a line popped up.

"Sign your name," Miss McCarthy whispered.

His brows furrowed. "Sign it with what?"

"Your finger." She pointed her own in the air and wiggled it. Yes, that explained everything so well.

Nicholas touched his finger to the box and a black dot appeared. He pulled his hand away and examined his fingertip. Where had the ink come from?

"Sir?" The woman behind the desk was giving him that *look* again. At this rate, he would end up in an asylum.

Quickly, he ignored his concern and curiosity, touching his finger to the box and scribbling his name. It was messy, as his title did not quite fit on the line. He handed the magic box back to the woman and she glanced down at his signature, her brows on the move again.

"You didn't have to put your title." Miss McCarthy shook her head.

"Alright," said the woman. "I think that's everything. They'll take you back in just a minute."

Nicholas tensed. Take him where?

"Relax." Miss McCarthy leaned closer to him. "They'll take you to another room. For privacy. The doctor will make sure you don't have any brain damage. Just don't say anything weird."

"What constitutes as weird?"

Miss McCarthy pursed her lips for a moment. "Don't say anything at all. Answer any questions directly if you have to. You'll be fine."

She didn't seem all too convinced of her own words. Could Luke not come with him?

He glanced to the seating area where the duke and Katherine sat. Luke appeared to be sleeping. Some help his friend was. Nicholas could be dragged off, and the man would be none the wiser.

A few minutes later, a nurse appeared and gestured for Nicholas to follow her. They proceeded down a long corridor and into a tiny room with strange instruments and another illuminated box. The nurse did a number of things she referred to as *checking his vitals*, and it took every ounce of effort he possessed not to react to her invasive prodding, particularly when the cuff she placed on his arm squeezed so tightly his fingers tingled.

"Everything looks good," she said far too cheerfully. "Now, I'll leave you to change into your gown and then we can take you for your CT scan."

"Change into my what?"

She pointed to the thin pile of fabric sitting next to him. "Remove all your clothes and put on the gown. I'll be back in a few minutes."

He watched her leave, his mouth hanging open again. Once the door had closed he lifted the fabric and stared at the long gown with a grimace. He was meant to wear this? In public? He ran hand through his hair. What had he gotten himself into?

Katherine

KATHERINE SCRATCHED AT THE DARK GREEN CUSHION BENEATH her as she took in the room. Empty chairs surrounded her, and the only sounds were occasional dings and Maggie's voice as she spoke with the woman behind the counter. The *waiting room* was practically empty given the late hour, which had proven a gift with how much of a fuss Lord Keswick had made upon their arrival. The marquess had insisted he was well and did not require an examination, but Maggie was relentless.

The duke sat next to Katherine, his head leaned back against the wall and his eyes closed. She wondered if perhaps he had fallen asleep. They had been at the hospital for some time now, and her own eyes wanted to rest. She glanced at the clock on the wall.

Ten o'clock. It certainly was not the latest she had ever stayed out, but after traveling through time, her body was exhausted.

Maggie's voice trailed over to Katherine, and she noted a slight hint of alarm in it. The staff had been curious about Nicholas and his injury when they arrived. Maggie claimed Nicholas had stumbled, hitting his head on the sidewalk as a result. That was untrue, of course, but Nicholas had played along with an unamused scowl.

Maggie slunk into the chair next to her and heaved a sigh. "That was difficult. They had so many questions, and I couldn't exactly tell them Nicholas was from two hundred years in the past." She kept her voice low. "I think we're in the clear, though. So long as the hospital gets their money, they're happy."

So long as Nicholas was well. That was all that mattered.

A woman entered the room through a set of double doors, Nicholas trailing behind her. He seemed well, albeit slightly agitated. Katherine breathed a sigh of relief.

The woman escorting him wore a pale blue shirt and pantaloons, and her blonde hair was styled neatly at the back of her head. She came to a stop in front of them, and her lips lifted into a warm smile. "Hello, I'm Dr. Jenson. Are you here with Mr. Betham?"

Doctor? This woman was a *doctor?*

"Yes," answered Maggie. "How is he?"

"I am fine," grumbled Nicholas, shooting her another scowl. "As I told you before."

Dr. Jenson's eyes glittered with mirth. "There doesn't seem to be any critical damage. His CT Scan came back clean. We can either keep him here for observation, or we can release him to you. He'll need someone to keep an eye on him the next few days in case he has a concussion. I assume you are a relative?"

Maggie whacked Luke's leg, causing his eyes to fly open and him to sit up abruptly. "He's his cousin. We'll definitely keep an eye on him.

Nicholas needs supervision."

The marquess crossed his arms, narrowing his eyes at her.

"Yes, we shan't let him out of our sights," added Luke.

"Perfect. I just have a few things to go over with you, and then he can be discharged." The doctor stared at Luke expectantly.

"Go ahead," said Maggie softly. "We'll wait here for you."

Luke nodded and followed the doctor and Nicholas to the receptionist desk where the woman began explaining symptoms to watch for and which ones were worrisome. Their conversation faded into a murmur as Katherine's thoughts turned and a spark settled in her chest.

"Women can become doctors?" she asked.

Maggie shifted to face her. "Doctors, surgeons, astronauts—women can become whatever they want nowadays." She tilted her head, grinning. "Even mathematicians."

"How extraordinary. I can hardly comprehend the notion. I wish it were the way of things in my time."

Maggie's smile faded. "Katherine, I know things are different in 1815, but that doesn't mean you have to hide your interests. You should pursue them no matter what others think. The world has changed, but that change didn't happen on its own. If no one ever broke the rules, they would remain the same, never altering for the better. Change can't happen without people who are willing to defy expectations."

Katherine shook her head. "What you suggest is logical, but those who go against expectation are typically outcast. I cannot afford that."

Maggie placed a hand on Katherine's shoulder. "I'm not saying you have to upend every rule. Just don't hide your talents and interests. If more people like you let those things shine, it will become the norm, a beacon that encourages more people to be who they are without fear of judgment. Change often starts small. Let those around you see the beauty in your talents, whatever they may be, and if they can't appreciate them, maybe they don't deserve to be in your life anyway."

Maggie rose, leaving Katherine alone with the empty chairs. Was her friend right? Katherine didn't need to be some well-known mathematician. All she had ever wanted was to pursue her interests without being chided or needing to avoid the topic when conversing with others.

Could she really make a difference by not hiding? She had always told herself she needed to be more like Mama, to fit into the small mold society had created. But what if she refused? Would the freedom be worth the repercussions?

She would never know unless she put forth the effort to try.

California, 2023

Nicholas

Nicholas shook his head, though why he bothered to protest after what felt like hours of disagreement, he may never know. The attire of the future was hardly to his liking. A single shirt and the absence of a cravat made him feel...vulnerable. He swore to never complain about the neck cloth again. He had oftentimes yanked the wretched thing from his person after a long day, but that had always occurred in his home where no one, save his mother and servants, would see him.

Perhaps it was not the clothing that made him uncomfortable, per say, but the vast amounts of information he had experienced in the past few hours alone. Miss McCarthy's driving had drastically improved after several sharply rounded turns and the doctor's mention of his nausea continuing. Nicholas had never seen Katherine blush so much in such a short time, nor had he ever experienced the amount of heat radiating up his own neck and into his ears. Although loath to admit it, he hadn't minded the proximity or the opportunity to offer Katherine his assistance.

Not that he could assist her to any great length when he, himself, was being thrown against the car door every few minutes.

Nicholas turned, inspecting the way the strange blue pantaloons looked on him in the looking glass attached to the wall. They were comfortable, he had to admit, but...

Luke's reflection appeared next to his own. "What are you, some debutante? You look fine."

"This does not feel right...nor look in any way appeasing to the eye."

"Should I take offense given you are dressed the same way I am?"

Nicholas scoffed. For whatever reason, modern fashion suited Luke. Even donning what resembled something more in line with what someone of servitude would wear, Luke retained his regal air. But the man had always possessed a commanding presence. Perhaps it was due to him embracing his impending title at a young age rather than wishing to drown it in the nearest river.

"Have waistcoats gone completely out of fashion in this century?" Nicholas asked. Something more formal would make him less uncomfortable.

"I do not believe so. Maggie mentioned I would require a fitting for our wedding. She also mentioned something called a *tux*. Regardless, I imagine it would cost a fine note."

The statement made Nicholas wince. Miss McCarthy was the one paying for this, and that fact did not sit well with him. He had but a few shillings in his pocket, and Miss McCarthy had responded to his question about banks and whether his fortune remained intact with barefaced amusement.

Nicholas tugged at his shirtsleeves. "I detest saying so, but this will do well enough."

"You shall grow accustomed to it. The ensemble felt quite normal for me after a week."

"I do not intend to be here that long."

Luke shrugged. "Then I suppose you must simply deal with it. We cannot parade you around in clothing that is two hundred years old. Too much attention."

Attention, Luke had told him, was not wise. The last thing Nicholas had concerned himself with was how dangerous traveling to and from the future might be—until Luke had recounted his and Miss McCarthy's encounter with a secret organization out to get their hands on the time traveling pearls. As if he needed more to worry over.

The pearls responsible for Luke and Miss McCarthy's journey rested in Luke's pocket. He'd brought them along on their trip in an effort to keep Maggie's father safe. Likewise, Nicholas had refused to allow Katherine to carry the pearls. He might have agreed to spending two days in the future, a decision sealed further by Miss McCarthy's insistence to keep an eye on him per the doctor's orders, but he would not be taking chances with becoming stranded should someone steal them.

Nicholas changed back into his waistcoat and pantaloons. Having settled on his new attire, he and Luke shuffled to the opposite side of the store to the *women's section* where he felt wholly out of sorts and quite certain no honorable man had any business venturing. Luke agreed, if the redness of his ears was any indication. They both kept a firm gaze on the floor most of the way, but that did not stop Luke from interrogation.

"Why have you not heeded my advice?"

Blunt. Impertinent. And the last topic Nicholas wished to discuss.

But, his time with Luke was limited. Whether he wanted to converse on such matters held no weight against the fact that he needed to put his thoughts to words. He needed his best friend and the advice Luke was sure to offer.

"I have missed my chance. Katherine is engaged."

Luke halted next to a circular display of heavy coats with fur-lined collars. Fur coats were not abnormal, but Nicholas had never seen one that showcased a rainbow of color. What sort of animal did that hail from? It was dyed, of course, but who would wear...

An image of Lady Garrick promenading about the ballroom with her peacock feathers flashed across his mind, making his lips twitch. Katherine's mother might enjoy the attention such a bizarre fashion statement would bring.

"Engaged?" Luke sputtered. "To whom? I do not recall anyone courting her...besides your poor attempts, of course."

Nicholas shot him an incredulous look. "The failure is hardly a fault of mine, of which you are well aware. Lord Emerson proposed, and the banns have been read once."

"Does she care for him?"

"Not with any sort of deep affection."

Luke nodded slowly and lifted his finger to his chin to accompany his contemplative expression. "Then you have time, yet."

"No." Nicholas continued forward with aggressive haste. Luke's white shoes, which Nicholas only now noted looked completely absurd and odd with their splashes of orange and the strange markings, tapped against the floor silently, unlike his own brown Hessian boots that created a distinct sound.

"Why not, Nicholas? She is not married. You could change her—"

"No!" He halted and ran a hand through his hair. "You know how Society will treat her should she call off her engagement. The rumors and gossip...I will not subject her to that. I cannot."

Nicholas knew full well what the *ton* did to those they made the victim of their wagging tongues. Though cordial to his mother within her presence, the gossip had not ceased since the moment she eloped with his father. The rumors of their rushed nuptials still frequented ballrooms, and the negative attention had often left his mother lonely and lacking in the friendships she once knew. Everyone had abandoned her the moment she disappeared with his father, even her own family.

And he had no doubt that Katherine would be dealt a similar experience should she call off her engagement to fall into a courtship with him. Her reputation would never fully recover, especially given the state of his own.

No. He would never ruin her like his father had ruined his mother. He would not be like him. No matter his feelings for the young lady, his selfishness was not worth so great a cost.

"Perhaps if you spoke to Emerson about the matter," said Luke. "He has always seemed reasonable, and if he were to call off the engagement, Katherine's reputation would not suffer so tremendously."

"To what end, Luke? Lady Garrick will no sooner allow me to court Katherine than she would become a scullery maid, and Lord Garrick can be convinced of nothing, save his wife give him permission. I believe the man fears her more than anyone."

Luke folded his arms. "And Katherine will reach her majority in nigh on a year, at which time she will not require her father's consent. Wait them out if you must."

"You have an answer for everything, don't you?"

Luke lifted a shoulder. "I presume you would not have offered me all the details if you did not wish for my opinion and advice."

"That may be, but you have forgotten the detail of greatest import—Katherine would need to *choose* to wait. She would need to choose me."

His stomach twisted. For that to happen, he would be required to profess his feelings to her. What would Katherine think of such declarations? He had begun falling for her the day they met in the garden—spent years waiting and watching, lovesick to the point of insanity. A confession would likely scare her away, and even if it did not, he was not sure he could live with the consequences of interfering with her engagement.

For all the façade of being the cad Society deemed him, he could not pretend losing Katherine would not crush him. Perhaps he would never marry. No one else had ever caught his attention the way she had.

Nicholas's steps grew heavy and slow. Luke walked next to him in silence, keeping the same pace as they weaved through displays of clothing.

"Ah, there they are," said Luke.

Nicholas followed his gaze to where Miss McCarthy and Katherine were sorting through a rack of pantaloons, their expressions filled with joy. Women enjoyed shopping in any era, so it would seem.

Katherine caught his stare, and her smile widened until it met her eyes. She waved to him, bouncing a little on her toes as she did so. Warmth raced through his appendages, a deuced reaction he wished he could control.

"Lord Keswick! You must come offer me your opinion."

Gads. This was a bad idea, he well knew, but how could he deny her?

Luke chuckled next to him and lowered his voice as they approached the women. "You worry she would not choose you if given the chance, but I suspect she would. She likes you, Nicholas. It is plain as day. She needs only to realize what it means."

His traitorous heart leapt, and Nicholas quelled the hopeful thoughts seeping into his mind. They had no place in there or in his heart.

Katherine stepped out from behind the clothing rack and gestured over herself. She had chosen a pair of dark green pantaloons that fit snugly against every inch of her and a thick cream-colored top that, fortunately, covered the more curvy parts of her torso. It did not, however, stop his mind from imagining what those curves would look like.

She took in his expression, which he could only fathom appeared ridiculous, and her cheeks tinted. "It is different, but I find I quite love how comfortable the ensemble is. What do you think? Do I look like a modern lady?"

She looked like an angel fallen directly from Heaven, but he dare not say as much. In fact, his tongue seemed incapable of words at all.

Miss McCarthy grabbed Katherine's arm and gave it a squeeze. "Your outfit has had the desired effect."

Katherine turned to her. "You think I shall fit in now? That is a relief. I would not want to be responsible for drawing attention to us when you and Luke are working so hard to avoid it."

Nicholas knew a twinge of jealousy at her use of Luke's Christian name. He had taken to calling her Katherine, though she'd never granted him permission, but she had continued to refer to him as Lord Keswick. Perhaps that was for the best. She flustered him enough as it was.

"That's not the effect I was referring to," said Miss McCarthy. The woman's eyes settled on him, and her mouth twisted into a grin. "I think

Nicholas will agree that the outfit looks very nice on you."

He fought the urge to scowl. He did not need Miss McCarthy playing matchmaker and would not give in to her prompts. "As Katherine has stated, the outfit will help us avoid unwanted attention. I believe that is the *effect* that matters."

Katherine dropped her gaze to the floor, clearly put-out by his response. His chest constricted. She had wanted his compliments, and in his attempt to evade Miss McCarthy's designs, he'd hurt her.

Miss McCarthy chided him with her eyes and jutted her chin to the pile of clothing draping his arm. "I see you've found some things. If we're finished, then we should get going. Come with me so you can change, Katherine."

He swallowed, all too aware of those watching him, but leaned close to Katherine's ear as he whispered, "You look lovely no matter what you wear."

Her lips lifted slightly. "Thank you, Lord Keswick."

"Nicholas." Gads. What was he doing?

Katherine's cheeks turned rosy, but her smile erupted fully. "Thank you, Nicholas."

He pulled away and cleared his throat. For the longest of moments, Katherine stared at him, her expression drawn tight as one he recognized. She was thinking—contemplating something deeply—and his curiosity burned.

She came to whatever conclusion that had eluded her, and without warning, grabbed his hand. Neither of them wore gloves at present, and although the contact was briefer than a heartbeat, she may as well have set him on fire for the way flames seared across his skin. He fought a desire to pull her into his arms.

Katherine squeezed his hand. His muscles tensed with the restraint it required not to succumb to the impulse, and they did not loosen until Katherine had released him and walked away.

"I must recant my earlier declaration," said Luke once the ladies were out of sight. Nicholas turned to face his friend. The man wore an all-too-satisfied expression that, had they not been on good terms, Nicholas would have used his fists to remove. "She would accept your pursuit without question."

Nicholas scowled. "You and Miss McCarthy are enjoying this far too much. Katherine is engaged, and I am not her suitor."

"Ah. Is that why you call each other by your Christian names?"

The memory of Katherine's soft voice speaking his name sent a shiver up his spine. "That—Miss McCarthy calls me Nicholas, too. It means nothing."

"Maggie calls you Nicholas because, in the modern world, everyone calls everyone by their given name. It is considered normal, not the exception. But if the address is not evidence enough, shall we discuss Katherine holding your hand? That is to say nothing of the way she was looking at you."

Heat crept up the back of Nicholas's neck. "I do not wish to discuss it."

"Very well, but that does not change the fact that it happened."

"It was a gesture of gratitude, nothing more."

"I thought you did not wish to discuss it?"

Nicholas crossed his arms. "You know, I am starting to wonder why I missed your company at all."

A hearty laugh rumbled from Luke, and he stuffed his hands into his pockets. "Because you need someone to ease you out of your state of denial."

Nicholas scoffed. "I need no such thing."

Luke said nothing more, but his everlasting smirk spoke volumes. They waited for the ladies to reappear from the dressing room, and Nicholas buried his agitation, a trying task.

Two days. He need only endure this for that short amount of time. So long as Katherine refrained from touching him, he *might* stand a chance.

Chapter II

California, 2023

Katherine

After a long evening of riding in the strange carriage, Katherine sat on the edge of her bed in their *hotel* room, picking at the fold in the white blanket. The muffled sound emanating from the water closet suggested Maggie had begun her *shower*. Maggie had asked Katherine whether she wanted one, but the idea of trying the strange bath was daunting at present. The future was, truthfully, a bit overwhelming, especially given the state of her muddled thoughts.

They had parted with the gentlemen following dinner, but even with their absence, Katherine lingered on their time shopping for clothing. She had tried a number of things, from brushing her hair to cleaning her teeth with the strange paste that came out of a tube. Even the television had not held her interest for long. Nothing provided enough distraction to outshine what she had done.

What had she been thinking? To touch a gentleman, hold his hand in such an intimate manner, and more specifically, a gentleman who was not her intended?

Mama would surely die of apoplexy if she found out. Given her disdain for the marquess, she would regard this situation with the utmost disgrace, and perhaps Katherine would have agreed with her under normal circumstances. She had followed the rules of society with care since her come out, always obedient to her mother's wishes and instruction. Indeed, it had been Mama who first suggested a courtship between Katherine and Lord Emerson.

The match was sensible in every way, and yet...

She yearned for more than sensible, though what, she could not entirely say. The idea of love had become a notion long lost to her with Mama's insistence that she marry a man of title. Why engage her heart when she only needed to find someone tolerable and possessed of enough pounds per year to ensure a comfortable future?

For two Seasons, she had kept her heart from forming an attachment. She had secured an engagement to a man who had no desire for their marriage to be anything more than a convenience, a notion that had not bothered her.

Until now.

Why did her heart ache for something she had never wanted before? And why did she suddenly feel hollow thinking about her upcoming marriage to Lord Emerson?

She folded her arms. The answer was simple—Lord Keswick must take all of the blame.

She felt drawn to the man for seemingly no reason. Ever since their conversation near the churchyard, she had not succeeded in putting him from her mind. She enjoyed his company above all other men of her acquaintance despite having never been given much time with him. Mama had ensured that.

Their journey to the future presented an opportunity to come to know one another better. Surely that must be the only reason she desired to hold the man's hand? Nicholas was, in a way, her guardian at present. She trusted him to keep her safe, and that alone must claim responsibility for the ease she knew in his presence, for the longing to be near him.

Longing? Good gracious.

Maggie exited the water closet, pressing a towel to her wavy brown curls. "You're awake? I thought you might have fallen asleep. You've had an eventful day. Time travel is exhausting."

"I cannot disagree with that," said Katherine. "I am afraid my thoughts would prevent any resting at the moment."

Maggie passed her bed and came to sit down next to Katherine on hers. "Do you want to talk about what's bothering you?"

Did she wish to? Katherine was not one to confide in others, but perhaps Maggie could help her find clarity.

"I am engaged," she began slowly, but the remainder of her words fell in quick succession. "That should make me happy. My intended is a man of title. He has a handsome fortune, and my life with him shall be comfortable."

Maggie tilted her head. "But?"

"But I...well, I do not know how to explain it. I suppose indifference would be less puzzling than this strange ache I feel. It is as though I have lost something—something very dear to me—but I cannot know what."

"Lost something?" Maggie hummed, tapping a finger to her mouth. "And how is this ache when you're spending time with Nicholas?"

Katherine shrugged, though the pointed question bothered her. Why would this woman suspect Nicholas had any effect on her at all? They had been in the future for less than a day. "He has the ability to distract me from the ailment. That is the only way I can think to describe it. He is the reason I questioned my engagement in the first place."

"Oh?" Maggie's lips lifted slightly, and the knowing look in her eyes left Katherine unsettled. Why did they appear as though they possessed secrets?

"He asked me—rather impertinently, I might add—whether I was in love with Lord Emerson. I cannot decipher what he meant by asking me such a thing, and despite my best efforts, my mind insists on lingering on it. I had not possessed even the smallest amount of doubt before that, nor had I hoped for a marriage consisting of more than pleasant companionship."

"And now you hope for more? I can't see that as a bad thing, Katherine." Maggie shifted to face her more fully. "A marriage should be more than a stale agreement between two people. Why not marry a man you care about, build a life with someone who will share in your happiness? With someone who won't restrict your studies?"

Because Mama insisted love would not provide for one's well being. Love would not keep the candles burning or food on the table. She proclaimed love a fickle insensibility that would fade. She and Papa certainly harbored no such affection for one another.

"You are fortunate," whispered Katherine. "You have found a man who quite obviously adores you, a man of wealth and title."

Maggie shook her head. "A man who also gave all of that up to be with me. His fortune is in the past, and our life will be full of hard, manual labor. You're right—I'm very fortunate. That's the thing about love. It usually comes with a price, but anyone who has found it knows it's worth every dollar."

"Dollar?"

"I guess you would say pound. Or shilling? I'm not familiar enough with your currency to make an accurate conversion." She chuckled. "Either way, love is a gift. You shouldn't set the possibility aside for convenience."

Maggie made a valid point, and Katherine decided that she would address the issue with Lord Emerson upon her return. The man had not wished for their marriage to be more affectionate, but why not give themselves a chance? What if they could find love with one another?

Her stomach twisted into a knot. The idea of falling for Lord Emerson struck her as impossible. They had taken rides together and managed pleasant conversations. He had been a perfect gentleman, yet she felt nothing but indifference toward him. Would their marriage reflect their courtship? In all her time with the man, not once had she been pressed with a desire to kiss him.

Katherine stood, donning a smile that was entirely forced. "I should like to try taking a shower."

Maggie nodded, and Katherine gathered a change of clothes before heading to the water closet. The warm water would silence her unwelcome thoughts for a time.

At least, she hoped it would.

THE NEXT MORNING, KATHERINE STOOD IN FRONT OF THE LOOKING glass, studying the way her modern outfit hugged her body. Never had she imagined she would wear pantaloons, but they had already grown on her.

The memory of Nicholas looking her over while they shopped yesterday brought heat to her cheeks. Certainly she had noticed men eyeing her before, but there was something different about the way the marquess stared at her. And then there was his sweet compliment that she looked lovely in anything.

For the briefest time, she had allowed herself to consider what those things might mean, but she had doused the conclusions her mind wished to draw. If Nicholas had been interested in her at all, he would have put forth an effort to court her. She had been out in society for two years, and they had made one another's acquaintance long before that, plenty of time to consider her a proper candidate for a wife.

He had never approached her with such intentions. They had never danced in those two years, and their conversations had been sparse. Mama could be blamed to an extent for that, but the truth was Lord Keswick simply had no desire to begin a courtship. She would do well to be content with that knowledge, considering she had become engaged to another man, yet the realization sparked a pang in her chest for which she could not name the cause.

Maggie's reflection appeared next to her in the mirror. "Would you like help with your hair? We have time before we have to meet the men for breakfast. I could curl it."

Katherine shook her head. "I could not ask that of you."

A grin swept over Maggie's face. She grabbed Katherine by the wrist and tugged her toward the water closet. "You didn't ask; I offered."

Katherine held perfectly still while Maggie wielded her curling tongs like a weapon, a strategic look upon her face as she appeared to debate which strands of hair to style first.

"There," said Maggie, stepping back to admire her work. "You look gorgeous."

Katherine tilted her head from side to side, watching the soft curls bounce with the movement. She did prefer her hair in spirals to the straightness it naturally assumed. "Thank you. I am wholly impressed with your abilities. I could never have achieved this style on my own."

Maggie swatted at the air. "I've had years of practice using an iron. Besides, I'm guessing you usually have a maid to do your hair for you?"

"Yes, though watching you almost makes me wish to learn." It would be nice to have the skill to style her own hair instead of being stuck with whatever coiffure Mama instructed her maid to create.

"Should we go down for breakfast?" asked Maggie, an eager spark in her eyes.

"Very well," said Katherine.

She followed Maggie down the long corridor to the strange moving box. Katherine clutched the railing when it dropped, fearing it would descend without her if she did not hold on. She was not fond of the instability she felt riding the elevator.

They entered the lobby and found it empty but for the woman behind the reception desk. Maggie and Luke had repeatedly mentioned the need for remaining inconspicuous. Thus far, they had traveled back roads through less populated areas. What Maggie considered small towns completely enthralled Katherine. Everything about the future was mesmerizing, and while she understood the reason for avoiding the bigger cities, she wanted to see more.

The two of them filled odd plates made of what Katherine could only describe as a thick paper with muffins, sausage, and eggs. They sat down at one of the square tables near the window, and Katherine immediately began eating to stop the way her stomach growled in anticipation.

Maggie glanced at the clock hanging above the sideboard and sighed. "They're late. I bet they couldn't figure out how to set the alarm and overslept."

Katherine chose not to respond. She would be a hypocrite for doing so when *she* would not know how to *set an alarm*.

The rapid tap of Maggie's finger against the table betrayed the woman's unease. Katherine swallowed the food in her mouth. "Do you wish to check on them? I am perfectly fine to sit here for a few minutes on my own."

Maggie pursed her lips as if considering the offer. "Are you sure? I don't like the idea of leaving you by yourself." Her voice dropped to a whisper. "The future can be a confusing place for someone unaccustomed to our craziness."

Katherine chuckled. "Perhaps, but I can handle breakfast on my own for a time. I promise to remain here until you return."

Another minute passed before Maggie gave in. She rose from her seat with a sigh. "I'll be right back."

Katherine nodded, and Maggie scurried toward the elevators. The woman hid her concern well, but Katherine did not blame her for feeling restless without Luke and Nicholas about. If there truly was an organization after the pearls, it was best they stayed together as much as possible. She hoped, however, the concern was unnecessary. Perhaps those desiring the time travel beads had given up after the encounter Maggie and Luke had described.

A tall man with dark hair entered the lobby. Katherine dropped her gaze to her food, but she could still see his movement out of the corner of her eye as he perused the sideboard. She hadn't minded being without Maggie when she was alone in the breakfast room, but now her pulse raced.

A silly reaction.

The man sat down a few tables away from her, and Katherine finished the last few bites of her breakfast, all too aware of his presence. Once her plate was empty, she shifted slightly to obtain a better view of her silent breakfast companion.

He was staring directly at her, the food on his plate completely untouched. His dark eyes pinned her, and she could not look away. The coldness in his expression sent an icy shiver through her body, and the urge to flee the room nearly had her feet moving of their own accord.

Katherine smiled, but the man's features remained unchanged, and she quickly turned toward the window. Why was he staring at her so unabashedly? And more importantly, why did instinct tell her this was not a man she wanted to be alone in a room with?

Chapter 12

California, 2023

Nicholas

N icholas heard the squeak of closing doors and tripled his pace down the hallway. If he hurried, he might catch the...what had Miss McCarthy called it? An elevator? He was uncertain he trusted the contraption, but for whatever reason, that only made him wish to ride it more.

Luke had left the room ahead of him not a minute before, eager to meet his intended for breakfast. His friend was deeply enamored, enough so that he willingly gave up everything to be with Miss McCarthy. His wealth, title—even his own family. And despite those sacrifices, Luke had never appeared happier.

Nicholas stopped in front of the metallic doors and pressed the button like he had watched Miss McCarthy do last night when they arrived. The *hotel* was nothing like the inns he had boarded at during travel in his time. The place was exceptionally clean and lavish by comparison.

The door slid open, having yet to make its journey to another floor, immediately revealing the two lone figures inside. Miss McCarthy jumped away from Luke, dropping her hands from around his neck. Her cheeks tinted a deep shade of red.

Luke simply looked annoyed.

Nicholas gaped for a moment. He certainly had not expected to find *that* behind the doors. Best to make use of the situation. "Have I interrupted?" He stepped inside, not bothering to hide his grin.

"Yes," said Luke flatly.

"My apologies." Nicholas shuffled to the buttons and pressed the one with a *G*. It lit up, and he knew a desire to press all of the others just to see them do the same.

So he did.

"What are you doing?" asked Miss McCarthy.

Nicholas shrugged. "I thought you wanted more time alone."

"We aren't alone. You're in here."

It was mischievous of him, perhaps, but after Miss McCarthy had teased him so openly yesterday, he would not feel guilty about it. "Again, my apologies, but you needn't stop on my account."

"I needn't refrain from getting you back, either," she muttered as the doors closed again.

Nicholas chuckled. Last night, the men and women had parted ways, their rooms next to each other. Miss McCarthy and Luke had lingered in the hallway, and Nicholas assumed they had engaged in a similar sport to the one he'd encountered moments ago. He, on the other hand, had been investigating what Luke later explained to him was a microwave.

It had plenty of buttons for pressing as well.

The elevator lurched upward, making Nicholas's stomach drop to somewhere near his knees. He held onto the railing behind him and leaned back.

"Where is Kat—Miss Garrick, this morning?" he asked, though why he bothered to hide his use of her Christian name, he did not know. Luke and Miss McCarthy had heard him use it the day before.

Miss McCarthy smirked, the incorrigible woman. "She and I went down for breakfast, but since the two of you were taking so long, I decided to check on you. Luke assured me you were on your way when I found him outside the elevator."

"You left her alone?" Nicholas was not overly fond of that notion. They were in the future, after all, an era neither of them were familiar with.

"It's breakfast. I'm pretty sure Katherine can handle eating by herself for a few minutes."

Nicholas bit his tongue. She was right, of course. He had no reason to worry so much.

They proceeded to stop at three floors, each time the doors sliding open to an empty hallway. Miss McCarthy took a deep inhale whenever they closed, which gave Nicholas great satisfaction.

Until they started going down.

His stomach appreciated descending far less, and his fingers tightened around the metal railing.

"Something wrong?" Miss McCarthy asked, her eyes narrowed on Nicholas.

"Not at all. Perfectly well." Lies.

She pushed herself away from the wall as the doors closed once again, a slight smile playing on her lips. "I always liked elevators as a kid. Do you know what I would do?"

Nicholas was uncertain he wished to know the answer, if the glint in her eyes was any indication. His lack of enthusiasm did not deter Miss McCarthy, however. When the elevator dropped again, she jumped, and the entire compartment shook with her heavy landing.

"What the devil are you doing!" He gripped the railing so tightly his hands hurt.

"Having a bit of fun."

"Maggie." Luke's face had paled somewhat, and Nicholas was grateful his friend felt as uncomfortable about the jumping as he did. The woman would not entertain Nicholas's pleas for her to cease such clearly dangerous ideas of *fun.*

Miss McCarthy sighed and leaned back against Luke. "Alright, I won't do it again."

They descended in silence, and when the doors opened on the floor where they had started, Katherine appeared in front of them. Nicholas's breath hitched. She wore another pair of pantaloons that left no curve to the imagination, and it took great restraint for his eyes not to roam over her.

"There you all are." She stepped into the elevator. "I had gone back to the rooms, but no one answered when I knocked."

"You can blame Nicholas," said Miss McCarthy. "He decided we need to pay every floor a visit."

Katherine's brows furrowed, but she did not press for more details.

"Did you sleep well, Miss Garrick?" Luke asked.

"As well as can be expected, I imagine. My mind remained restless. There is so much to take in, after all."

"I can sympathize. I bombarded Maggie with a thousand questions every night the first few days."

Miss McCarthy tilted her head back and glanced up at him, her brows raised. "The first few days? You still bombard me with questions."

Luke kissed her forehead, and she smiled contentedly when he brushed the hair away from her face. Women, Nicholas had noted, often wore their hair free of pins in the future, and some sported unusual styles he'd never before seen. The receptionist downstairs last night had even dyed hers purple, which had been a thorough shock and made him stare far longer than he should have. Luke's elbow into his abdomen had been required to break the trance.

Katherine had her hair down today as well, the curled golden locks draping over her shoulders in waves that did nothing to decrease his desire to touch the strands.

Nicholas swallowed when she positioned herself next to him. Katherine had receded into a state of shyness since she held his hand in the clothing store. He wondered if she regretted the intimate gesture. He'd certainly been unsuccessful at removing the sensation of their bare hands touching from his memory and likely never would.

Or wanted to, for that matter.

"Good morning, Katherine," he finally managed, meeting her gaze with a smile.

"Good morning, Lord Keswick."

"Nicholas," he corrected.

Her expression brightened, twisting his insides into knots. "Nicholas." Her gaze perused his form, and he tugged at the hem of his shirt under watch of her considering eyes. What did she think of his donning of modern clothes?

As if able to read his thoughts, Katherine leaned closer as the doors shut to yet another floor that was not their destination and whispered, "You look handsome no matter what you wear."

She said it without coyness, for Katherine was hardly an expert in flirtation, but the genuine sentiment made his heartbeat erratic all the same. The woman *meant* it. She thought him handsome. Somehow, he minded modern apparel far less with this knowledge.

"Thank you," Nicholas whispered.

The elevator finally found the ground floor, and with the ding of arrival, the four of them exited the tiny compartment. They had breakfast at the hotel, a young family their only company in the room, and gathered their belongings before setting out to the car. Miss McCarthy claimed they would likely arrive in Los Angeles late that afternoon, and Nicholas was eager to witness the grand city she had described to them.

The scenery had changed over the last day from one heavily forested to one with sparse vegetation. The air had grown dry as well, and Nicholas's lips felt perpetually in need of moisture. They had yet to see much of modern civilization, as Luke and Miss McCarthy insisted on taking what she called *the scenic route*. From what Nicholas could gather, it meant a longer journey over less used roadways. He could hardly blame them after what they had both gone through.

Nicholas buckled his seatbelt and tapped his pocket, assuring himself it was not empty. Both pearls still rested there.

He glanced at Katherine out of the corner of his eye. She sat directly next to him, oblivious to the notion that the middle seat making her less sick was a lie. Perhaps he should tell her for propriety's sake, but he had no desire to do so. And what difference did their proximity make, anyway? No one from the *ton* would ever know.

Nicholas shook his head, ridding himself of the dangerous thoughts. Society's presence or no, he would conduct himself as a gentleman. It would be far too easy to get swept away in the loose rules of the future.

And his heart could not afford to be taken out to sea with the tide.

They spent most of the day in the car, stopping only for a quick meal at noon before continuing on their way. It was not the grandest way to experience the future, but considering the precautions Miss McCarthy and Luke were taking, it was the best that could be done. Katherine seemed unbothered by the lack of opportunity, her gaze constantly fitted to the window with a look of wonder dancing within her brown eyes.

He considered trading seats with her so that she might have a better view, but doing so would steal the moments she leaned close, gifting him a whiff of whatever futuristic soap she'd used as she peered past him at the sights beyond the glass.

They stopped at a *gas station* so the car could be refueled, and when Miss McCarthy re-entered the carriage holding a thin box in her hand, she heaved an irritated sigh.

"What is the matter?" asked Luke once she had sat down and inserted the keys.

The conveyance hummed to life, and Miss McCarthy placed the box between them. "It's Diana. She insists we come to her apartment first and then go to dinner."

Diana? Nicholas had no idea who that was or how Miss McCarthy had been subjected to her insistence while she was inside the gas station.

"You do not wish to see her?" asked Luke.

Miss McCarthy shook her head. "It's not that. I hadn't planned to expose you to Diana's overly intrusive interrogation so soon. I thought we would settle in at my Mom's first."

"It cannot be so bad as that. A short visit and dinner with your best friend cannot possibly require such furrowed brows." Luke lifted his hand and brushed his thumb over the supposed furrowed brows, and Nicholas turned his attention to the window. He often felt as if he were intruding with how openly infatuated the two of them were with one another, to say nothing of the kiss he'd interrupted in the elevator.

"You underestimate Diana's enthusiasm," said Miss McCarthy. "It's compounded by the fact that it isn't just you." She turned in her seat to face Nicholas and grimaced. "Diana has already asked if you're hot."

"Hot?" asked Nicholas.

"She's referring to your looks," explained Luke. "Hot means very handsome."

Ah. A much more bearable topic and one that would hopefully cease their gestures of adoration for a moment.

"Pray tell, what was your answer?" Nicholas lifted a brow, not bothering to temper his smirk.

Miss McCarthy turned around and cast her gaze out the front window. "I ignored her."

His grin widened. "Are you embarrassed to admit you find me dashingly attractive, Miss McCarthy?"

"There are only two people in this car, besides myself, that I would call attractive. Luke is very handsome, and Katherine has exquisite eyes."

Well, he should certainly be offended...and would if he actually cared what she thought of his appearance.

"She thinks *I'm* sexy," said Luke, amusement lacing his tone. "It's the accent."

Miss McCarthy faced him and rolled her eyes. "I like you for more than your accent."

"Thank heaven for that as I am not the only British man in the world. But since we are on the subject, you never *did* tell me what it is you appreciate about me...physically."

Miss McCarthy's face turned a very dark red.

Gads. Nicholas had no desire to listen to this conversation. He started to say as much when Katherine interjected, "What precisely does sexy mean?"

For several long moments, everyone remained silent. Luke broke the awkwardness with a chuckle. "Yes, my dear Maggie, do tell her precisely what it means."

Miss McCarthy scowled at him and then turned to face Katherine. "If you find a person sexy, it means you have a desire to...to—"

"Kiss them," Nicholas blurted. He had a good idea what *sexy* meant, and a desire to kiss them was not it. He had no reason to protect Katherine's innocence. She was engaged and would discover the truth of things soon enough, but he had been unable to stop himself all the same.

Miss McCarthy appeared nothing short of relieved at Nicholas's intervention. "Exactly. Kiss them."

Katherine's brows knitted, and her gaze shifted to Nicholas. She studied him, and the deep contemplation she exhibited with her furrowed brows and tilted head made his heart race. Was she...was she deciding whether she found *him* sexy?

"Well," said Miss McCarthy, tapping her fingers rapidly over her little box. "I believe I'll tell Diana she can formulate her own opinion once we get there."

Nicholas shifted on his seat, causing the belt to dig into his shoulder.

"You may tell your friend that my looks do not matter as I am to be here for only one more day. Perhaps not even that. It would be best if we returned to our own time."

"You can't leave yet," said Miss McCarthy, the words almost pleading. "A good night's rest is best before time hopping. And besides, the doctor said we were supposed to observe you in case of concussion. Right, Luke?"

Luke passed her quick glance, his brows raised. "Of course."

Suspicious, indeed.

"That reminds me." Miss McCarthy held up her box. "Would either of you mind if I took your picture? If you intend to return to eighteen fifteen tomorrow, I would love to have something to remember you by." She glanced at Luke. "Both of us would."

"Picture?" asked Nicholas, narrowing his eyes on the box.

"Do not worry over it," said Luke. "Cameras are completely harmless. Think of them as instantaneous portrait makers. Like an artist trapped in a box."

Nicholas rubbed his forehead. He wished to know how the machine worked, but something told him he would not comprehend an explanation even if one were offered. So, he settled on agreeing to Miss McCarthy's request. Katherine agreed as well and appeared far more enthusiastic to have her portrait taken with the little box.

Miss McCarthy held it close to her face. "Alright, the two of you scoot a little closer together."

Nicholas swallowed before his heart could jump out of his throat. "I beg your pardon?"

"Just for a second." Miss McCarthy swatted at the air as if the breeze she created would shift him in the right direction. "You can suffer being uncomfortable for that long."

The problem was he would not suffer at all. He would enjoy it, and that was a dangerous thing, indeed. Keeping his distance yesterday had been difficult enough, especially when Luke and Miss McCarthy seemed intent on matchmaking. Had Katherine not been engaged, Nicholas might have appreciated their meddling, but circumstances being what they were, his friends were encouraging something that simply could not be.

Burying his frustration, Nicholas shifted slightly closer to Katherine. She smelled differently today, no doubt due to the strange modern soaps she used, and while the fragrance remained appealing, Nicholas found he missed the soft floral scent she usually carried.

"Maggie, your father claims the camera adds ten pounds. Said so when he was watching the news." Luke tapped his finger to his chin, his expression thoughtful with a hidden hint of mischievousness. "Do you suppose that's true? Nicholas is overly concerned about the figure he cuts."

Added pounds? What the devil did that mean? And he was not *overly* concerned about his figure.

Only averagely concerned.

Miss McCarthy shrugged. "Sometimes. Would it kill you to smile, Nicholas?"

"It may if it encourages the camera to add ten pounds," Nicholas snapped, still uncertain whether Luke had been teasing him. "I shan't do anything that might put my delicate *figure* at risk."

"Don't be a drama queen. The camera doesn't *actually* add ten pounds. The wrong angle just makes it appear that way."

"What a comfort that is."

Luke's betrothed glared at him over the top of her box. "Smile,

Nicholas. It isn't as though I'm stealing your soul."

"You continue to be the voice of encouragement, Miss McCarthy."

Warmth enveloped his left hand, and Nicholas turned to find Katherine beaming at him. Her fingers gave his a squeeze. "If you're scared, you may hold my hand. I shan't let the box steal your soul."

There was a sparkle in her eyes, a mischievous one. She was teasing him.

No—she was *flirting* with him. He'd never seen Katherine do so with anyone. What did that mean? *Did* it mean something? Either way, he would not let the moment go to waste.

His mouth lifted into a wide smile. "How fortunate I am to have you as my protector."

A clicking sound drew his attention.

"Well done, Katherine. I got him." Miss McCarthy lowered her box and grinned with satisfaction.

"Got me?" asked Nicholas. "But I was not facing forward."

Miss McCarthy rotated in her seat to face the window. "Still got precisely what I wanted, and don't you dare complain." She glanced over her shoulder, and her gaze dropped briefly to where Katherine held his hand before she turned back around. The car hummed to life when she inserted the key, and she guided the contraption onto the road.

Meddlesome woman. He hated to admit she had done him a favor, even if that favor was one he should not want.

He glanced down at his hand, tucked securely within Katherine's smaller one, and fought the urge to intertwine their fingers. How long would she hold onto him? Would she remain that way if he made no effort to move? The longer they sat there with their hands—which he was keenly aware were touching without gloves again—warming each other, the more his heart pounded. Minutes ticked by, and it was not until Miss McCarthy pulled onto a road crowded with more cars that Katherine finally slipped her hand away.

She did so slowly, her cheeks displaying a rosy hue. "Has your soul remained intact?"

"You have successfully kept me safe. I am forever in your debt."

Katherine's eyes searched his face, though what she was looking to find, he couldn't say. Her brows furrowed slightly, but she said nothing, lost to her thoughts as he knew her often to be. He recalled the hint of mischievousness that had settled in her warm eyes when she'd flirted with him. It had vanished now, but he would remember it so long as he lived. Katherine had never teased him with such coyness before—or any man, to his best knowledge—and it raised questions his mind had no business asking.

He remained in close proximity to her, aware of every movement she made. Even her breaths did not escape his notice when each inhale caused her arm to brush against his own.

Not for the first time, he resented the idea of returning home. Here in the future, he had opportunities that eluded him in 1815. Lady Garrick would never allow him this close to her daughter. He had never had so much time, and yet so little. Two days would not be enough.

No amount of time would *ever* be enough.

California, 2023

Nicholas

The road filled with more cars, and Nicholas could only assume they approached their destination. He watched out the window as the scenery shifted to an endless stretch of buildings. After expressing his awe, Miss McCarthy assured him they had not quite reached Los Angeles.

Nicholas brushed away her implications, for how could a city be much busier than what he already saw outside his window?

He had never been more wrong.

Buildings of unfathomable height stretched into the sky. What must be thousands of homes and all manner of businesses passed by so quickly he hadn't the time to take them all in. The road became so crowded with cars that he felt a sliver of anxiety. Luke gawked out his own window, clearly just as humbled by the scene. Los Angeles was beyond description.

"This," Nicholas began, unsure how to put his observations into words, "is far more than I expected."

"I cannot disagree," said Luke. "Are all cities of the future like this?"

Miss McCarthy chuckled. "I guess not all. Many are smaller, but some are also larger."

"Larger?" Luke and Nicholas both questioned at the same time.

"Yeah. I believe Tokyo has the largest population."

Katherine leaned forward, her eyes shimmering with excitement. "How many people do you suppose live there?"

"Hmmm, let's find out." Miss McCarthy grabbed her small box and held it out to Luke. "Hold down on the circle button for me, please," she instructed once he had taken it.

The box beeped.

"What's the current population of Tokyo, Japan?" asked Miss McCarthy.

To Nicholas's utter surprise, a feminine voice responded. "The current population is approximately thirteen million, with an estimated thirty-seven million in the surrounding metropolis."

"Thirty-seven *million?*" Nicholas's mind had no way of processing such information. "What is the world population?"

Luke held down on the button again, and Miss McCarthy relayed Nicholas's question to the woman in the box. She answered with an astounding eight *billion.* Billion! It seemed impossible, but the view out his window washed away any notion the statistic was incorrect.

"May I try?" asked Katherine.

Miss McCarthy nodded. "Of course."

Luke showed Katherine what to do, and she spent the next several minutes asking the woman trapped inside the box questions. They began as statistical inquiries but eventually progressed into random queries about the most random aspects of the future. Regardless, the information fascinated Nicholas, and he smiled watching Katherine's insatiable enthusiasm.

According to the clock at the front of the car, they had maneuvered through the busy streets of Los Angeles for nigh on three quarters of an hour. Miss McCarthy guided the car down a narrow street and parked in front of a two story brick building.

She heaved a sigh and leaned forward to rest her head on the wheel. "We're here, and I'm exhausted."

Luke rubbed his hand in circles on her back, and Miss McCarthy whimpered contentedly. By no means had they arrived in their relationship easily, but it was clear to Nicholas they had found their way to happiness despite the challenges before them. For time travel was, by his estimation, the grandest hurdle any couple could possibly face. Luke had given up everything for the young woman, and Nicholas knew his friend held no regrets. He had never seen the duke so happy.

"Shall we go inside and rest?" asked Luke. "I think we are all looking forward to a respite."

Miss McCarthy scoffed. "None of us will find rest with Diana, but yes, we should go inside."

Luke grabbed the two portmanteaus from a compartment at the back of the car and together they walked to the door on the bottom level of a wide structure with the number *278* on it. One knock was all it took before it flew open. A woman with long brown hair wrapped Miss McCarthy in a tight embrace, jumping wildly up and down with a scream.

"You're here! *Te extrañé, chica.* We have so much to talk about." She released Miss McCarthy and faced Luke. "You must be the duke. Maggie has told me all about you, but she will have to tell me most of it again since I thought she was crazy the first time and didn't commit the information to memory."

Miss McCarthy turned to Nicholas and answered his unspoken question. "No one believed I'd traveled through time when I first returned. Well, almost no one."

Her friend swatted the air. "Whatever, you can't blame me. I mean, *time travel.*" She glanced over Luke and nodded. "At least you came back with a fantastic souvenir to prove you'd been there."

"Diana," Miss McCarthy ground through gritted teeth.

"Technically, I did not come back with her," said Luke, his expression all amusement. "I was delayed."

Diana held up her finger, and her lips curled. "Right. You were lost in customs for a few months."

Luke tilted his head from side to side. "I've no idea what customs is, but lost is an accurate word to describe my four months of misery."

The woman leaned close to Miss McCarthy, and her dark brown brows lifted to the top of her forehead. "I like him, Maggie. You picked a good one." Her attention shifted to Nicholas, and the way her eyes raked over him made his stomach knot. "And you must be Nicholas."

He gave her a polite bow. "A pleasure, Miss...?"

"Just Diana."

Nicholas attempted to keep the unease from his expression. He had no desire to be overly familiar with this woman whether it was customary in the future or not. He had not even taken to calling Miss McCarthy by her Christian name.

"A pleasure, *Miss* Diana. You may call me Lord Keswick. Thank you for allowing us to encroach on your hospitality." There. Perhaps that would be enough for her to comprehend his wish to retain propriety. Miss Diana grinned. "I think I like you, too. *Lord Keswick.*"

DIANA'S APARTMENT WAS SMALL—TOO SMALL FOR NICHOLAS'S LIKING due to it forcing more proximity with Diana. The entryway, which was little more than a few square feet in size, immediately led into what resembled a tiny drawing room with two settees and a forest green chair. Across from the furniture, a desk with a large black box, thin like the one Miss McCarthy used for taking pictures, displayed images that moved.

More than moved—they looked real.

Nicholas's jaw dropped. He was vaguely aware of the conversation happening around him, but his attention could not be swayed. How did they get people inside of that thing? The inn they had stayed at last night had possessed one too, but Luke had refused to show him what it was. Now he understood why. It threatened to overwhelm his mind.

"You have lost him, I'm afraid. I did not take the time to show him the TV at the hotel." Luke placed a hand onto Nicholas's shoulder. "Diana has convinced us to spend the night and says you and I are to sleep out here. The ladies will take the bedchamber. She has but one."

"Bedchamber," said Diana. "Why does it sound so much more...*enticing* when he calls it that." She wafted air to her face with an invisible fan.

"Diana," Miss McCarthy chided.

"What? It's true. Bedroom doesn't sound nearly as sexy."

At this, Katherine's gaze shot up from the floor. "Rooms can be sexy?"

Miss Diana opened her mouth to respond, but Nicholas cut her off. "I am quite fascinated with your picture box. Would you tell me more about it?" He gestured to the desk, while simultaneously giving Diana a look he hoped conveyed the previous conversation had come to an end.

"The TV?" asked Diana. "I don't have a clue how it works, technically speaking." She grabbed something from the arm of the settee and pointed it at the picture box. The images shifted to a new background and people.

Nicholas gaped.

Diana grinned, and a mischievous glint flickered in her eyes. "Would you care to see the rest of the apartment, Lord Keswick?"

He would very much like to see more. Modern machines and inventions fascinated him, but spending any amount of time alone with Diana was bound to make him uncomfortable.

So he turned to Katherine. "Would you care to tour the apartment with me?"

Her lips lifted into a hesitant smile. "I would be glad to accompany you."

Flutters filled his stomach at her endearing meekness. He offered Katherine his arm out of habit, and only when he caught Diana staring did he wonder if such customs were nonexistent in the future. Now that he thought on it, he hadn't seen Luke escorting Miss McCarthy around in such a way since they arrived.

"I believe we shall stay here." Luke grabbed Miss McCarthy's hand,

and she squealed when he pulled her down onto the settee into his lap.

Nicholas wrinkled his nose, but the expression faded the moment Katherine's hand settled in the crook of his elbow and sparks fired through his arm. He cleared his throat. "If you would lead the way, Miss Diana."

Diana's eyes narrowed, but only briefly. "Follow me."

The woman led the way into the kitchen where she proceeded to describe the room with thorough detail. Nicholas reluctantly released Katherine. It would appear silly for him to stand in the kitchen with her on his arm. Then again, perhaps it appeared that way to Diana, regardless.

He could admit Diana's dark hair and eyes made her a handsome woman. She exuded an attractive confidence that many gentlemen would find appealing. Her skin held a warm tone, unlike the many ladies of his acquaintance whose color was often exceptionally pale by comparison. It suited her, though.

Once Diana had finished her detailed tour of the tiny kitchen, they followed her down a hallway with doors leading to a privy and a bedchamber. He insisted there was no need to see the latter. They'd had enough discussion about sleeping quarters already.

Katherine remained quiet through it all, and Nicholas fought the urge to draw her closer, to abandon Diana and her tour to have a moment's respite from the woman's attention.

His desire was granted when Diana asked them to give her a moment to make use of the privy. "Just wait here, and then I'll show you the backyard."

The door closed, leaving him and Katherine alone in the hallway. Katherine released his arm and approached the painting that hung on the wall. It was nothing exquisite, but she studied it all the same, her brows drawing together as her expression turned pensive.

She was beautiful, especially when lost to deep thought. For the first time, he found himself with the opportunity to discover what she was thinking without interference from his friends or her mother, and he intended to seize it.

California, 2023

Katherine

The painting of the sea should have calmed her, but being alone in the hallway with Lord Keswick left Katherine anxious in a way she was unaccustomed to feeling. How the man could comfort her one moment and make her exceedingly unsettled the next, she did not know. Perhaps he was not responsible at all and merely reminded her that their time in the future approached an end.

She had promised Nicholas they could go home after two days. He was right to worry about the gossip their absence would cause. What if it ruined her engagement to Lord Emerson?

Her stomach twisted, but it was not with concern. Part of her *hoped* this venture would lead to an end in her betrothal. How could things have changed so much so quickly? She should be happy to have gained the attention of a man of title, to have been offered for. Why was it no longer enough?

Lord Emerson was a good man and a fine match, she told herself. The reminder did nothing to erase the dread swirling inside her. If she were no longer engaged—

No. She would not allow her thoughts to explore the notion. She *was* engaged, and she should focus on contriving a story to recount upon their return. Inventing something that would sound realistic without endangering either of their names would prove difficult.

Her stomach grumbled, and she pressed her hand to it as if that would stop its demands.

"Someone is hungry."

Nicholas's deep voice startled her, and she spun around with a squeal. One foot caught on the other, throwing off her balance. She lifted her hands to catch herself before hitting the floor, but a strong arm wrapped around her waist and settled her against the wall next to the painting of the seaside.

"My apologies," said Nicholas. "I did not mean to frighten you."

"Perhaps I should apologize. It is miraculous that my growling stomach did not scare *you*."

His mouth twitched. "I would like to think it would take more than that to make me cower in fear, unless you have wolves hidden in there?"

"Certainly. Ravenous wolves who clearly require dinner soon if they are to remain amiable."

"Ah, so now I know how to appease Katherine Garrick. Feed her wolves. A handy bit of information should the occasion arise that you are less than amiable."

She tilted her chin to look up into his eyes. Their color held more blue today, though green still dominated the stage. She wondered if Nicholas's eyes changed color with the weather or his mood. Her brother, George, experienced such changes, his blue coloring often fading to a stormy gray.

"Is something amiss?" Nicholas whispered the question, searching her expression. Only now did she realize how close he stood and that his hand still rested on her waist. She could feel the warmth from his touch seeping through the thick fabric of her sweater.

Heat flooded her cheeks. "No, nothing. I was only admiring your eyes." Another wave set her skin aflame. "What I mean is that I find their change in color fascinating."

She dropped her gaze, and it landed on the spot where his hand rested on her hip. Nicholas immediately released her, as though she'd brought the placement to his attention. He cleared his throat and backed away a pace but said nothing.

After several long moments, she dared to look at him again. He was tapping his fingers against his thigh and staring down the hallway. How she wished to know what he was thinking. She often wondered if there could be more between them than friendship, but at times he seemed eager to keep her at a distance. His actions utterly confused her, but she convinced her mind not to linger on them. What did it matter when she was meant to wed someone else?

It should not, yet she was finding it increasingly difficult *not* to wonder—to imagine what being courted by Nicholas Betham would be like. How it would feel to have his lips pressed against hers.

Drat.

She clasped her hands in front of her, dousing the imagery. "Perhaps we might discuss our plan."

His brows furrowed. "Our plan?"

"Yes. Unless you have changed your mind about returning home soon?"

"I have not. I believe it the best course. We will be under scrutiny as it is."

She nodded despite the urge to beg for more time. It was no longer about seeing the future, though that did hold a great deal of appeal. She *needed* time to sort out her thoughts and feelings. More importantly, she wanted that time to be spent with Nicholas, an admission that was causing her a great deal of doubt and frustration.

But staying was not what the marquess wanted, and she dared not attempt to persuade him.

"What shall we tell our families when we return?" she asked.

Nicholas folded his arms, and the sleeves of his shirt tightened against them, revealing the curves of his muscles. She tried not to stare, but the man was making it impossible not to admire him. First his eyes; now his arms. Heaven help her. Perhaps going home truly was for the best.

"I have been giving it some thought," said Nicholas. "Our story must be believable, but we must also be certain it does not leave room for anyone to question your reputation."

"*Our* reputations. Yours is as important as mine."

His lip curled upward with his chuckle, the expression only highlighting his strong jaw-line and high cheekbones. For goodness sake, why must he be so handsome?

Or *sexy*, as Maggie had termed it, for Katherine certainly had the desire to kiss him.

"No, your reputation is far more important in addition to being salvageable," said Nicholas.

Katherine crossed her arms to match his and scowled. "I do not believe you are a rake."

"Is that so?" He smirked, and drat it all if the expression didn't make him more handsome.

"Am I incorrect in my declaration?" she asked.

"No, but you will find few who agree with you."

He sounded amused, but she had given this a great deal of thought. Nothing gave evidence better than personal observation, and she had not seen anything to suggest Nicholas could claim the title of a rake. "A theory does not have to be widely supported to be the truth. How much of human progress was made because someone believed differently than everyone else? Society is wrong, and you can prove it to them. You need only discover the source of the rumors and set them to rights."

Nicholas released a long exhale through his nose. "I know the source, and applying to the person's good nature has led to Fiddlestick's end. Nothing can be done for my reputation, but I refuse to allow yours to be tarnished, especially by me."

She wished to argue with him, to tell him it was not too late to paint a different picture—the correct picture—but he continued before she had the chance.

"We were abducted and, after three days, managed to escape our captors."

"Abducted? By whom, and how when we were in the duke's study? It is not as though he keeps scoundrels about the estate."

Nicholas tapped his finger on his pursed lips. He had fine lips.

"A fair point. Perhaps you were in need of fresh air, and I escorted you to the veranda. We were abducted there."

"That will do, but for what purpose were we abducted? Our nonexistent scoundrels never asked for a ransom or demanded an exchange for our return."

He held up a finger. "I have it. One of my business ventures went south. The blame fell to me, and these scoundrels sought their revenge. You were merely an innocent taken to ensure no one alerted the constable."

"So the scoundrels never wanted me?"

"No. Yes." His brows knitted together. "Do you *want* the scoundrels to want you?"

She lifted a shoulder, far too pleased with the game they were playing. "I suppose it depends on what sort of scoundrels they are. Perhaps they were pirates."

"Pirates?"

"Certainly. And they took me hostage to assist them in their search for lost treasure. My talent with numbers would prove useful in analyzing the island—one off the coast of Spain, most likely—for the best places to look."

The corners of Nicholas's eyes crinkled. "And for counting the discovered bounty, I presume? These particular pirates were not good at mathematics."

"Precisely; they were terrible mathematicians."

"I see. You were the target and I the innocent bystander?"

She could not stop herself from grinning. "Yes, and the pirates hit you on the head, thus incapacitating you. But they did not successfully knock you out, as they had thought, and you followed them."

"Ah, I am to be the hero, then?" He waggled his brows, making her laugh.

"Do you *want* to be the hero?"

Nicholas hummed, his expression a façade of contemplation. "Quite honestly, I would have preferred to be the pirate who abducted the beautiful mathematician."

Her heart doubled its efforts, and she attempted to ignore the effect his coquettish remark had on her. "I'm afraid that would not work in this instance, unless the pirate intends to return me home."

Nicholas's smile widened. "Of course. He is an honorable pirate, after all."

"Honorable, but terrible at mathematics."

"No, he only pretended to be terrible at mathematics to procure a reasonable excuse to abduct you."

Katherine nibbled her lip. She had been enjoying their game up until now. Not that Nicholas's attention was undesirable, but his words confused her. Did he truly think her beautiful, or was this nothing more than entertainment for him?

She looked down at her clasped hands and fiddled with her fingers. "And why did the pirate want to abduct me if not for finding treasure?"

He was quiet for a moment, and when he finally spoke, his tone had changed. "Because by doing so he hoped to claim the greatest treasure of them all—your heart."

Her breath grew stale in her lungs. Was Nicholas still the pirate they were discussing? He stared at her with no trace of tease, but surely he could not mean the things he said. He had never attempted to court her, never hinted that he wished to do so.

Katherine had always possessed a blind eye to flattery and its implications. Surely Nicholas's words could be nothing but harmless flirtations that lacked depth of feeling.

But why did that knowledge pain her heart so much?

Nicholas

SOMETHING HAD SHIFTED IN KATHERINE'S DEMEANOR AFTER HIS last comment, that much Nicholas knew. He'd gone too far with his flattery, a near confession, in truth. He did believe her heart was something of a treasure—an unobtainable one forever out of his grasp. Admitting his feelings would do neither of them any good, though, and he would do well to steer clear of topics that would lead him to divulge deep emotions that could never be fully expressed.

The door to the privy opened, and Diana stepped out. "Should we continue our tour?"

"Yes—"

"No, thank you—"

Nicholas looked at Katherine. He was ready to be done with their so-called tour, but apparently she was not. "I am happy to continue if that is what you wish."

"I suppose I do."

That did not sound at all convincing, and guilt settled in his stomach.

His choice to reveal too much of himself had chased away the ease between them. He needed it back.

Diana's eyes darted between them, and she tilted her head with a pensive look. "Alright, then. Follow me."

They walked slowly, Katherine at his side and Diana in front of them, down the narrow hallway. Nicholas thought to offer Katherine his arm, but the uncertainty of what had passed between them prevented him from doing so.

When they arrived in the kitchen again, Diana glanced at him over her shoulder. " So, are you dating anyone, Lord Keswick? Someone as handsome as yourself must have his pick of women."

"Dating? If you wish to know if I am presently courting anyone, then the answer is no." And not for lack of trying with one woman in particular.

Diana stopped and laid her hand on his arm. "I don't suppose you would consider staying in the future? I can think of a few friends who wouldn't mind getting to know you."

Nicholas gave her a tight smile, resisting the urge to pull away from her. "A lovely sentiment, but I'm afraid I must return. Though you are welcome to visit anytime."

"Shame I don't possess pearls that would allow me to do that," said Diana.

"A terrible shame." It wasn't. Nicholas had no desire for Diana to visit him, but playing the game of faux flirtation was one he knew how to win. Society expected it of him given his reputation, and when the *ton* expected something, it had a way of transforming a person whether it was their true character or not.

Nicholas glanced at Katherine and found her looking at him—or more specifically, the hand Diana still had on his arm. There was a great deal of emotion in her expression, and he could hardly sort it all out. Disappointment certainly stood at the forefront, but there was hurt hidden in her brown eyes.

Had he caused that? His stomach sank.

"So." Miss Diana drew out the word, her attention set on him and Katherine. "What do the two of you think of the future?"

The question seemed to pull Katherine from her thoughts, and a smile appeared on her lips. "It is amazing. I cannot believe how much things have changed. I wish we could stay longer. There is so much to see."

The disappointment in her tone niggled at him. He wished they could stay longer as well. Not only was the future fascinating, but he longed for more time with Katherine. His interactions with her would be vastly limited once they returned, and soon, they would nearly cease altogether.

But they could not remain in the future. He had an estate to look after and a title to pass on. Luke may have gotten away with handing the dukedom over to Edwin, but Nicholas did not possess that convenience. He had no siblings. The duty to marry and continue his family line rested on his shoulders.

And Katherine had Lord Emerson waiting for her.

"I know how exciting it is here," Nicholas said in a sympathetic tone, "but would you not miss your family if we stayed?"

Katherine sighed. "I would miss them—I *do* miss them. You are right, of course; we must return. I can only fathom how worried they must all be." Her eyes widened, and she pulled in a sharp breath. "Your mother! She is likely out of sorts with worry."

Nicholas shook his head. "My mother may worry, but my greatest concern remains that the two of us disappeared together."

"You are still concerned for our reputations."

He nodded. "Two days is a long time, Katherine. Plenty enough for rumors to spread."

Her gaze dropped to the floor, and Nicholas noted the change in her features. More disappointment than fear, but why?

"Yes, Lord Keswick. And as you have stated before, you would not wish for our names to be tied in that way."

Nicholas swallowed. He had said those words, but only now did he realize how they must have sounded to her. She believed him against such an intimate connection, and he was, but merely to keep her reputation unblemished. Katherine was engaged. Too much time in his company would not only jeopardize that but also attach scandal to both of their names. His own was less concerning as the *ton* already viewed him as a rake, but he had vowed to never ruin a lady's reputation. He would not become his father. Even during his attempts to gain permission to court Katherine he'd worried the inescapable rumors would damage her. Had the Garricks approved, the *ton* might have considered him reformed, at least, but without their permission, the damage would have been insurmountable. It was that reason alone he had not addressed Katherine directly with his wishes of courtship.

"Katherine, when I said—"

"I think I could use some air," said Katherine.

Miss Diana averted her gaze. "There's a patio just through the kitchen. And a tiny yard." She gestured in the direction of said place, her brows tight with what Nicholas believed to be confusion.

"Thank you," muttered Katherine. She swept past them and did not stop even when he called after her, asking if she would like company. "No, thank you." She tossed the words over her shoulder, and Nicholas felt a stab of guilt. He hadn't thought his insistence to keep their names from mingling would have offended her. He certainly hadn't meant them the way they were interpreted.

"Well." Miss Diana crossed her arms. "Are you going to go after her? You've apparently butchered something, but I'm not really sure I understand what."

"I have not butchered anything. And your ridiculous flirtations did not help matters."

Diana rolled her eyes, but she did him the courtesy of lowering her voice. "I was trying to get a reaction out of her, you dolt. You're obviously head-over-heels. I wanted to know if she was, too. I gave up for real flirting with you the second I stepped out of the bathroom and saw the way you were looking at her."

"My apologies," replied Nicholas with a sarcastic tone. "It is rather difficult to tell the difference, what with you asking me to stay and court your friends."

"As if I would have ever let my friends date you. If you stayed, I'd keep you for myself."

He fought a shudder. "I think not."

"Glad we cleared that up. Now, will you go after her already?"

"I do not need anyone interfering in my business." He gave her a pointed look he hoped conveyed a warning to cease with her interference. These matchmaking efforts, well-intentioned as they were, did not help him. They made things decidedly more difficult.

Still, he needed to explain to Katherine what he'd meant—that he did not find the idea of their names together distasteful. Quite the opposite.

"If you will excuse me." He walked past her but not quick enough to miss the look of triumph on Diana's smug expression. He was ready to go home.

California, 2023

Nicholas

Nicholas paused at the door. The tiny veranda was comparable to the car in size and had a black, metal railing around three sides. The fourth remained open to a set of stone-like stairs that gave way to a path leading through a fenced area of rocks and odd-looking plants with spiky needles. Katherine stood at the railing, staring out over the grass with her back to him, her arms wrapped about herself. She inhaled, and the breath shuddered on the way out. He wanted nothing more than to enfold her in an embrace, to reassure her in every way he could not.

He'd bungled things with his words, but he suspected Katherine had departed for more reason than that. Diana's flirting bothered her. At least, he believed it had. Katherine's actions indicated a certain amount of jealousy, but to what depth, he was unsure. Regardless, her reaction filled his thoughts with questions. If she was jealous, could it mean she...

Nicholas shook his head. Such thoughts would only wound him further. He walked across the veranda and stopped behind her, whispering. "Katherine, are you well?"

She turned around, and he noted her glazed eyes.

"I am"—she heaved a sigh—"frustrated."

"Diana—"

"Not with Diana. I am frustrated with myself, with my lack of understanding."

He hadn't expected that answer, and he reared back slightly. "Your lack of understanding?"

"Yes. I do not understand flirting."

Nicholas laughed. He should not have, but the sound came out before he could think. He started to apologize, but Katherine's giggles stopped him. She covered her mouth with her hand until they subsided.

"How ridiculous I am." She shook her head, sending strands of her blonde hair tossing against her face. "I cannot comprehend even the most basic social interactions."

"You have managed well enough till now. It should not matter." Should not, but he knew the *ton* would disagree with him.

The sun had nearly set, leaving only a spray of color to streak the horizon. Katherine drew in a deep breath and looked up at the sky, unwittingly entrapping his gaze with her loveliness. "So many lights make the stars difficult to see. I like the future, but I would miss counting them. It calms me." She leaned against the railing and gripped the top as she peered over. "I might count the rocks, but that is hardly the same."

Nicholas chuckled and stepped forward to stand next to her. "Ah, but the rocks shall take offense hearing you say such things."

She turned to face him with a lifted brow. "The rocks would be offended?"

"Jealous of the stars who so fully captivate your attention. For it would be a grand life, indeed, to be the recipient of your time and focus. I shall take a grain of jealousy for myself."

Katherine tilted her head, her expression taking on her usual analytical front. She studied him in a way that made him internally squirm. What did she see? What conclusions did her mind draw of his character? He may never know; asking her personal questions only ever served to deepen his attachment. He could not afford to do so, not when she would soon be tied to someone else, thus shattering his heart with no hope of recovery.

"You are flirting with me," she said finally. Her voice was like a reverent whisper, soft and uncertain.

"Yes, I was."

Her lips turned down in a frown. "Why?"

"I..." How was he to answer? Katherine had never recognized his flirtations before today, and now she had called him out on it.

Evidently seeing his distress, she turned to face the lawn. "Forgive me. You must think me quite the saucebox with my constant questions."

"Not at all." Nicholas hummed, reconsidering his answer. "Well, I suppose you do fit the definition, but I do not mind in the slightest."

Her smile filled his insides with fluttering feathers. The night needed no moon or stars when she was capable of illuminating the world around her. He would miss having her light in his life, a candle doused far too soon and lost to the shadows. Or perhaps taken to shine where he could no longer see it.

He tensed when her hand settled on his arm. There was no coyness as there had been with Diana, only pure curiosity. What was she thinking?

"If you truly do not mind, then I must ask you to explain flirting to me. I trust your honesty."

He had changed his mind. He did *not* wish to know what she was thinking. "Explain?"

"Yes. I do not understand the idea of flirtation. Is it not meant to gain the attention of someone of interest? To *show* one's interest?"

"It does hold that purpose oftentimes."

"Then why do men flirt with so many women at once—no, not just men. Women do so as well. Diana has flirted with both you and Luke today."

Nicholas ran a hand through his hair and stopped at the back of his neck, attempting to rub away the heat building there. "Flirting is simply an enjoyable way to interact with others. I suppose I cannot speak for women, but men often flirt to pass the time—amuse themselves—and yes, to show their interest in a lady."

Her brows furrowed as she chewed on this response, and he waited on bated breath. She dropped her hand from the railing and turned to face him fully. "How does one determine which sort of flirtation is being offered?"

Nicholas taped his fingers against the metal bar. How did one tell? He'd never given it much thought. Most of the flirtation he received had been vain and shallow. "I suppose a man interested in more than amusement might use a different tone, or their teasing may be different than what they typically offer."

Katherine's nose scrunched. His answer made little sense to himself let alone to someone completely uneducated in the art of flirtation. But how could he better explain?

"I want you to demonstrate," said Katherine.

He stilled. "What?"

"Show me the difference between flirting for amusement and flirting out of genuine interest." His face must have reflected some degree of horror because she stepped closer and grabbed his hand. "You are the only man I would ask such a thing of, and I need to understand."

He should be flattered that she would trust him with this—value his character high enough to make the request. And he was, but...

No. He absolutely could not do this. It would be the death of him. It would lead him to say and do things he very well should not say or do.

"Please," she whispered. "I shall never ask another impertinent thing of you again."

He took in a slow breath, and all the while, Katherine's pleading eyes worked on his resolve. Gads.

"If I must, but know that my flirting is bound to be different than another man's flirting, and doing so on command will have less effect." It would, he instructed himself, because if he were to flirt without restraint...

He simply could not.

"Thank you, Nicholas." She squared her shoulders and released his hand. "What is something flirtatious you would say for amusement?"

He thought for a moment and then cleared his throat. "Good afternoon, Miss Garrick. Lovely day for a walk, is it not?" When she returned a confused expression, he leaned closer, catching the scent of her soap. "Pretend it is a sunny afternoon."

She caught on to his intention of play-acting and smiled. "A lovely day, indeed, Lord Keswick. The sun is delightful after our recent bout of rain."

"Ah, 'tis true, but not nearly as delightful as your smile."

"Thank you—oh! That is very subtle."

Nicholas chuckled. "Subtle was my intention, yes."

"I see. Now show me how you would do it if you were interested in courting me."

If he were interested. If only there were any question to his desires, then he might not find this situation so stressful. "I...well, I would..." He swallowed and met Katherine's gaze. Her brown eyes penetrated him to his core. They provoked him. Consumed him. Drowned him. He could not disabuse her of the idea of asking him impertinent questions, and he found in that moment, as he so often did, he had no desire to disappoint her by remaining silent. He had done many foolish things in the past, but this moment was about to trump them all. "I would tell you how sunlight catches the golden flakes in your eyes, giving them a depth so mesmerizing that it steals my breath. I would tell you how your smile makes my world brighter even on days when the sun cannot escape the clouds."

Her cheeks filled with color, and the desire to keep the endearing shade in them fueled him to continue. "If I wished to simply flirt without consequence, I would meet your gaze across a crowded ballroom, offer a charming smile, and look away. But if my intentions were to take on a deeper note, I would meet your gaze with stilled breath and hold it until the lack of air finally forced my lungs to expand."

He took her hand gently in his own and brushed his thumb over her bare skin. "If I wished to flirt with you purely for amusement, I would greet you by bringing your hand to my lips and leaving a quick kiss on your gloved knuckles." He performed the gesture, keeping his sight firmly on her face. "But should I wish to convey more, I might wait until not a soul were watching and leave the same at your exposed wrist, slow and tender, lingering there until I was certain the touch would forever haunt you."

He should stop; he knew he should. This was not how a gentleman behaved. His sense of honor warred with his desire and ultimately lost. Nicholas dropped her hand and took a step closer. He wrapped an arm around her waist and pulled her to him. She gasped softly, and her hands came to a rest on his chest. Surely she could feel the harsh beats beneath his shirt, his heart threatening to break free of its prison. Surely she would put a stop to his advances and push him away.

But she did not.

Katherine stared up at him, anticipation dancing in her coffee brown eyes. She held his gaze with a look of firm resolution that did not waver even as he slid his hand to the small of her back. He lifted the other to her cheek and noted her subtle shift as she leaned into his hand. "If I wished to show you my deepest affection, I might steal you away to the gardens and hold you like this."

His gaze dropped to her lips, slightly parted and inviting. He could take them for his own, and Society would never be the wiser. He tilted his head, eliminating a few more inches from between them until little remained, and whispered, "I might even kiss you."

California, 2023

Katherine

K atherine had never expected a love match. Marriage was, according to her father, nothing more than a business agreement between two people. Happiness need not be in the equation, let alone any notions of *love*. Her parents certainly held little affection for each other, after all, but the two of them were content with their circumstances.

But right now, Katherine had never been surer that her parents had applied the wrong solutions to their marriage of convenience. Could two people who had agreed to tie themselves to one another for the sake of wealth and title become something more? She had never considered it, but then, she had never thought much about love at all until Nicholas Betham questioned her about loving Lord Emerson.

Thank goodness for the strong arm enveloping her waist, for the way Nicholas was looking at her made her knees wobble. His steady gaze ignited something akin to fire in her chest.

"You might kiss me?" she whispered, willing him to close the remaining space between their lips and deliver on his statement. She wanted him to kiss her—heaven knew she did. It would be unlike anything she'd ever done. No experience told her this. More like an instinct, something deep within that assured her just as it proclaimed this was right.

His fingers splayed over her back, sending a shiver up her spine, and the warmth of his breath tickled her cheek when he spoke. "I might..."

Something shifted in his expression, as though he had come to some realization.

Katherine grabbed a handful of his shirt and pulled, but Nicholas strained against it. His brows furrowed, and disappointment threaded through her. His arm fell away, and he took her hands and gently pried them from his clothing. The soft squeeze he gave them before releasing did nothing to appease her heart.

Nicholas backed away two paces. His throat bobbed with a hard swallow. "I hope I have demonstrated properly enough."

Too properly if she were to be honest. Had that all been for her benefit? She had asked him to show her the differences in flirtations, but it had turned into more than that...at least for her. Perhaps he had not felt the charged air between them.

Nicholas Betham was known by the *ton* as a rake. It had taken Katherine some time upon entering Society to grasp what exactly that meant. To her knowledge, the man should enjoy the pleasure of drink and the stealing of hearts he had no intention of keeping.

The man before her seemed none of those things. Nicholas had been given the opportunity to kiss her without any repercussions and had forgone it. Either he was not the rake everyone believed, or he simply had no interest in her.

Perhaps both.

"I believe I understand," said Katherine. "Thank you for...informing me of the difference. You are a good friend, Nicholas."

Friend. The word tasted bitter on her tongue. She needed to gain control of her muddled emotions. The marquess did not want her, and even if he did, she was engaged to Lord Emerson. She had accepted the man's proposal without hesitation. She'd had no reason to say no, but Nicholas's question had snaked its way into her thoughts and made her doubt the decision.

She felt more confused than ever.

Nicholas reclaimed the distance he had put between them and took both her hands. She gasped, and her heart sped into an unhealthy rhythm.

"Katherine, I need you to understand. When I said I did not wish for our names to be discussed in the ballroom—to be connected—I did not mean..." He heaved a sigh and looked away. "I would never forgive myself if I ruined you," he whispered, keeping his gaze focused on something beyond the veranda. "Society has painted me as a rake, and any young woman seen spending too much time in my company is at risk of gossip. Especially one who is engaged. The *ton* loves a good scandal."

He started to pull his hands away, but Katherine gripped them. Nicholas tilted his head, a mixture of emotions she could not read twisting his expression.

"What do you believe?" she asked. "How would you paint yourself?"

"I wish to be seen as a gentleman...as a decent man who strives to be honorable." His focus dropped to the ground, and she could see the pain he hid, his mask thinly veiling it as he spoke. "But I fear I will always be seen as quite the opposite. I do not wish to be like my father."

Katherine had heard talk of the former Lord Keswick and his character. Her mother certainly did not approve of him. The man was known for taking mistresses and cared not how young they were or if his actions ruined them. According to her mother, Nicholas was the same. Until recently, Katherine had never questioned the declaration.

"I was not acquainted with your father, but I do feel I know you. Well enough to determine your character is exactly what you wish it to be. You are a good man."

He turned away, and without thinking, she pressed her palm to his cheek, bringing his gaze back to her. "An honorable man who deserves to be painted in the best light."

"That means a great deal to me." He choked on the words, his glazed eyes catching the last of the dimming sunlight. She wanted to wrap her arms around him, offer him comfort or perhaps—

Nicholas placed his free hand on her neck. His eyes roamed her face, full of uncertainty, hesitation, and a flicker of fear. But then he leaned forward, and she froze when his lips brushed against her cheek, tender like the gentle stroke of a butterfly's wings. Heat seared through her, as did the desire to pull him close. Her body, mind, and heart all wanted more.

He lingered next to her ear, his breath caressing her skin with a whisper. "Thank you, Katherine."

Once he had pulled away, Katherine managed to inhale. She'd spent hundreds of hours in Lord Emerson's company, and not once had she felt like this—never lost the ability to breathe. Not once had she thought to kiss him or wish beyond measure for him to kiss her.

If only Nicholas felt the same way, saw her as more than a friend.

"We should go back inside," said Nicholas. He squeezed the hand he still held. "Miss Diana will be insufferable as it is; worse if we stay much longer."

Katherine laughed, packing her emotions and thoughts away for later. "She may expect more of your attention."

"More than I wish to give, I assure you. I would much rather remain out here with you."

Her stomach fluttered. *Flirting,* she told herself. It was only more flirting, and not the kind that suggested he was interested. Nicholas had shown her what *that* would be like.

She shook those images away. "Thank you for instructing me. I fear I overanalyze everything and it often leads to confusion rather than understanding."

"You enjoy numbers and equations. An analytical mind is crucial for such an interest. There is nothing wrong with—"

"People are not like numbers, Nicholas." She leaned against the rail and sighed. "People are complicated. Society may set rules but even they do not always dictate how a person will act or respond to a given situation. Numbers are easy. They follow patterns; they obey principles and laws without fail. They do not leave room for guessing as to how others feel...what kind of flirtation is being offered."

"Your inability to comprehend is a gift, Katherine."

She scoffed. Surely he was not serious? "How could that be a gift?"

"Because it affects the way you present yourself. What everyone sees is who you truly are. There's no disingenuous presentation, no façade, no pretending. You leave no one to guess at your true nature." He leaned closer. "You are honest in everything you say."

"I am a social nightmare according to my mother."

"No. You are beautiful." He tucked a strand of her hair behind her ear, his knuckles brushing over her cheek. A shudder wracked her body. Was this more flirting? He lacked the twinkle she often saw in his eyes. His stoic expression said he had no intention of teasing her, but he could not mean to flirt with genuine interest.

Could he?

She pushed down her irritation. If only she understood people as easily as she understood numbers.

"Lord Emerson is a fortunate man," said Nicholas, his tone carrying an underlying sadness that left her further confused.

"Lord Emerson barely knows me. If he is like most of society, he will not appreciate my follies any more than my mother does."

"Is that why you wished me to explain things? You fear what he will think of you?"

She had never confessed her concerns to anyone out loud for fear of being mocked. She knew the expectations set by her family, by society, and could only hope to change her disapproving ways before the marriage. But confessing those concerns to Nicholas did not leave her feeling the fool, but rather understood. Listened to. He would not judge her for her folly. He never had. "I do not want to offend Lord Emerson or bring dishonor to his name. Embarrassing him in public concerns me as does how he will respond. So, I have put myself to studying people, hoping I will learn to be perfectly sociable...to be a good wife."

Nicholas's frown deepened. "You need not change anything about yourself to be a good wife. Lord Emerson will understand in time. He will *love you* in time. How could he not?"

How could he not? The words echoed through her mind, and she longed to believe them. Nicholas spoke with such sincerity, yet he did not love her. The admission constricted her chest with disappointment, an emotion she knew should not be there.

She closed her eyes, willing her thoughts to veer away from the unfamiliar pain. "I wish I was confident that my impending marriage could be built on more than an agreement; the idea of a love match had never been a consideration until…"

Until Nicholas had asked her if she loved Lord Emerson. Until she had seen the way Luke looked at Maggie, as though she were the most precious treasure in his life. Until Katherine realized what she had deprived herself of by accepting Lord Emerson's offer.

She heaved a sigh. "Regardless, watching Luke and Maggie has proved helpful. I can at least recognize flirting now. They are constantly doing so with each other."

"Can you?" Nicholas grinned, and her heart stuttered. Something in his eyes promised mischief, but she welcomed it—welcomed his attention and the way it made her feel.

She lifted her chin. "I can. Certainly better than before at the very least."

"Perhaps you need a test."

"A test?"

He nodded. "A test to see if you notice my flirtations."

Heavens, this was a terrible idea. She already had feelings she could not quite sort out. Nicholas flirting with her would make things worse—

more confusing. On the other hand, she needed to practice if she had any chance of being prepared. With only two weeks remaining until her wedding, time was not a luxury she could enjoy.

"Very well, but I shall pass. I always took the tests from my governess quite seriously."

His smile returned. "I have no doubt." He pushed away from the rail, and his increased proximity did nothing to calm how anxious she felt for accepting his challenge. He rubbed a hand over his chin. "I will proceed once we return to our time. I shan't flirt with you anymore in front of Diana."

He offered his arm. They walked back inside the house, and Katherine dreaded the moment when he would let her go. Things were different when she was close to Nicholas—different in a way she could not explain.

"There you two are." Diana had taken a seat on the settee across from Luke and Maggie. "I was starting to wonder if I should check on you."

Nicholas's arm tensed beneath her fingers. "We managed quite well without you."

"I'm sure you did." Diana smirked, which only seemed to irritate Nicholas further given the way he shifted on his feet.

Did she think that they had kissed? Katherine's face heated. Diana would be disappointed right alongside her.

Diana stood. "Well, now that you've...finished, what do you say we get some dinner?"

"Someplace inconspicuous, Di," said Maggie. "We've kept under the radar so far, but I don't want to take any chances."

Katherine bit her lip. They had stayed out of the eye of would-be pearl hunters...probably. She hadn't forgotten the man who watched her at breakfast and the eerie feeling she got with him there. He had not followed Katherine when she left to find Luke, Maggie, and Nicholas, and for that reason alone she had kept the strange encounter to herself. Perhaps she had been overly suspicious.

"I promise," said Diana. "I know the perfect place."

California, 2023

Nicholas

Saddles and Spurs—that was the name of the inconspicuous place Miss Diana had chosen to have dinner. Nicholas supposed it was, given how few people were currently inside the building. Last night Miss McCarthy had fed them *fast food*, which Nicholas quickly learned was prepared with the kind of haste a man running from a constable might display and then delivered through a window. The food itself was interesting, but not something he'd readily request from his cook at Ravenhall, and he wondered if tonight's meal would be different given they had actually gone inside and sat down at a table.

The five of them took up a spot in the back of the building, empty tables and chairs surrounding them. Luke sat next to Miss McCarthy and

Katherine at Nicholas's side while Diana seemed content to take the space between the two women. A glossy sheet of strange, thick paper was placed in front of him by a young man with wiry red hair and an abundance of freckles. He was young, not more than seventeen if Nicholas had to guess.

"What would you like to drink today?" the young man asked.

"Root beer," said Miss McCarthy without pause. She turned to Luke, a mischievous smile crossing her lips. "Should we order that all around?"

"I, for one, shan't ever drink root beer again." Luke turned his attention to Nicolas. "You are free to give the stuff a try, but I would advise you to take small sips."

Small sips? Curiosity provoked Nicholas to request the beverage, and to his surprise, Katherine did the same. Luke asked for water, which made Nicholas more suspicious of the entire situation, and Diana requested lemonade.

The young man returned a few minutes later, placing a glass with a dark-colored liquid in front of Nicholas. He heeded Luke's advice and took a small sip. The drink left a tingling sensation on his tongue, much like soda water, and the sweetness far exceeded that of the ratafia often served in the ballroom.

"It is not terrible but certainly not my drink of choice."

"I like it," Katherine stated matter-of-factly and then took another drink of her own. Nicholas smiled when she smacked her lips together. She was enjoying her time in the future. Luke's revelations about the pearls and those who sought them still set him at unease, but he had no intention of relieving Katherine's lovely face of the happiness it displayed. He'd promised her two days.

"Good afternoon!" A plump man stared down at them with a wide grin, holding his rounded stomach with one hand and resting the other on his hip. "I'm Eugene, the owner of this establishment. Have you come for the challenge?"

"What sort of challenge?" asked Luke.

"Why, the Monster Saddle challenge, of course! Two strapin' men like yourselves could handle it, I bet. One two pound burger on a nine inch bun loaded with the works and a side of my Mama's hand-cut fries. Finish it all in an hour, and your party's meal is on the house. Plus"—he jutted his chin toward the back wall—"you get inducted onto the Wall of Fame."

Nicholas had learned from his meal of fast food the day before what a burger and fries were. He had handled that with ease enough. Surely this could not present as much challenge as the man implied.

"And if we fail to finish?" asked Luke. His brows raised in obvious interest yet his tone gave nothing away.

Eugene shrugged. "Then you pay for the meal and suffer embarrassment in front of your ladies. Forty bucks is all it costs. What do you say?"

Luke turned to Miss McCarthy, and she held up her hands. "Your choice, but if you and Nicholas intend to have a duel of gluttony, us women should offer something to motivate your success since it will pay for our food as well."

She had that twinkle in her eyes again. Nicholas hated that twinkle.

Luke grinned. "What did you have in mind?"

Miss McCarthy hummed for a moment, but her expression lacked genuine contemplation. The woman knew *exactly* what she would offer. She pointed to an elevated platform at the other side of the room. "If you finish the whole thing in the allotted time, I'll kiss you on the karaoke stage in front of everyone."

"Deal," said Luke without so much as a second thought.

Nicholas looked heavenward. What an enamored fool.

"That is an excellent idea." Diana turned toward Nicholas, and the look of expectation in her eyes left him completely unsettled. "I'd like to offer some motivation, too."

No. Absolutely not. He would not be accepting any kisses from Miss Diana.

She chuckled at what he could only assume was pure horror in his expression. Miss Diana shifted her attention to Katherine. "There are two of us, though, so I suppose Lord Keswick will just have to choose who he'd rather have a kiss from."

Blasted woman.

How was he to answer that? Naturally he'd prefer Katherine, but she was off-limits. Engaged. Intended for another man in a few weeks time. He could not kiss her.

"I am happy to participate." Katherine's voice was quiet, and she refused to meet his gaze. Her cheeks filled with a soft pink that betrayed her embarrassment to even make the offer.

He couldn't let her do this. He'd almost kissed her once already; a second temptation would kill his resolve completely.

"You needn't participate if it makes you uncomfortable," Nicholas rushed to say. "I can manage without more motivation."

It was food. That would prove satisfying without a reward.

Katherine considered him for a moment, her head tilted and her lips pressed tightly together. He tried not to stare at them, but it did little good. His mind began imagining things it should not imagine.

"It would hardly be fair if everyone but me contributed," said Katherine. "I insist. A kiss on the cheek is more than manageable."

Nicholas tapped his fingers against his thigh, failing to douse the thrill that shot through him. Well, if she insisted, then he could hardly tell her no. He had kissed her cheek, after all. "Are you certain?"

She nodded and offered him a careful smile. "So long as you will not take offense to the gesture?"

Offense? He had never been less offended by anything in his entire life.

"Offense is hardly the word I would use," said Luke.

Nicholas glared at him.

"Sounds like Nicholas has made his choice," said Diana with far too much satisfaction. "I'll just have to be a cheerleader."

Eugene clapped his hands with a thunderous bang. "Fantastic! I'll see to the orders, and we'll get something for ladies as well." With that, he trotted off, his eagerness evident in his steps.

The longer Nicholas waited for his *Monster Saddle*, the more uneasy he became. He wanted to impress Katherine, though how impressed she would be by him gorging himself, he couldn't say. Still, the thought of receiving a kiss, even one that merely graced his cheek, was more than enough to lay abandon to how ridiculous this whole thing had become. He likely should avoid earning a kiss entirely, but a peck on the cheek was harmless enough.

He shifted on the bench, uncertain the last thought was accurate. Katherine's touch did things to him—reason aplenty to abstain from situations where any part of her made contact with his body. *She is engaged*, he reminded himself. A kiss on the cheek would mean nothing.

"Here ya go!" Eugene held his arms out wide as two servers placed enormous platters in front of Nicholas and Luke. "As the owner of this fine establishment and a five-times champion myself, I wish you the best of luck."

Nicholas's eyes rounded. "I am to eat all of this?" He had never eaten this much in one sitting, and his confidence wavered. The burger was at least twenty times the size of the one he'd consumed yesterday.

The owner held up a finger. "And you must do it within one hour."

"Right." Nicholas glanced at the mound of salted potatoes. "And those as well?"

"Those as well." The man called to the worker standing behind a tall counter. "Gerald! Start the clock!"

If Luke held any uncertainty about the challenge, his expression did not portray it. The duke dove into the meal the moment the owner shouted for them to begin. At first, Nicholas took on the strategy of shoving as much food into his mouth as quickly as he could, but the endeavor became hindered by his curling stomach.

He might be sick before this was over.

The few other people who were in the establishment gathered around to watch. They cheered, many of them downing what Nicholas guessed was alcoholic beverages. Luke ate slowly but with a stoic expression that Nicholas envied. The former duke had always hid his thoughts and emotions well, which made him exceptionally formidable at cards.

Not that Luke often indulged in gambling. Nicholas refrained from such behavior as well, but the rumors floating through the ballroom would suggest otherwise.

"Fifteen minutes!" Eugene yelled.

Nicholas swallowed a large bite and closed his eyes. He was unsure his stomach could hold all of this. In fact, he was quite certain it could not, yet for some reason he continued to stuff pieces of bread and meat into his mouth.

He finished off the last of the burger at the five minute call. That left the fries, and simply looking at them made him wish to cast up his accounts. Luke had slowed considerably as well, his expression finally reflecting some discomfort.

"You've got this!" Miss McCarthy shifted closer to Luke and squeezed his shoulder. "Almost finished."

Nicholas pressed his fist to his mouth. He only had a handful of fries remaining, but...

"You can do it, Nicholas!" Katherine's petite fingers settled on his arm, and an explosion of heat coursed through him. "You mustn't give up now."

No, he most certainly mustn't. His eyes drifted to her lips, briefly, but the reminder of what awaited him was enough. He grabbed the remaining potatoes and swallowed them with a minute to spare. The crowd erupted into a commotion of screams and hoots. Luke finished what remained of his platter and more noise followed. They had done it.

Eugene clasped Luke on the shoulder as the crowd dispersed. "Well done, boys. I'll give you a few minutes to digest, and then the ladies can offer their contribution before we take your picture."

Nicholas leaned back in his chair and lifted his gaze to the ceiling. "I shall never do that again. What in heaven's name were we thinking?"

"About your impending reward, I'd imagine," said Miss McCarthy.

Nicholas tucked his chin and narrowed his eyes at her. "Perhaps I was merely hungry."

"Hungry, I have no doubt. But not for food." Miss McCarthy waggled her brows.

Ridiculous woman.

Eugene returned and with far too much enthusiasm escorted them to the raised platform across the room. Luke stepped up onto the stage first and offered his betrothed a hand to guide her into his arms. Without a moment's hesitation, his lips eagerly descended on hers, and they slipped into a passionate kiss that made the other customers whistle and clap.

Somehow it both lasted too long and ended too soon, for now it was Nicholas and Katherine's turn. A wave of anxiety swept over him. For the second time today, he was doing things he knew he should not. This kiss would be his undoing.

He took to Katherine's side and leaned close to her ear. "You are under no obligation to do this if you have changed your mind."

Katherine grabbed his hand and started up the stairs to the stage, pulling him along behind her. His heart raced. It was a simple kiss on the cheek. Nothing more. Katherine had agreed to this only because she wished to participate, and he would not make more of it than that.

They stopped center stage, and Katherine turned to face him. The crowd's excitement did nothing to curb the tension building between them. Nicholas tilted his head to one side and bent at his midsection, offering his cheek. He kept his gaze on the crowd. He told himself it would mean less if he did not look into her eyes while she kissed him, but it was a lie. The sensation, should it be anything like he imagined—and he fully anticipated it to be—would irrevocably undo him.

Every day spent thinking of her, every moment watching her in the ballroom just out of reach, and every rejection he'd accepted from her parents—*everything* he'd endured would be made worthwhile by one simple kiss on his cheek.

The crowd cheered them on. Katherine's subtle shift on her feet caused his muscles to constrict with anticipation, and he closed his eyes.

Warmth spread over both sides of his face, coaxing his eyes open, and Katherine's petite hands guided him to face her fully, her soft voice filling his ears. "Nicholas."

He took in every speck of color in her eyes amidst the sea of brown. The flakes of gold there sparkled in the light pouring from overhead. He still needed to ask Luke how the odd candles worked, but the thought was put from his mind when Katherine lifted slightly on her toes, bringing her lips even closer to his.

He tried to turn his head, but her hands kept him from doing so. She studied his face, and his breath caught when her gaze landed on his mouth. Surely she would not *kiss him* kiss him? He certainly wanted her to, perhaps more than he'd ever wanted anything.

But what would he do if she did?

California, 2023

Katherine

The persistent chant of the crowd became drowned by the loud thumping of Katherine's pulse in her ears. She stared at Nicholas's lips, and the desire to feel them on her own consumed her. It was as if every part of her wanted to feel the warmth of his skin against hers. *Needed* to feel it.

She brushed her thumbs over his face. His eyes fluttered, and his throat bobbed with a hard swallow. Did her touch affect him the same way his did her? Did he feel the same sense of urgency and desire?

She could not know for certain without asking him, and doing so in front of a crowd did not seem fair. He would never confess to such a thing with this many listening ears. Perhaps she could deduce his feelings without words.

Holding her breath, she leaned closer, her eyes set on his face, waiting for any reaction that might change her course. Nicholas's hand lifted to her waist, and warmth seeped through her clothes despite the gentle pressure he applied. He did not push her away but rather drew her closer with a subtleness she questioned was reality.

Her mind wanted to analyze every movement, every line in his expression, but her body had ideas of its own and, without her expressed permission, eliminated the gap between them. Her lips landed on his, and Nicholas went completely rigid, the fingers at her waist digging into her side. The crowd demanded he return her kiss, but he did not heed them, leaving her to pull away with burning cheeks.

Nicholas had not wanted her to kiss him so intimately.

Regret pooled within her. What had she been thinking? How improper he must think her to force an unwanted kiss on him.

Katherine backed away, and Nicholas's hand fell loosely to his side. She averted her gaze, unable to stand his wide-eyed expression of horror any longer. What a fool she'd acted.

Against her better judgment, she peeked over at him. He had plastered on a forced smile and was staring out over the dispersing crowd. Once most of the people had returned to their tables, he took her hand gently, avoiding eye contact, and guided it to his elbow. "Allow me to assist you down."

Katherine nodded, but he likely hadn't seen her acceptance given how he refused to look at her. Ever the gentleman, he escorted her off the stage, and she released his arm the moment they reached the bottom. He sighed heavily and closed his eyes.

"Are you well?" she asked, sidling closer to him so only he would hear.

Nicholas looked down at her. "I feel as though I have eaten ten courses, but otherwise, a picture of good health."

He smiled, and she relaxed somewhat. "That is good."

Nicholas studied her expression for a moment and then gently took her hand. Why must hers fit so perfectly in his? She gave no resistance as he led her through the crowd to a corner where they could avoid being overheard so easily. Still, he whispered. "Are *you* well?"

"No. Well...." She nibbled on her lip. It was best to be done with it. "I am merely concerned that you are upset with me for kissing you in such an untoward manner."

He looked affronted. "Upset?"

"You appeared displeased when I did so, and I—"

"Katherine." Nicholas turned to face her fully and took her other hand so he was holding both. "I am certainly not upset with you. Your kiss was unexpected, yes, but you needn't apologize for it. We had agreed beforehand."

"I agreed to kiss you on the cheek and cannot blame you for reacting so stiffly. I haven't the experience of kissing anyone, cheek or otherwise. Perhaps I did not do it correctly." She wanted to believe that was the reason for his poor reaction, but she suspected her gesture had appalled him. What must he think of her? She was uncertain she wanted to know, and it was easier to cling to her lack of experience as the reason, unlikely as it was. "I have never witnessed a proper exchange of affection until tonight when Maggie kissed Luke. What makes a kiss satisfactory?"

"I..." Nicholas's brows furrowed, and his thoughts seemed at war, keeping him from responding. Her question was impertinent, and she'd promised him hours ago there would be no more of those.

She could add lying to her unending list of poor qualities.

But she wanted an answer all the same. She had never considered flirtation or kissing as an art that should be studied in order to execute them properly. Should she not know how to do these things as a woman about to become a wife? Lord Emerson would expect both, would he not?

That was all this had been. She needed to ensure she could be a proper wife. For Lord Emerson. Her intended.

She rushed to continue when Nicholas remained silent. "You needn't worry that I shall take offense. I could tell my kiss provided you little pleasure, but I beg of you to answer my question. I shan't know how to do better, and I trust you to be honest with me."

"Honest?" Nicholas swallowed, and for whatever reason he appeared more worried now than he had on the stage. Drat. The poor man looked positively horrified.

"Forgive me. I should not have asked you such a thing." Perhaps she should flee to the car before she could say anything else that would put her upbringing into question.

She began to step away, but Nicholas's hold on her hands tightened. "There is nothing wrong with your kisses, Katherine. My response was purely due to surprise and...restraint. I assure you, if you weren't presently engaged, I would have..."

The admission, or near admission, made her pulse race. Nicholas Betham had wanted to kiss her on that stage, only he'd been too honorable to do so. The realization both filled her with guilt for having put him in the situation and thrilled her. Perhaps she *had* mistaken their exchange on the veranda. Was it possible Nicholas had been genuinely flirting with her and not simply educating his friend in the art because she'd asked?

It should not matter. She was engaged, as the marquess had just reminded her. Yet on the stage, Lord Emerson had been far from her mind, perhaps not in it at all. Nicholas must think her the worst sort of lady, throwing her affection at him when she was meant to marry another man in a matter of weeks.

Her heart sputtered. Affection. Until now she had not admitted it fully to herself. Somehow she had developed a *tendre* for the marquess. Somehow he had changed the way she viewed marriage and misaligned all her hopes for the future.

Which was why she needed him to finish his statement. "If I were not engaged, would you have kissed me back?"

His green eyes pierced her, unrelenting yet cautious, but his words were firm with a confidence she could not question. "Undoubtedly."

Nicholas's gaze dropped to her lips, and desire gripped her. If only he would forget her engagement as she had, just for this moment. Just long enough to press his lips to hers.

But if she had learned anything with confidence during their journey to the future, it was that Nicholas Betham was not the rake everyone believed him to be. Twice he'd had the opportunity to kiss her and chose not to do so. A rake would not have hesitated. A rake would not constantly concern himself with maintaining her reputation.

Mama was severely misinformed.

"Are the two of you alright?" Maggie's question startled Katherine out of her thoughts. She, Luke, and Diana had joined them away from the crowd. "The owner wants to put Nicholas and Luke's picture on the wall. He's gone to get his camera, but I think it might be best if we go."

She glanced behind her. The establishment had become more crowded as the evening dragged on, thus reducing their ability to remain inconspicuous. With all of these people here, someone might take notice—

Katherine gasped when her eyes landed on a familiar face. Staring at her from across the room was the same man who had watched her at breakfast. Her pulse quickened as his dark eyes bore into her. She'd had a terrible feeling about him that morning and brushed it aside. But now...

"We need to leave," she said, turning quickly toward Maggie. "There's a man here who's watching us."

Maggie's face paled. "Watching us? What do you mean?"

"I saw him this morning while I ate breakfast. I thought perhaps he was just grumpy with the way he scowled, but it cannot be a coincidence that he is here now. The odds of that are close to nothing."

"Agreed," said Luke just as the owner returned holding a tiny black box. Before Eugene could speak, Luke cut him off. "We need to leave. Is there another entrance to the building?"

Eugene's brows furrowed. "Sure. Through the back, but—what about your pictures!"

They neared a dark corridor, and the owner's pleas blended with the chatter and music. Luke led Maggie by the hand toward a glowing sign that displayed the word *exit,* and Katherine, Nicholas, and Diana followed. A door at the end of the hallway opened to the outside, and the moment the chilly air filled her lungs, relief washed over Katherine.

Luke kept his hasty pace. "Let's get to the car."

"Where are we going to go?" asked Diana, her tone filled with concern and unease lining her expression. "If they've pursued you this far, won't they follow us back to my place?"

The question stopped Luke in his tracks, and he scrubbed a hand over his face. "She is right. We cannot go back there. At least not together."

Diana gave him a pointed look. "I'm going with you guys."

"It will be safer if you do not. They are not after you."

Maggie grabbed Diana's arm, her tone and expression pleading. "Please, Di. Go home, lock the door, and I'll call you once we're safe. Promise."

With reluctance, Diana agreed. Luke escorted her to the street where Maggie said Diana could catch a cab while the rest of them waited in the alleyway for him to return with the car. Katherine leaned against the brick exterior of the building and drew in a slow breath. Perhaps the man had yet to realize they had escaped, but he would not remain ignorant for long.

Luke returned within minutes and assured Maggie that Diana was safely on her way home. "The car is out front. Let's go before—"

"You're discovered?"

The deep voice emanating from the street sent chills down Katherine's spine. The same man who had been watching them inside stood in their path of escape. The street lamp revealed that his scowl was gone, replaced by a smirk that heightened his dark features and the foreboding ambiance he emitted.

Luke positioned himself in front of Maggie, and Nicholas did the same for Katherine. The security their barriers created did not last, however. The door they had exited through minutes before opened, and two men entered the alley, successfully boxing them in.

"Who are you?" asked Luke.

The man at the head of the alley crossed his arms. "Landon Atton. I can't say I know your friends"—he looked pointedly at Katherine and Nicholas—"but I need no introduction to the two of you. I know Miss McCarthy quite well, having watched her for a number of years. You, *Your Grace*, were an unexpected surprise, but I believe I have your character down fairly well based on the information Gerard sent us."

"Gerard?" Luke's brows formed a deep frown. "You were the person he claimed to be working for."

"Guilty," said Landon. "I had hoped my cousin could manage the task assigned to him without assistance, but...well, we know how that ended, don't we? Naturally I had to ensure he wouldn't talk to anyone while in prison. That required me to cash in some favors I'd hope to save, and losing a family member is never easy. A sacrifice to our cause."

"You had Gerard killed?" asked Maggie.

Landon shrugged. "I keep a tight hold on the information revolving around my efforts and an even tighter hold on those privileged with it. A small ring of people I trust. But Gerard failed me. Once arrested he became nothing more than a loose end."

Katherine shuffled closer to Nicholas's side. This man was mad, willing to murder his family to get what he wanted. She glanced behind her. The two men who had exited the building had narrowed the gap between them.

"I'd prefer to do this the easy way," said Landon, checking his watch as if he had someplace to be and this was nothing more than a friendly discussion with acquaintances. "Hand over the pearls, and you're free to go."

Luke tucked Maggie closer to him. "I doubt that. You have just informed us what you do with loose ends, and I would wager that is the label you've given us."

Landon hummed, nodding as if amused. "It's a shame you aren't more dim-witted."

He lifted his hand and snapped his fingers—a signal that set the men behind them into action.

Chapter 19

California, 2023

Katherine

Katherine barely had time to inhale before Nicholas's arm wrapped about her waist, and he positioned her next to Maggie. Luke faced Mr. Atton while the marquess protected them from the men approaching in the shadowed alley.

"The moment you have a chance," whispered Luke. "I want the two of you to run for the car."

"What?" Maggie gripped his upper arm, but it didn't draw Luke's attention away from Mr. Atton.

"Please just do as I said."

Katherine swallowed. The duke wanted her and Maggie to escape without them? Could she do it? Could she leave Nicholas behind?

Instinctively, her hand flew to his arm. He glanced at her over his shoulder, not longer than a second before returning his focus back to the men. "All will be well, Katherine. Do as Luke instructed. He and I will be right behind you."

She struggled to believe him, and that would make convincing her feet all the more difficult.

Nicholas swept forward, and her hand slid from his arm. He took with him her warmth and security, and she held her breath as he raised his fist. The first man dodged, and the second caught hold of Nicholas's wrist. He twisted it, cocking Nicholas's arm at an odd angle, and the marquess groaned.

Behind her, Luke had moved into action, shifting from side to side as Mr. Atton drew closer. With the duke preoccupied, Nicholas would have no assistance.

Katherine turned to face him and discovered he'd maneuvered out of the man's grasp. With a sweep of his leg, Nicholas sent one of them to the ground with a heavy thud. The second threw a punch, and Nicholas evaded, firing one of his own back at the man. The hit landed square on the man's jaw, and he stumbled backwards into the brick wall.

"Now!" Luke's shout startled her, and warmth encompassed her wrist. Maggie pulled her forward, and they slipped past Luke and Mr. Atton, who were in a deadlock with Luke pinned on the ground beneath the man.

"Get to the car!" shouted Luke.

Maggie dragged Katherine forward. Her mind ordered her feet to resist but they carried on without permission. She could not stand the thought of Nicholas or Luke getting hurt, but what help would she really be in a bout of fistcuffs?

They reached the car, and Maggie tugged on the handle. "No, no, no. Luke must have locked it."

"And he has the keys?" Katherine guessed.

"Of course he does." Maggie groaned and tugged frantically again. On the third pull, the door gave, and Maggie nearly toppled over. Luke's hands caught her waist and steadied her, and Katherine spun around to see Nicholas jogging toward them, his hair disheveled but no signs of injury on his person.

Thank heaven.

Luke guided Maggie onto the front seat, his gaze never falling from the alleyway. "Get in. I am driving."

"You?" asked Nicholas, still catching his breath. "Do you even know how to work this contraption?"

Luke scowled. "Well enough. I drove it closer to the alley, did I not?"

"Oh, yes. That builds my confidence." Nicholas shuffled around the front door and, placing his hand on the small of Katherine's back, coaxed her into the back. He sat down beside her and closed the door. Katherine started to scoot to the other side so she could also be near a door in case a hasty escape were required, but Nicholas's hand gripped her wrist before she could move more than a few inches. His pleading green eyes flicked to the window where three dark figures raced toward a black car. "Please stay in the middle."

Whether he asked because he wanted her close or merely out of obligation as her present guardian, she was inclined to obey. She reached for the safety belt, but before she could clasp it in place, the car lurched forward. Her shaky hands fumbled over the two pieces as Luke swerved onto the street.

"Luke," said Maggie, clutching his arm. "Keep in mind you don't have a license yet."

"I have not forgotten but am currently preoccupied with not dying." He steered the car around a sharp corner, throwing Katherine into Nicholas, both pieces of the safety belt still in her hands.

"Allow me," Nicholas whispered, so close to her ear that shivers ran down her neck. He took the buckle from her hands and clicked it into place with ease. How could he be so calm? Her heart threatened to burst out of her chest.

Maggie turned and looked past them out the back window. "Luke."

"I know. I see them."

Katherine dared a glance over her shoulder. The black car followed behind them, groaning as it gained ground.

"Blast!" Luke smacked his hand against the wheel used for steering. A car the color of the sky had caused them to slow. "I cannot go around. There are too many vehicles."

"Lu—" Nicholas lurched forward when something rammed the car from behind but threw out his arm to prevent Katherine from doing the same. The belt dug into her neck and stomach, inciting a burning sensation across her skin. The car jolted again, and Nicholas braced himself on the seat in front of him. "Do something, Luke!"

"Would you prefer to drive?" Luke responded with irritation.

"Not if you want to live."

"Then do be quiet."

Katherine smacked into Nicholas's side when Luke jerked the car into another lane. Nicholas wrapped his arm around her shoulder, pulling her close, and she balled a handful of his coat in her hands. She had little else to hold onto, and the constant swerving nauseated her, but tucked against the man at her side she felt secure despite it all.

With another jerk, the car pulled back onto the right side. Katherine peeked over her shoulder. The black car had passed the blue one and was gaining proximity by the second.

"Luke, there's a stoplight ahead," said Maggie with an urgency that knotted Katherine's stomach.

"I am aware," said Luke.

"It's yellow."

"Mmm, hmm."

Katherine hadn't the slightest notion what the color meant, but Luke was not *stopping* at this so-called stoplight. Quite the opposite.

"Luke!" Maggie gripped the armrest of her seat, her eyes wide.

They passed beneath the overhead light, which had changed from yellow to red before they reached it. To the left, a monstrous carriage with more sets of wheels than Katherine could count barreled toward them. The shrill of a horn tore through the air, and Katherine buried her face into Nicholas's side, pinching her eyes closed.

Coming to the future had been a mistake.

Nicholas

THE HORN BLARED SO LOUD NICHOLAS COVERED HIS EARS WITH HIS hands. Katherine buried her face into him, clutching his arm with an iron grip. Other cars voiced their disapproval, but after several moments, the

when she fit so perfectly in his arms. Once they returned to 1815, he would no longer have such an opportunity.

"Katherine," he whispered, rubbing his hand up and down her shoulder. "It's time we went home."

She sat up slowly, and he noticed her eyes were red and tear streaks lingered on her cheeks. The entire situation had been terrifying, and while he and Luke had escaped unscathed, it did not mean that another encounter would have the same result. His concern for Katherine's reputation only took second to one other thing—her safety.

Nicholas lifted a hand to her cheek and brushed his thumb over the tear trail there. "I know you wanted to stay longer, but—"

"I am ready to go home." Her voice was soft, resonating with the fear displayed in her wrinkled forehead and watery eyes. He wished he could smooth it away as easily as the tears.

Nicholas assisted her out of the car. Miss McCarthy rummaged through the portmanteaus in the back and found the clothing they had traversed time in. She directed them to what she called a *bathroom*, which was nothing more than a public privy that had clearly been neglected by whatever servants were in charge of its maintenance.

They changed in separate sides of the small building, Miss McCarthy assisting Katherine, and within minutes they were ready for their return trip home.

"Nicholas, before you leave," Luke began. "I have a request to ask of you."

Nicholas turned to face his friend, and a hollowness settled in his chest. This time, he would have the chance to say goodbye, but he wondered now if that only made things more difficult. "Of course. Anything."

"The pearls must be kept hidden. You have seen first hand what they are capable of doing, and you have also witnessed what those who desire them are willing to do."

Nicholas placed his hand on Luke's shoulder. "I do, and I promise to help Edwin keep them safe."

Luke nodded. "Look after my family. And please tell Edwin that I am happy—that I miss him." He swallowed, and his gaze flicked to Katherine. "It was good to see you, Katherine. Stay safe, and keep this one out of trouble for me."

Nicholas scoffed. "I am never trouble."

Miss McCarthy placed herself between them and offered Nicholas an envelope. "This is for you. Open it once you have returned to your estate."

"Very well." Nicholas accepted the envelope with narrowed eyes but did not question her further, slipping the parcel into the inside pocket of his coat before turning toward Katherine. "We should lie down. I would prefer to not fall over this time."

She nodded, and they found a patch of grass out of sight of anyone else wandering the park. Katherine flattened onto her back and adjusted the skirt of her dress to cover her legs and feet properly. Nicholas joined her on the ground, laying close enough that their arms brushed.

"Are you certain the two of you will be well?" asked Nicholas, directing the question to Luke. "Those men will likely continue looking for you."

"We shall manage," said Luke. "Once they realize you and Katherine are gone, I imagine they will leave us be. We no longer have anything they want."

"Once you're ready, all you need to do is say 'I want to go home'.

The pearls will take the lead from there." Miss McCarthy wrapped her arm around Luke's. "We'll leave you to it. I can't say for sure, but I believe the pearls won't work with non-travelers around. I didn't pass out until after Luke left the room, anyway."

Luke scrubbed a hand over his face. "Yes, because the notion of time travel isn't insane enough, it must only occur when no one is around to witness."

Miss McCarthy chuckled. "I didn't make the rules."

"If I ever find out who did, they will be getting an earful from me." He looked down at his intended, and a wide smile erupted over his face—the one that confirmed he was not the least bit sorry for all he had given up to be with her. "And a thank you."

The look they exchanged was evidence of their deep adoration. Nicholas averted his gaze. At least he would no longer play the intruder on such moments.

"Stay safe," said Luke. "Best of luck to you both."

They said their final goodbyes and left Nicholas and Katherine alone in the shadows on the grass. Nicholas drew in a deep breath, willing his heart to calm. This had been so much easier when he was not expecting to be transported through time. The anticipation curled his stomach.

He rolled to his side to face Katherine. "Ready?"

"Yes. I am nervous, though."

"You needn't be nervous. We have each other. All will be well." He hoped.

Nicholas wrapped his hand around hers. This may well be the last time he ever did so, at least with this sort of intimacy, and he hated the thought. With their return to 1815 came the loss of something wonderful. An opportunity he never thought to have yet had not lasted long enough.

He dug in his pocket, withdrew two small beads from inside, and handed one to her. "Shall we say it together?" She nodded, and he squeezed her hand. "On the count of three, then. One, two..."

Nicholas clenched the pearl until it made his palm ache.

"Three." He tightened his hold on Katherine's hand, and together, they spoke the words that would take them home.

Blushe Justice

Oxford, 1811
Four years previous...

Katherine

The strong arms about Katherine's waist loosened and fell away. Lord Branbury took a quick step backwards, placing distance between them as people entered the garden. His face twisted into one of concern, a reaction she did not understand. He had been incredibly kind to her and her lady's maid, Cecily, offering to help them find their way out of the maze of flowers and plants, but something akin to regret now lined his features.

Footfalls pounded against the stone pavers. Her mother barreled her way through the group of men and women they had been touring the gardens with and stopped at her side, the beading on her dark yellow gown catching the last bit of fading sunlight. She gripped Katherine's arm with an iron hold, her tone and expression frantic. "Are you well? What happened?"

Katherine patted her mother's hand. The woman had a knack for overreacting, especially where Katherine was concerned. Her social blunders, as Mama called them, occurred frequently enough that it was nothing short of a miracle the woman had not succumbed to a fit of the heart.

"I am fine, Mama. Cecily and I merely lost our way in the gardens."

"Lost your way?" Her gaze flicked to Lord Branbury, and the glare she shot him made the man tense. "And who is this *gentleman?*"

Murmurs filled the air around them. Several onlookers, including her uncle and his wife watched the scene with furrowed brows. Her and Cecily's disappearance had gained more attention than Katherine had realized, and the thought of being the topic of so much discussion made her stomach churn.

"I wish to know that answer as well." Katherine's father marched toward them, his eyes narrowed. He stopped in front of Lord Branbury and folded his arms. "I believe I can wager a guess. You look much like your father."

Lord Branbury winced. "It seems I have no need of introducing myself, as you are already acquainted with my family."

Katherine's father grunted. "Everyone knows Lord Keswick. I'd also wager most would prefer not to know him."

Her mother's grip on her arm tightened. "You are Lord Keswick's son? That explains it all, then."

"Mama, that hurts." Katherine pried her mother's fingers away. "What do you mean that explains it all? Lord Branbury offered to assist us."

"Assist you?" Mama scoffed and shook her head. "Assist you into a compromising position, perhaps. I have no doubt that was his intention."

Lord Branbury's face paled. "I assure you, my lady, that was never my—"

"You have been caught in the act. Do not deny it when we came upon you with my daughter in your arms. Learned the practice of ruining young ladies from your father, I am sure." She turned to Papa. "Do not simply stand there! Do something."

"Shall it be pistols at dawn, then?" asked Papa, though the question seemed addressed to Mama more so than Lord Branbury. Papa was not known to be a man of renown shot, and the idea of him dueling for Katherine's honor appeared to rattle her mother. Mama looked between the two men with pensive frustration.

Lord Branbury shook his head, panic riddling his expression. "Please, sir. I meant no harm. I swear it."

Katherine placed herself between her parents and Lord Branbury. She would not let this come to a duel. The entire thing was beyond ridiculous. "Lord Branbury was escorting us to the garden entrance. I became distracted by..." She would not tell Mama it involved a book. "I became distracted and caught my foot on the rocks around the pond. Had Lord Branbury not acted, I would have fallen in."

Papa turned his attention to Cecily, and her maid's voice quivered when she affirmed the truthfulness of Katherine's words. "'Tis what happened, sir."

Mama pursed her lips. "Then I suppose we owe Lord Branbury our gratitude." The words were laced with nothing that would convey gratitude. Lord Branbury seemed to recognize their disingenuity, for he closed his eyes and sighed.

"Very good, then." Papa gestured to the garden path behind them, a fair amount of relief relaxing his form. "I believe it is time we leave. Come, Katherine."

He turned and started down the path. Katherine met Lord Branbury's gaze, and he offered her a sad smile. She would not have him think her ungrateful for his act of service. And for her parents to accuse him so thoroughly in public! She may not have the most graceful decorum, but she did not understand how this encounter had shown her family in the best of light, either.

"Thank you, Lord Branbury," she said, dipping into a curtsy. "I apologize for the...inconvenience." If one could call it that. Pistols certainly would have been more than inconvenient.

"You are most welcome, Miss Garrick." His voice was soft, almost dejected.

It pained her to hear him that way when moments before he had been so full of life, smiling and happy. Her mother's accusations and cold disposition had sucked that all away from him. She understood the feeling, having often experienced it herself over her sixteen years of life.

But she had also learned there was little to be done about it.

She followed her father away from the remaining crowd, Cecily's light footsteps and the swish of her skirts echoing behind her. Just before rounding the corner of a hedge, Katherine turned to look over her shoulder. Mama had moved closer to Lord Branbury, and although she could not see the woman's face or hear their conversation, his expression said more than words.

He flinched, and her mother spun around. She stormed toward Katherine and took her by the arm without a word, practically dragging her along the garden path.

"Mama, what did you say to Lord Branbury? He looked rather put out."

"Do not concern yourself with that man. He's a rake if I ever saw one."

Katherine bit her lip. "A rake? Are you certain?"

"Indeed. His father cares not one whit about the women he ruins. The apple never falls far from the branch. Mark my words, Lord Branbury will have a reputation before the next Season begins, and I shall make sure everyone knows of his despicable ways."

"Despicable? Mama, Lord Branbury has done nothing to deserve—"

"Enough, Katherine. You are yet naïve to the ways of men. You must trust me in this matter."

She trusted her mother's experience, of course, for her own was severely lacking. She had not yet come out in Society, and the rules and expectations often escaped her understanding. Her mother said she spent far too much time with her nose stuck in the pages of books, which was likely a correct notion given how often Katherine ventured to their library at home. She found numbers and equations fascinating and far less complicated than trying to understand people.

But what of Lord Branbury? The man had been kind, offering his time without hesitation and even protecting her from getting drenched. What about his actions suggested him deserving of ill reproof? She could think of nothing. Perhaps she would never understand, but that was why Mama's guidance was to be heeded.

Once her mother had taken a seat inside their carriage next to Cecily, Papa handed Katherine in and joined them. He rapped on the ceiling, signaling for the coachman to set them on their way. Several minutes passed in silence, only to be broken by her father's light snores.

"Katherine, you must take better care when you are out." Mama turned her gaze upon Cecily, and the scrutiny made the poor young woman cower in her seat. "You hold responsibility for this. Why did you venture so far from our group?"

"Do not blame Cecily," said Katherine, her tone sharp. "It was my idea, and I was not to be persuaded out of it. No harm—"

"No harm?" Mama squared her shoulders, her regal posture giving her the air of a queen. "Had you already come out there may well have been a great deal of harm accomplished. Your reputation is fragile, Katherine. To be seen alone with a gentleman in a compromising position, especially the son of a scoundrel, would not bode well. You would be ruined. Our name blemished. No one would want you, and the rest of your days would be spent as a spinster with nowhere to go, living off of nothing more than the good will of your family."

"I told you, Mama. Lord Branbury only kept me from falling in the pond."

Mama scoffed. "It would not surprise me if he led you to the pond with the intention of entangling your feet. A perfect excuse to put his hands on you."

"That is simply untrue." Was it not? Perhaps Mama was right.

"You are to steer clear of the earl," said Mama. "I will not have our name tarnished. Is that understood?"

"Yes, Mama. I understand."

But she truly did not.

Chapter 21

Suffolk, 1815

Katherine

The rustling of leaves drew her eyes open. Katherine stared up at the sky, visible between the bare branches of the tree limbs hanging over her. Gloomy, gray clouds painted in fluffy streaks added to the way the cold nipped at her nose. The ground beneath her felt like a bed of ice though it was devoid of snow.

She exhaled, and her breath rose in a wispy puff like smoke from a fire. How good it would feel to stand next to the hearth now, allowing a warm blaze to thaw her frozen limbs. She could hardly feel the fingers inside her right glove. The left, however, was wrapped in a blanket of heat. In fact, her entire left side felt significantly warmer.

She turned her head, and her nose brushed against the fabric of Nicholas's coat. It smelled like orange and leather, a pleasant mixture that made her stomach flutter in ways a scent should not. His chest rose and fell with his steady breathing, and the small cascade of sunlight breaking through the overcast made his skin glow, reflecting off the moisture that had settled on his cheeks. He had shaved that morning, leaving his face clean of visible stubble. She wished to stroke her fingers along his jaw, just to see if any evidence of it remained.

She pushed herself into a sitting position to get a better look. Slowly, she lifted her hand and, using only her pointer finger, trailed it along his chin all the way to his ear, feeling no resistance on the smooth surface. She moved to his forehead and swept the strands of his hair—a very light brown with hints of blond—to one side, and then followed the contour of his jaw to his lips.

Her finger paused at the corner of his mouth. There was nothing proper about her exploration of his face, but she couldn't deny the desire. She ran her finger over his upper lip and imagined, not for the first time, how it would feel to be properly kissed by Nicholas Betham.

A flurry of anxious energy flowed through her. She should concentrate on something else. He had a fine, rounded nose with a sprinkling of freckles on the tip. She counted seven of them there. His cheek had a few more, five and six respectively, to be exact, and below his eyes—

His *open* eyes.

Flames seared across her cheeks as she took in the green depths staring up at her. She withdrew her hand, pulling away from him, and bit down on her lip. What had she been thinking?

Nicholas sat up, and his soft voice enveloped her like a blanket. "Are you well?"

She nodded, keeping her gaze trained on the dry, leaf-covered ground. She had certainly stared at his face for long enough already. "How do you fair?"

"I am well but admittedly was better before you ceased touching my face."

Another wave of embarrassment pricked her skin. "I thought you were sleeping."

A low chuckle pulled her gaze back to the source of her chagrin. "Certainly I was, until you brushed the hair from my forehead."

Heavens. He was aware of her touching his lips, then. Her face could not possibly grow any hotter.

"Why did you not say something?" she chided though she could hardly blame the man for this awkward situation. *Her* fingers had caused it.

He shrugged but maintained that mischievous smile of his. "I was enjoying it too much to interrupt you."

Her heart attempted to leap from her chest, and she willed it calm. She could not let his words affect her. "You are flirting with me already, are you not? Testing me?"

His smile faltered. "Of course. Merely testing you, though it seems I have no need to do so. You have called me out enough times to pass." He shifted to his feet and offered her his hand. She accepted it, and he pulled her from the ground. "We should go. I recognize this area. It's part of Windgate Estate, perhaps a quarter mile from the house."

"And what shall we tell the duke? Do you think he knows about"— she lowered her voice, fearing that someone might be listening even this far from the massive estate—"time travel?"

"Luke assured me that his brother is aware of the pearls' unusual abilities. Speaking of which." He held out his hand, palm up. "I would prefer to carry them both as a precaution."

She tilted her head. "The people after them are in the future. You don't think they would use Maggie and Luke's pearls to come to our time?"

"You can never be too careful, and as I gave Luke my word, I would prefer not to risk your safety even if the chances are slim."

She placed the small bead she still clenched into his palm, and Nicholas tucked it away inside a pocket in his waistcoat. The notion that someone might attack them here on the duke's estate sent a shiver down her spine, racking her body with a violent shudder.

"You are cold," said Nicholas, his voice carrying concern.

She shook her head. "No, it is just the thought of someone coming after us. I have no desire to be involved in another chase."

"Even so, I can tell you are freezing. The color of your lips is disconcerting."

She lifted her hand to her mouth. "What color are they?"

"Blue." Nicholas shrugged out of his coat and threw it around her shoulders, successfully engulfing her in his scent. "Put your arms in; you'll be warmer."

She did as he instructed, her mind too fuzzy to argue. "Thank—"

Before she could finish, he pulled her to his chest. His arms encircled her, and his hands rubbed up and down her back, leaving trails of warmth wherever they went. Tucked away like this, basking in the heat radiating from him, she realized how cold she had truly been, though only some of the warmth she was experiencing could be attested to the actual temperature. Being in his arms felt right. Safe.

And she was beginning to think that Nicholas Betham thought of her as more than a friend. Now that she understood the reasoning behind his refusal to kiss her, the doubt had faded. This man cared for her, at least to an extent. She felt it in every touch. Every look.

But she belonged to someone else, and given the circumstances, Nicholas would not kiss her. Whether that was a testament to his lack of deep affection or his honorability, she could not say.

His hands moved to her shoulders and worked their way up and down her arms. Katherine rested her forehead against him, just below the folded cravat tied around his neck.

Cold air washed over her when he pulled away. His knuckle tipped her chin up, and she met his gaze. His green eyes wandered over her face before settling on her lips, and her heart stuttered.

"That color is much better." He brushed his thumb over her lips, and her knees nearly gave out. Perhaps she should allow them; Nicholas would undoubtedly catch her, thus placing her back in his arms.

His hand dropped before she could make use of the idea, and he took a step back. "Come. Let's get you out of this weather."

There was a certain soberness to his expression and voice that hadn't been there moments before, replacing the softness and concern. They were in 1815 now, and propriety demanded they obey the rules of society. She would be better off forgetting the time they had spent together in the future, to sever the strange intimacy that had grown between them.

She would do so with reluctance, but the memories, Katherine suspected, would never fade. Nicholas Betham may not have ever wished to court her, but she could not deny the way she felt around him. The man had stolen a piece of her heart, a piece she had never intended to give away.

Nicholas

HE SHOULD OFFER KATHERINE HIS ARM, AS ANY GENTLEMAN WOULD, but keeping space between them seemed more important right now. Spending the last several days with her had deepened his affections to a dangerous level. Being in her presence had grown into more than a desire. It was a need, one that he would soon not have the ability to satisfy. Not returning her kiss after his giant meal had taken every ounce of self restraint he possessed.

"We have yet to decide on a story to tell my mother. I am uncertain the pirates will do." Katherine lifted her skirts to step over a lichen-covered log. Nicholas wondered if she missed wearing pantaloons. It had certainly shocked him to see so many women donning them, and he was not entirely sure how he felt about it. Katherine had said she found them comfortable, though.

"I suspect the pirate story may be lacking," said Nicholas. "Did you have any other clever ideas for us to consider?"

"Not one. I think your original plan may be best. We should go over the details so our stories match when we are undoubtedly asked."

Nicholas agreed, and they memorized their fictional abduction while traversing across the duke's estate. They discussed everything from the number of captors to what the men wore, how many meals they were given to the particulars of their escape—all of it needed to be concise and memorable enough that they would not forget.

An impossible task.

Katherine heaved a sigh, twirling a brown, shriveled leaf between her fingers. "I shall never remember all of this. Two days worth of details for an event that never happened. I see now how easily gossip is spread about the *ton*, always changing and rarely accurate to what actually occurred."

"But that is what makes the gossip so enjoyable for the pickthanks. Whatever they can twist and bend to suit their amusement shall receive the most attention, and therefore, the most alteration from the truth. They need only a small, good seed to begin with, and from there...well, the better the repast, the fatter the pig."

Katherine tightened Nicholas's dirt brown coat around her when a soft breeze swept past them, stirring the few dead leaves clinging to the branches above. "Many could do with skipping a few meals. Why can people simply not mind their own lives? I needn't know everything about everyone."

A full laugh rumbled from his chest, and his reaction brought a wide smile to her face.

"If only society shared your way of thinking." Nicholas kicked a rock and sent it rolling forward. "It would certainly be easier to redeem oneself after a mistake."

Distant memories filled his thoughts—a garden, a lovely young lady, and a troublesome pond surrounded by rocks. Everything had changed for him that day. Before then, he had never held a *tendre* for a woman. Before then, he had not fallen so far from Society's good opinion, the rumors of the *ton* yet to stain his reputation.

You will stay away from my daughter. Lady Garrick's words, laced with a threat he hadn't understood at the time, rang in his mind. He had not stayed away, at least not indefinitely, and with every attempt to be near Katherine, the rumors had grown.

Katherine clasped her hands in front of her, nibbling at her lower lip. She seemed lost to her own musings. When she finally spoke, her tone was soft with compassion. "Nicholas, what mistake do you speak of that has all of society convinced you are a rake?"

He stopped walking and turned to face her. How could he answer? He had long suspected Katherine had no idea how that day in the garden had affected the course of his life. She remained ignorant of how his actions to rescue her had caused both his affections and her mother's disdain to deepen. She likely had no inkling that Lady Garrick was the source of the rumors that plagued him.

And he would not tell her. She was engaged to Lord Emerson. The truth simply did not matter.

He forced his lips upward.

"You needn't concern yourself with my problems, Katherine."

"But—"

"You have returned!" A feminine voice cutting the air with an almost squeal drew their attention. The head housekeeper, Mrs. Bielle, rushed down the garden path, the two-story manor looming behind her, its dark red bricks as intimidating as they were beautiful set against the gray sky.

Katherine gave her a little wave, but the woman did not stop when she neared, instead scooping her into a warm embrace.

"It is wonderful to see you," Mrs. Bielle whispered loud enough for Nicholas to hear. She pulled away, her lips twisting into a mischievous smile. "I cannot wait to hear all about your journey to the future."

Chapter 22

Suffolk, 1815

Katherine

Where Katherine stood, the stone pavers split into three separate paths. Rose bushes separated each one, their branches now bare, but she could imagine the plethora of color that would bloom into display once spring arrived. She had never spent much time on the ducal estate, given that Luke had not been one to hold grand balls or provide social activities, but her imagination filled in the missing details of the barren landscape.

Nicholas paced in front of her, his fist to his chin and an annoyed look on his face. Mrs. Bielle had taken a seat on one of the stone benches positioned at the split between two of the paths. Her eyes followed the man with glittering amusement.

"You shall wear a trough into the ground if you do not cease," said Mrs. Bielle, her words flourished with her French accent.

"Edwin will forgive me," snapped Nicholas. "After all, my frustration is certainly justified."

"You did not have a good trip, then?" The question sounded innocent enough, but one glance at Mrs. Bielle's face told a different story. The situation entertained her, judging by the smug grin she wore.

Nicholas halted and glared at her. "That is not the point. How do you know about the pearls and time travel? Did Luke tell you? Did you know he was still alive?"

Mrs. Bielle lifted her chin. "What difference does it make how I know? But the answers are *no* and *yes*."

A growl not fit for a gentleman rumbled from Nicholas's throat. It sounded more like a lion than anything. "If Luke did not tell you, then who did?"

The corners of the housekeeper's eyes crinkled. "No one."

The marquess ran both hands through his hair, leaving the strands in charming disarray. "No one? How...nevermind. You knew Luke was alive? Why the devil did you not say something!"

Mrs. Bielle narrowed her eyes. "Watch your language, young man; there is a lady present. His Grace knew about the time travel beads, and so did Miss Garrick." She turned to Katherine, and the smug grin she donned turned into a pleasant smile. "She knew about the pearls before Maggie even left our era. But regardless, why would I mention anything that would make me sound touched in the head?"

"Fine. You offer a fair point." Nicholas began his hasty pace across the garden path again, this time with his arms folded. "I cannot believe Luke did not tell me. Did I not deserve the truth?" He halted again, turning his attention to Katherine, his expression pinched with realization. "You knew about them. Did you know Luke was alive as well?"

"I knew nothing for certain," she replied. "I hoped as much, of course, but I confess the notion that either Maggie or Luke had traveled through time...well, I had my doubts."

Nicholas groaned and resumed his march. "Am I the only one who knew *nothing*?"

"You have the truth now," reminded Mrs. Bielle. "And you received a nice gallivant through time. You can hardly be upset, especially given the wonders it has done for your relationship."

"Relationship?" Nicholas scowled. "With whom? Luke?"

"Of course not. With Miss Garrick."

Nicholas stopped so quickly he nearly toppled over. Heat crept into Katherine's cheeks. What did the housekeeper mean by such a statement? Suggesting their relationship had *changed* implied she had been observing them before all of this, but what reason would the housekeeper have to do so?

Fire burned in Nicholas's eyes, the ravenous sort that would disintegrate anything its path. "*Miss Garrick* is engaged. She and I are friends, nothing more." He winced at the conclusion of this declaration, and Katherine found her heart reacted in much the same manner. It felt strangled, tied with a ribbon like one tied a bonnet on an exceptionally windy day.

Mrs. Bielle pursed her lips. "That complicates matters, I admit. Even I did not foresee that bit of detail."

Nicholas cocked his head and gave her an incredulous look. "Did you leave the pearls on Edwin's desk on *purpose*? To play matchmaker?"

The housekeeper scrunched her nose, rows of wrinkles forming between her brows. "Well, I should think that obvious. I ushered you inside and shut the door."

Nicholas threw his hands up with exasperation. "Why must everyone interfere in *my* business? I can handle my own affairs."

Mrs. Bielle tutted her disagreement which only earned her a fresh scowl from Nicholas. The mixture of emotions warring inside Katherine prevented her from adding a word of any kind on the current topic of discussion. Perhaps she might have felt grateful had the marquess not displayed so much irritation and disgust at the mere idea of forming a deeper connection with her.

The thought caused a twinge in her chest. It should not have mattered. As the marquess had so clearly stated, she was engaged. They were only friends and could never be more than that, but it was Nicholas's objection that pained her the most. The admission was accompanied by the agonizing realization that, at some point in the last week, Nicholas Betham, Marquess of Keswick, had wriggled his way into her traitorous heart. Perhaps the man could claim the definition of a rake in one sense— he had stolen her heart with no intention of keeping it.

A cold, sharp wind stirred the dried leaves on the path and whipped her skirts against her legs. Katherine tightened Nicholas's coat around her, but the air dug through the fabric, sending a wave of shivers through her limbs.

It had been easier to stay warm when she had walked next to Nicholas through the woods. The movement alone had kept her blood circulating, and their conversation, easy and carefree, had warmed her in other ways. Now she had neither, and the harsh reality of winter threatened to freeze her solid.

"W-we should g-go inside." Her teeth clattered, and she wondered why no one else seemed affected by the cold. Nicholas was keeping warm with his aggressive pace across the path, of course, but Mrs. Bielle, who was certainly not young in years, appeared completely undisturbed by the nipping air.

Nicholas turned to face Katherine, and the frustration drained from his expression only to be replaced with concern. He shuffled to her side and placed his gloved hand on her cheek. Even through the black leather she could feel the heat radiating off him. He tilted her chin, his eyes almost analytical as they surveyed her features.

"You are turning blue again. We should get you inside."

"Y-you know how to fix it." She attempted a demure smile, but her quivering lips prevented it.

He seemed to recognize her efforts to flirt despite this, however, and chuckled. "I think a fire and cup of chocolate might be better this time."

She disagreed but had no intention of telling him so or displaying her disappointment.

"Yes, we should get the two of you to a fire." Mrs. Bielle approached them, and Nicholas dropped his hand. She directed her words at him, for which Katherine was grateful. Her mind needed a moment to recover from the repeated exposure to Nicholas's touch. "His Grace will want to know of your return. If you would escort Miss Garrick to the drawing room, I shall inform him and send for chocolate."

Nicholas gave her a firm nod and offered Katherine his arm. She took it, and he drew her near. Her heart took on a robust rhythm, and she fought the urge to lean into him. *He merely means to keep you warm,* she told herself. He was concerned...as her friend.

They entered the house from the veranda. Inside, the temperature was far more pleasant, and the escape from the chilly breeze immediately gave her respite. Her lips ceased to quiver, and the uncontrollable clattering of her teeth fell silent. Still, Nicholas kept a tight hold on her. She thought to pull away, to put some distance between them given the way her body reacted to even the smallest touch, but her attempt to do so was thwarted when his muscles tensed to keep her near.

She shuddered, and Nicholas tilted his head to look at her. "You'll be warm soon. And then the real challenge comes."

"You mean telling my mother? Are you as terrified of recounting our false tale to her as I am?"

His eyes rounded in mock horror, and he placed his free hand over his heart. "More terrified than I have ever been in my life."

Had he been serious, that would have been saying something given the events of the last two days.

They passed through a set of mahogany doors, and the warmth emanating from the brick hearth beckoned her. Nicholas guided her to it, and she heaved a contented sigh. The crackling and dancing flames were soothing. She had missed the comfort a fire could bring. Not a single place she had been to in the future had been heated by fireplace. Maggie had mentioned *vents* and *central heating*, but Katherine had decided the hot air coming from the floor was simply magical. Still, there was nothing like curling up on a chair with a book in front of a roaring fire.

Nicholas released her arm and smiled. "Better, is it not?"

"Yes. I did enjoy the future, but this—the familiarity—I have missed more than I thought I would." She ran her fingers along the smooth surface of the mantle, following the wood grain. A clock rested there, along with a few other trinkets and nicknacks that appeared to have been collected from traveling the continent. She assumed they belonged to Luke, as Edwin had not likely had the opportunity to venture beyond England.

Then again, everything on the estate now belonged to Edwin by default.

"It is nice not to feel constantly overwhelmed," said Nicholas.

"Or be chased by a carriage without horses."

He tugged at his waistcoat. "Or wear unfashionable clothing."

Katherine scowled. "I liked the clothing. It was very comfortable. And you said I look beautiful no matter what I wear, or were you simply flirting with me?"

"Yes—no." His cheeks tinted, the glow of the fire accentuating the color. "I did say that, and I meant it, flirting or no. I simply wanted to convey that gentlemen's attire in the future was not necessarily to my tastes."

"Would you prefer the garb of a pirate, my lord?"

He sucked in his cheeks, but it did not prevent the smile forcing its way free. "Certainly, with a large, black hat and a white feather to adorn it."

"What of an eye patch? You would look particularly roguish with an eye patch."

Nicholas reared back with a look of surprise. "Why, Miss Garrick, I am both shocked and flattered." He narrowed his eyes playfully. "Are you flirting with me?"

She shrugged a shoulder. "I did learn from the best, did I not?"

"The very best, undoubtedly."

They both stared at the fire, grinning. The silence that settled between them was tight like a string stretched to capacity and ready to snap. The tension made everything all the more confusing to Katherine.

How was it they could converse and tease so easily, and yet the marquess wanted nothing more from her than friendship? Was this not the same display she had witnessed from Maggie and Luke the last few days?

One thing she knew well enough, her heart had fallen for the man next to her. What was she to do about it? The banns had been read once and would be read again in a few day's time. After the third, she would wed Lord Emerson. Her engagement made the situation complicated, but if Nicholas had been interested, he would have courted her before.

Clearly his affection for her hadn't been deep enough to take that leap.

She shifted on her feet, deciding it best to push the unwelcome thoughts from her mind. "How do you suppose Mrs. Bielle knows about the pearls? If Luke did not tell her, perhaps His Grace did. Or she overheard something."

Nicholas placed his hand on the mantel and rested his forehead against his arm. The curtains in the nearby window were not drawn, but the overcast skies allowed little light to fill the room. The fire, however, created a contrast of shadows on his dark clothing and an ethereal glow on his skin, giving her a rather nice profile to admire.

Which she most certainly should not be doing.

"I like the woman," said Nicholas, "but Mrs. Bielle has always been a rather odd character—quite outspoken given her station. I suppose much of it is habit, though, with how often Luke and I required scolding in our youth."

"The two of you were troublemakers, then?"

"I can answer that." A voice, more tenor than Nicholas's, sounded from behind them. The duke stood just inside the door of the drawing room with a wide grin. "He and Luke were always getting into trouble while I was the perfect angel of a child."

Nicholas huffed. "That could not be further from the truth. You were getting into trouble right along with us if not causing messes on your own."

The duke crossed the room, and the firelight illuminated the deep maroon color of his waistcoat and gold buttons. He bowed to them both, and Katherine returned a curtsy. She was not well acquainted with the new duke, but he seemed kind, much like his brother.

"The difference resides in the fact that I rarely got caught," said the duke.

Nicholas folded his arms. "Did Luke and I get caught, or were we unceremoniously betrayed?"

His Grace chuckled. "I shan't respond to that. Besides, we have something far more important to discuss." The mirth faded from his expression. "Something involving a particular set of pearls and a journey through time."

Chapter 23

Suffolk, 1815

Katherine

Katherine learned the duke had, in fact, known about Luke's plan to fake his own death. He also knew about the pearls and their ability to transport one through time. The confirmation seemed to annoy Nicholas, if his sour expression were any indication, but he did not fall into another angry pace across the room. The marquess sat on the settee next to Katherine, leaning forward with his elbow on his knee and his chin propped with a fist.

They had spent the last hour divulging the details of their trip to the future—or Nicholas had, anyway. She had spent the time listening and enjoying the way her chocolate warmed her from the inside out with every sip.

A few minutes by the fire had warmed her enough to discard Nicholas's coat, though the temptation to keep it despite her limbs having thawed had taken some time to overcome.

The duke heaved a sigh. "So, Miss Garrick, you knew about the pearls and wished to go to the future for a visit. Did you not consider the danger you might put yourself in?"

She had considered it. Repeatedly. She had required an entire month to come to the conclusion that she simply could not live without knowing if the things Maggie had told her the night of the woman's disappearance were true. The idea of a world where women were free to make their own decisions and study whatever they pleased appealed to her soul in a profound way. Like a spiritual awakening of sorts.

And the future had not disappointed her. It had also been a great deal to take in—overwhelming, as Nicholas had put it. And dangerous.

Katherine smoothed the wrinkles from her skirt. "I gave it considerable thought. The notion of seeing the future did drive me to seek out the pearls, but I also wanted to know if the former duke and Maggie were...well, alive. Miss McCarthy is my friend."

The duke rubbed a hand over his face. He appeared tired, which only stirred guilt in her stomach. The man had likely dealt with much the last few days with her and Nicholas's disappearance on his property.

"I admit, knowing that my brother is safe and happy provides me with much needed relief, but I would ask that neither of you go rushing off for another visit again. Your absence has been kept quiet for the most part, but Lady Garrick is completely beside herself. I cannot tell you how deeply this has affected her."

More guilt roiled her stomach. "This entire thing was my idea. Nic—Lord Keswick knew nothing about the pearl's capabilities, and once we realized we had landed in the future, I begged him to let me stay for a few days. It was foolish, reckless even, but I cannot regret it."

She never would. The future had been spectacular, of course, but it was more than that. Two days in Nicholas's company had taught her something. She did not want to settle for a match without love.

But the realization had come too late. She had accepted Lord Emerson's proposal, for she'd had no reason not to before now. She could end the engagement, but her reputation would take a severe toll. Perhaps it was not entirely too late to find more with the man who would soon be her husband.

"No one is blaming you," said the duke. His gaze flicked to Nicholas, and his brows furrowed with sympathy. "You on the other hand...I am afraid Lady Garrick may have your head. She believes you abducted her daughter."

For a moment, Katherine wanted to laugh as images of Nicholas dressed in his pirate garb fluttered through her mind, but one look at his expression dampened any amusement she felt. This situation was serious, not only for her but for the marquess. His reputation had already taken a beating over the years, but that was not the worst of it. What if her mother demanded her father call Nicholas out to a duel? The illegality of such things had not stopped many a man from doing what they deemed as defending honor, and she could not bear to think on either of them getting injured.

Nicholas growled beside her. "How bad is it? Be frank with me, Edwin. Does the whole of Society have their tongues loose?"

The duke shook his head, which eased the tension building in Katherine's shoulders a little. "Lady Garrick asked the situation be kept quiet, though the constable was alerted to the matter. The servants were sent to search the grounds, but I trust my staff's discretion. They have always been loyal to our family."

"Of course Lady Garrick had no desire to make it known," spat Nicholas. "Heaven forbid I do the honorable thing and offer for Katherine's hand."

"You would offer for me?" Katherine blurted.

Nicholas turned to look at her, hints of offense filling his features. She hadn't meant to sound so surprised. Nicholas did not lack a sense of honor, and she had no doubt he would do the right thing by her should the situation call for it. No, her reaction to his words stemmed from eagerness rather than disbelief. Her cheeks ignited. "Forgive me, I did not mean to sound astonished. It is only that I would never expect you to marry me because of this. None of it is your fault."

The marquess relaxed. "I would offer for you regardless, but you needn't worry over the matter. Your mother quite despises me. She would only allow it if there were no other course, perhaps not even then."

He sounded so certain. True, her mother had never cared for Nicholas. The woman had made that exceptionally clear, but what Katherine did not comprehend was *why*. Clearly her mother believed the false rumors of the *ton*. Perhaps if Katherine explained the truth to her, she would not view the man so poorly.

The duke released a long sigh. "I should send Lady Garrick a message and put an end to her suffering, and one to your mother as well, Nicholas. She has told everyone you have gone to London on business. I presume the two of you have contrived a story? Speaking of time travel will do you no favors."

"We have," said Nicholas. "We were abducted by scoundrels after one of my investments went south."

The duke nodded his approval, but his gaze flicked between them. "You may have to work on your appearance. Keswick, you could pass with your hair the way it is, but I am afraid Miss Garrick looks far too fashionable for someone abducted by scoundrels."

Nicholas lifted a hand to smooth out his hair, and the duke chuckled. "You are not supposed to fix it, Keswick." He rose from the armchair and bowed. "I shall see to informing your families. In the meantime, make sure your story is without flaw."

Katherine stood so she could offer him a curtsy. "Thank you, Your Grace. Your help is most appreciated."

Once the duke had left the drawing room, Katherine moved back to the hearth. She stared at the dancing flames and marveled at the way they moved without restraint. Looking closely, the flames appeared to enjoy their freedom, but one step backwards revealed the truth. The fire was not free at all, confined within the stone hearth, a prison that only offered a façade of flexibility.

From the fire's perspective, it believed itself at liberty to move however it wished, but to the outside observer with knowledge of the truth, the embers were trapped in an inescapable prison.

How like them she felt. She had not believed herself imprisoned until she had learned what it was like to care deeply for someone, to have a glimpse at a future where marriage meant love and affection rather than a business agreement. Her heart had become trapped in a gaol of her own creation.

"Is something amiss?" Nicholas's calm voice whispered next to her ear, sending shivers down her spine.

She turned toward him but refused to meet his eyes for fear of what he might see in her own. "No. I was only wondering how to make myself appear more dishabille."

He hummed, and the way his gaze roamed over her made her exceptionally self conscious. It flicked to the hearth and back to her, and his lips twisted with a grin. "How fond are you of this dress?"

"Not overly. Why do you ask?"

Nicholas stooped over and ran his fingers through the ash coating the outside edge of the fireplace, leaving mounds of gray on his black gloves. He straightened, and Katherine did not miss the twinkle of mischief in his emerald eyes. "Because, while I may oppose using my time to ruin young ladies, I am not against ruining a dress, especially if it will make our story more believable."

He crouched in front of her and took the hem of her skirts. Repeatedly, he crumpled the ivory-colored fabric and rubbed patches of ash into it. He worked his way around her, sliding on his knees, and Katherine watched his every movement, occasionally reminding herself to breathe.

"Do you think that will be convincing enough?" she asked when he had made a complete circle around her.

Nicholas coated his gloves with soot again and stood. "No, not nearly enough."

His throat bobbed with a swallow as he slipped closer. The faint scent of leather and citrus washed over her, making her dizzy. Nicholas brushed his fingers over her sleeve, leaving a wide streak of gray as they slid up her arm. He didn't stop there, slowly ascending into the hollow of her neck where his fingers lingered, caressing her with a subtle warmth. His thumb rubbed in circles over her skin, and then he traced the ridge of her collarbone, leaving a prickling trail of chills as he went.

Her breath hitched when his other hand slid around her waist and climbed her back. Through every movement, Nicholas's gaze never left her face, carefully watching as if waiting for her to react. But she could not react; she felt paralyzed, yet ready to burst at the same time. Her heart beat frantically enough she wondered if her ribs would bruise. She had never enjoyed having a dress ruined so much in her life.

Settling on the small of her back, his hand applied just enough pressure to bring her a few inches closer. Both of his hands moved to her face and swept the loose strands of blonde curls behind her ears while he whispered, "We must do something with your hair as well."

A few nods was all she could muster.

His fingers slid through her hair, searching for pins. Gently, he tugged at one and loosened the strands of hair beneath. This he repeated for several minutes, his expression focused on the task. His shirtsleeves brushed against her cheeks, and each time he exhaled, his breath would tickle the tip of her nose. But she dared not move.

Not that she could with the spell he had her under.

Nicholas lowered his arms, his voice even as though the entire ordeal hadn't affected him at all. "There. Much better."

She highly doubted her appearance was in any way attractive, but for some reason she could not bring herself to care. The way he stared at her now, as if he saw nothing of her newly disheveled state, made her insides flutter.

"And what of you?" she asked quietly. "Should we not address your appearance?"

Nicholas chuckled. "I suppose I should defile my clothing as well."

He started to move, but Katherine darted to hearth and crouched. She soiled her gloves with as much ash as she could. If the marquess was allowed to touch her in the name of making their story believable, then she deserved the same courtesy.

Standing in front of him again, she ran a hand from his wrist to his shoulder, leaving behind a trail of gray. His muscles tightened beneath her touch as she followed the same path back down, applying more pressure to better stain the white fabric.

Her gaze flicked to his chest, and she considered running her hands down that part of him, too. Heat flooded her cheeks, and feeling overcome with a wave of shyness, she moved on to his face instead. After all, she had experience in that area.

She smudged the gray powder across his forehead. Nicholas's brows raised as he looked up, attempting to see what her fingers were doing. She smiled. "No need to worry. I promise not to make you too ghastly."

His throat bobbed again. "I do not particularly care how you make me look at the moment."

Katherine rubbed her thumb over his cheek, creating a patch right in the center before continuing toward his chin.

She paused at the corner of his mouth, memories flashing across her mind. His lips were far more inviting than his chin. She began to trace them, but Nicholas's hand caught her by the wrist.

Perhaps she had gone too far. Touching his lips the first time was improper. A second—on the same day, no less—was scandalous. Her fingertips still rested on his mouth, and for several moments, they stared at each other in that strange position. There was an internal struggle in his eyes she longed to understand.

Nicholas guided her hand to his chest and pressed it flat against him. His heart pounded beneath her palm, the rhythm as erratic as her own.

"Katherine," he whispered. His gaze fell to her lips, and the air evaporated from the room. He shifted closer, the movement almost so imperceptible she might have imagined it. But he was near—near enough all her senses were filled with him. Near enough that without the light glowing from the hearth, their shadows would have melded into one.

Yet not nearly close enough.

Voices echoed from the foyer. Nicholas pulled away just as recognition of her mother's frantic voice settled into her mind. The marquess took several steps backwards and turned away, but not before Katherine glimpsed the frustration and regret in his expression.

Why could the message not have taken but a few more minutes to be delivered? Nicholas had nearly kissed her.

Frustrated, she wiped her ash-ridden gloves down the front of her dress, adding to its ruination.

"Katherine!" A half shout, half squeal cut through the quiet of the room. Her mother barreled toward her, holding up her skirts. She pulled Katherine into a tight embrace that threatened to prevent her from breathing.

"You're alive," Mama sobbed into her shoulder. "My darling, I have been consumed with worry."

Katherine squeezed her. "You needn't worry anymore, Mama. I am home."

Suffolk, 1815

Nicholas

To Nicholas's great surprise, Lady Garrick had few words for him. Her glares certainly said enough, but she refrained from addressing him directly. She allowed him and Katherine to deliver their contrived tale of being abducted, and her only response was to pull her daughter into another tight embrace. He despised the woman, but her genuine affection for Katherine lessened his frustrations.

Lady Garrick pulled away from her daughter, her cheeks wet with tears. "Come. We must return home and get you out of these clothes. Your father will be glad to know you are well."

Katherine nodded. "Does Lord Emerson know of my disappearance?"

The man's name made Nicholas nauseous. It was, however, the reminder he needed. Had Lady Garrick not arrived when she did, he would have kissed Katherine, a mistake he could not afford. The interruption had irked him at the time, but he saw it now for the blessing it had been. Kissing Katherine would spell his demise. Once he had, he would never be able to kiss another woman. He knew it as surely as the sun rose each morning. Nothing would ever compare, and his heart would be forever imprisoned.

It may be already.

"Yes," said Lady Garrick. "He assisted in the search and has paid a call every day for news."

Katherine smoothed the wrinkles in her skirt, adding another streak of dark ash to her pale gloves. "I apologize for making you worry. I shall apologize to Lord Emerson as well."

"Though I do not hold you accountable, a few words asking for forgiveness would not hurt. Unharmed or no, the man could question your reputation given you vanished with"—Lady Garrick's gaze darted to Nicholas and away again—"well, we must hope he is willing to overlook that detail of your disappearance. It will not do for him to end your engagement under those pretenses."

How wrong it was for Nicholas to wish for such a thing, yet he could not deny that the possibility sparked hope within him. Not that Lady Garrick would ever allow him to court Katherine even if Emerson called off the engagement. She had proven that a hundred times over.

"Surely no one would think ill of me for being abducted?" said Katherine. "Why should I or Ni—Lord Keswick suffer for something beyond our control?"

The near use of Nicholas's Christian name had Lady Garrick's narrowed eyes on him again. Nicholas turned away to hide his smirk. If the woman knew how familiar he'd become with her daughter over the last few days, she might strangle him.

"Your understanding of society remains in need of work," said Lady Garrick to her daughter. "The *ton* would happily throw you to the wolves if it satisfied their need for gossip. That is why I have gone to great lengths to keep word of your *abduction* a secret. However, should Lord Emerson call off your engagement, I cannot say whether he will hold his tongue. People will demand to know the cause of your falling out, and if he does not provide an answer, they will surely apply one of their own making."

Edwin, who had remained silent since Lady Garrick's arrival, crossed his arms over his chest. "I know Lord Emerson fairly well. He's not a man known to gossip, and I believe him the respectable sort who would not intentionally harm a lady's reputation. I see no reason to concern yourself over the matter. Speak with him, of course, but judging by my conversations with him during our search, he seemed more worried about your well being than casting doubt on your character, Miss Garrick."

Lady Garrick smiled at him with approval, and Nicholas rolled his eyes. She would not have bestowed *him* that look if he had stated those sentiments verbatim.

The matron took her daughter's hand. "Regardless, I have every confidence you can appease the man's concerns to prevent such a disaster."

Katherine smiled, though Nicholas could tell it was forced. "I shall do my best, Mama."

"Good, because I have already sent him an invitation to dine with us this evening. Yet another reason for us to get you home." She dropped into a curtsy and thanked Edwin before leaving the room with Katherine in tow. The viscountess did not spare Nicholas so much as a glance, but Katherine did, and the brief exchange left him feeling sullen and miserable.

"What do you intend to do?" asked Edwin, pulling Nicholas from his melancholy.

"Do? About what?"

Edwin's brows lifted high on his forehead, the same teasing glint in his eyes that Luke had worn the last few days. "About Miss Garrick, of course. You are in love with her, and she's to marry another man."

"I am to do nothing." Nicholas crossed the room and placed his arm on the wall next to the window. The sky had darkened now, and the sun would soon set. How it felt as though the sun were setting on his life. His last opportunity to spend time with Katherine before she became another man's wife had come to an end. He should be grateful. Once she and Emerson exchanged vows, his connection to her would be severed completely. He would have no reason to hope, as pitiful as it had been to do so before. Would that not free him in some way?

At the moment, he felt nothing of freedom, but rather a torment that would never end.

"You will not fight for her, then?" asked Edwin. "Perhaps you do not love her as I thought."

Nicholas turned sharply to face him. "Do not love her? I have done nothing but love her for years. I have wanted no one but her. But every effort I put into the cause is thwarted, time and again, by her mother. She has convinced Lord Garrick that I am unsuitable, and he has repeatedly refused to give me his blessing."

Edwin's mouth hung agape for several moments before he responded. "You have asked for his blessing?"

"Yes. As I said, repeatedly." Nicholas turned back to the window and leaned his forehead against the cool glass, closing his eyes. "I have asked him every few months for over a year. Begged, Edwin. How long am I to continue before finally conceding? My heart cannot take much more of it."

"I had no idea." The sound of Edwin's footsteps indicated he had come to stand next to Nicholas. "I'm sorry this has been so difficult for you. Does Miss Garrick know of your efforts?"

"No. I never told her. Perhaps I should have, though I cannot say it would have made any difference. Regardless, it is too late now. I will not interfere with her engagement." He swallowed, the guilt rising within him like bile. "I should have never agreed to stay in the future as long as we did. We should have come back immediately. It was selfish, but I wanted time with her. I wanted to ensure her dream of seeing the future was realized. If Katherine's reputation is soiled because of me, I will never forgive myself for it."

"Emerson is a good man. I do not think he will back out of the agreement over this, but if he does—"

"He will not." Nicholas had to believe that, much as it killed him to do so.

Edwin heaved a sigh. "Either way, you should tell Miss Garrick. She deserves to know. There is time to change things. She could still choose you."

Nicholas shook his head. "No. That is precisely why I mustn't tell her. If she ended her engagement with Emerson to be with me, she would be ruined. No one in Society would accept her. She would be ostracized."

"You cannot know that for sure. Yes, the gossipers will take delight in the situation, and perhaps things will be difficult for a time, but society will forget the moment something more interesting happens."

"You're wrong. My mother is the perfect example of how wrong you are. She has never been accepted back into society after eloping with my father. *Never.* Everything spoken to her is a façade of politeness." Nicholas pushed away from the wall and paced the room. "I have watched her suffer for years, Edwin. I have seen the look in her eyes every time there is a jab, pointed or disguised, at her character. It haunts me. To know how lonely she is, to see the light in her dim, year after year, while the *ton* effectively casts her out...I cannot do that to Katherine. I will not watch her become a flicker of herself just to satisfy my own desires."

Edwin stepped toward Nicholas and stopped his pacing with a hand on his shoulder. "And what about what Miss Garrick wants? Have you considered that she may be willing to forgo Society's approval to be with you?"

"You believe she would willingly make herself miserable for me?" He scoffed. Even if it were true, he would never allow it. Katherine could not possibly understand what consequences would befall her, just as Edwin did not understand. Neither of them had seen how ostracization had changed his mother. Had hurt her. Katherine would resent him for it one day if subjected to the same.

"What I believe is that, by not telling her, you are taking away her choice altogether and will make yourself and her miserable in the process, likely for the rest of your lives. But I shan't argue with you about it further. We have other matters to discuss at present."

Edwin took a seat on the settee and looked at Nicholas with an expectation to do the same. Nicholas obliged, and with an irritated grunt, sank into an armchair with intricately carved wooden legs.

"Now," said Edwin, leaning forward with his arms resting on his knees. "What are we going to do about the pearls?"

Suffolk, 1815

Katherine

K atherine's breath stalled as she watched Lord Emerson alight from his phaeton through the drawing room window. She would need to add punctuality to his list of attributes, for at his current pace he would reach the front door at precisely two o'clock. Perhaps if she only focused on his good qualities, she might feel something for him besides regret. It was hardly fair to the earl.

Their butler, Mr. Merriwether, showed the man into the room. His tailor-made clothes were covered with a thick wool greatcoat that did nothing to hide his handsome form. He looked every bit the gentleman from head to toe. He even donned a genuine smile.

Last night at dinner she had requested to spend a bit of time with him today. Coming to know the man was the only chance she had of making more of their relationship.

Lord Emerson removed his hat and bowed. Katherine returned a curtsy.

"Good morning, Miss Garrick. How are you today?"

"Well, I thank you for asking. I hope my request has not stolen you away from important business."

He shook his head. "Nothing I cannot see to later. Your proposal that we come to know one another better certainly holds merit. I would like us to be on good terms."

Good terms. It was not the most promising declaration, but as Mama always said, a woman had to work with what she'd been bestowed. A little more flirting would be required, but at least no one besides Lord Emerson would hear her pathetic attempts.

Katherine grimaced. Her lady's maid, Cecily, would accompany them so that was not entirely true. She had never possessed a close relationship with the young woman merely because Cecily was adamant about being proper in her station. Katherine would have preferred to be friends.

Lord Emerson offered his arm. "Shall we take a walk through the gardens?"

"Yes, that would be lovely." She drew in a shaky breath. It was time to enact her plan. She leaned closer to him, fluttering her lashes in a most ridiculous manner. "But I shall task you with keeping me warm. It is rather cold."

A flash of confusion swept over Lord Emerson's face, but it faded quickly. He nodded, his lips lifting into a smile. Perhaps all was not lost.

He mirrored her, tipping his head next to her ear with a conspiratorial whisper. "I look forward to it above all else."

Did he mean it? Despite Nicholas's thorough demonstration, she still could not account for the differences in flirtations. If only the marquess were here to...

Drat! She must cease thinking about Nicholas. Why must that be so difficult?

Katherine took Lord Emerson's arm. "Then let us visit the gardens."

Only a few clouds streaked the sky today, and hopefully the warmth radiating from the sun would stave off the frigid morning air. Katherine tightened her pelisse tighter around her, exhaling a cloudy puff. Why had she not suggested an indoor activity?

Together they walked the path, Cecily trailing behind them. Having an audience did nothing for her nerves. Servants gossiped, their rumors spreading between households. If she butchered her flirtations, the entire countryside might know of it by tomorrow. Perhaps she could bring the maid into her confidence somehow.

Lord Emerson guided her down a narrow path, one shaded by the alder trees in seasons of lush greenery but now left directly in the sun. She longed for the scent of wild flowers that would grow between the knobbly trunks after the snows, but for now the stale cold air was all the season would afford her. Come spring, she would no longer live at her father's estate, likely relocating to the earl's townhome for the Season so he could attend to his duties in the House of Lords.

She swallowed, but it did nothing for her dry throat.

They were supposed to be talking—coming to know one another—yet the only sound was the birds fluttering between the trees. If she withheld her words, would he make an effort to converse? He had rarely done so before, and though it irked her, in a way, she also understood. She had never been chatty when out in society, mostly for fear of making mistakes she would later be scolded about.

Lord Emerson had been rather quiet through their entire courtship, as short and abrupt as it was, and she had come to understand him as a shy being who preferred his estate to balls. She preferred that, too. Perhaps she could make use of the commonality.

"Tell me, my lord," she began, turning slightly to gain a better view of his face, "what is it you do in your spare time?"

The earl removed his gaze from the path ahead briefly to glance at her. "I enjoy a good ride in the morning. Do you enjoy riding, Miss Garrick?"

She suppressed a smile. At least they were speaking. "I do. I am rather attached to my mare, Ophelia. She is a pleasant creature. I shall hate to say goodbye to her."

"Would your father not consider allowing you to bring her along?"

Katherine shrugged. "Perhaps, though I believe it was his intention to breed her. If he has yet to change his mind on the matter, he will wish to keep her here."

Lord Emerson's face twisted with surprise. Drat. Ladies did not speak so plainly about such things. "Forgive me for such an uncouth topic of discussion."

"There is nothing to forgive." He rubbed a hand over his chin, his gaze distant. "Should it come to that, I would be happy to purchase a horse for you. I have many in my stables, but you may choose a new one for yourself."

Her heart warmed a little. "That is kind of you. I would like that very much."

"Of course, I would require something in exchange."

Her stomach plummeted. "And what might that be?"

"That you promise to ride with me on occasion. As much as I enjoy it, the endeavor is often lonely. Serene, yes, but lonely. I never imagined anything could add to the beauty of my estate. I was wrong."

The way he smiled, the glint in his eyes—it brought a rush of heat to her cheeks. The earl was capable of flirting, then. What he seemed *incapable* of was touching her heart. She appreciated his effort and his compliments, but neither created the stomach flutters she desired. Was it wrong of her to expect them from her soon-to-be husband?

"You flatter me too much, my lord."

"I was under the impression you wished to flirt with me."

The heat searing her face burned hotter. "I *attempted* to flirt with you, but the art is lost on me. I cannot make sense of the rules—how to do so, when, or even what type is appropriate." The admission somehow offered her both embarrassment and relief. Lord Emerson may think poorly of her, perhaps even believe her a ridiculous chit, but it was better he understood who he intended to shackle himself to.

He remained quiet for several moments, settling them into a peaceful gait. When he turned to face her, he placed his free hand over hers.

There was nothing—not a single jolt of excitement or moment of breathlessness. In fact, she struggled against the urge to slip her hand away. She knew the reaction to be dramatic. This man did not deserve her disdain. The only transgression she could denounce of the earl lie in that he simply was not Nicholas.

Drat the marquess for turning her into a hopeless romantic.

"Miss Garrick, I shall not tease you for a lack of skill in this area, but I would like to know why you suddenly feel the need to offer flirtations.

We are engaged, and it was my assumption that you understood the nature of our relationship when I offered for your hand."

"You mean that it was to be a marriage of convenience?" She glanced at him, the little hope she'd clung to ready to shatter completely.

His dark brows knitted together. "Yes, one of convenience. That is not to say we should not seek to form a friendship, of course, but—"

"Is that all you wish to come of our marriage? Friendship?"

He bit down on his lip as though the question troubled him. "I am afraid that is all my heart can give. It has yet to recover from the last time I gave it away."

Her shoulders slumped. The man's heart had been broken. It became clear to her that she might never break down the walls he'd constructed. Time could heal, but would she be old and carry a multitude of wrinkles before they found some semblance of love? Perhaps she could have been content with believing he might someday give her the relationship she now wanted, but the resolve in his expression doused what remained of her hope.

"I am sorry to hear that," she whispered, for what more could she say? She understood, for the first time, what losing the person one loved felt like. The pang in her chest each time she thought of Nicholas, knowing they could never be more than friends, was the worst sort of torture.

"I truly am sorry, Miss Garrick. I hope you will not think ill of me for this, but I prefer to be honest with you on this matter."

She shook her head, fighting the way tears burned in her eyes. "You have nothing to apologize for, and I appreciate your honesty. It shall save you from my terrible flirting attempts, at least."

A light chuckle sounded from his chest. "They are not terrible. Amusing, yes, but in an endearing sort of way. I only wish I could return them with more sentimentality."

"I would never want you to do that which you are not comfortable with, my lord. Your willingness to be frank with me only increases my respect for you."

He gave her hand a light squeeze. "Thank you for understanding."

She did understand his reluctance, but it did not abate the longing in her chest. Everything had been much easier to accept when she remained ignorant of how it felt to love someone, to desire their company above all others. To kiss them.

"We should return you to the house, I think," said Lord Emerson. "You've had an eventful week."

She smiled but offered no words. Resignation had stolen them away.

Suffolk, 1815

Katherine

M r. Merriwether offered Katherine a bow when she entered the house, his wrinkled face full of genuine concern at the sight of her. He likely sensed her discontent, or perhaps it was etched into her expression. That the butler would take notice at all allowed her to relax. The servants at Rusgrove had always been Katherine's favorites. Many had been with her family for as long as she could remember whereas those serving at her father's property in Town had been hired within the last two years. There was something comforting about being surrounded by those of long acquaintance, even if most of them were far below her station and rarely exchanged words with her.

Would the staff at the earl's estate be as friendly? What if they hated her?

Her stomach knotted. She started for the stairs but stopped at the bottom when George appeared from the drawing room. He glanced over her and tilted his head. "Is something amiss?"

Drat. Could everyone see the effect her conversation with Lord Emerson's had on her?

"Quite well," Katherine lied.

George folded his arms and leaned against the railing of the staircase. "You forget, dear sister, that having known you my entire life gives me great advantage in recognizing your lies. Now, tell me what it is that bothers you."

Could she? George had always been the best sort of brother. Teasing, perhaps, but willing to keep her confidence just as she did for him.

She glanced at a passing servant and then grabbed George's hand. He followed her lead into a smaller parlor. His brows furrowed when she closed the door and released a sigh. "I do not wish Mama to overhear."

"You are quite distraught, then. Having noticed you have just returned from a walk with Lord Emerson, I can only assume he is the cause. Do I need to call fellow out?"

"No, nothing of the sort. It is only that I..." How could she possibly explain?

"You do not love him."

She glanced sharply at George, and his lips lifted, amused by her surprise.

He knew, as did her entire family, that her marriage would be one of convenience, but how had he suspected that was what burdened her thoughts?

"Something has changed," he said, his grin fading. "I can see it. You seemed fine with the engagement before, but now...you have doubts."

"Yes," she whispered, almost ashamed to admit it. But George was not like Mama. He would not judge or think less of her for it. "You are correct in your assumptions, but it hardly matters. Even if I were not engaged to Lord Emerson, Nicholas has never shown interest in courting me."

"Nicholas?" asked George. "You refer to Lord Keswick?"

Katherine pulled in her lips. Maybe this was too much, even for George. She was at a loss for words, uncertain how to explain herself. She could hardly tell George about her trip to the future; he would never believe her. How could she explain to him how much her feelings had changed in such a short time? How the marquess had earned her regard during their supposed abduction.

To Katherine's surprise, her lack of response prompted a laugh from George. He shook his head, a wide grin upon his face. "I cannot believe it. After all Mama's efforts to chase him away, he still managed to win your heart. I thought for certain he had given up."

"Given up? Whatever do you mean?"

George's expression sobered. "You do not know? Mama instructed us to all remain quiet on the matter, but I thought Lord Keswick would have told you."

She shifted on her feet, attempting to douse her impatience. "Told me what, George?"

Her brother frowned. "That he pays a call every two months or so like clockwork. I cannot count the number of times I have seen him here. At first I thought he had business with father, which is not entirely untrue,

I suppose. But his request to court you was always denied, though Mama was surely the reason for that."

"C-court me?" Katherine nearly choked on the words.

George nodded. "The man must be completely besotted. I am impressed with his determination. I would have given up long ago. Katherine, wait! Where are you going!"

"I must speak with Mama straight away." Katherine paused at the door, her fingers firmly gripping the knob. She turned to look at her brother over her shoulder. "I shall not tell her who informed me for it is clear she had no desire for me to know."

George gave her a commiserating smile. "Best of luck."

Katherine did her best not to storm down the corridor in search of Mama. Anger surged through her with a vengeance. She had known Mama despised the marquess, and while she'd never understood why and had learned to ignore her mother's constant warnings, this was beyond what her patience could endure.

How could Mama keep something like this from her?

A maid offered her a curtsy as she passed by, and Katherine spun on her heels. "Pardon me, but have you seen my mother this afternoon?"

"I believe she is in the blue parlor, miss."

"Thank you." Katherine continued down the hall until she reached the open doorway of her mother's favorite sitting room. Patterns of bluebells adorned the cream-colored wallpaper, giving the room an air of spring when the chill outside was anything but warm and inviting so close to Christmastide. The pop of color was extenuated by the navy rug covering much of the wooden floor, and near the window, her mother sat in an oversized armchair with a cup of tea.

Katherine drew in a deep breath, willing her growing angst to calm, but the effort did little good. Mama had always been rather controlling, but this...

She clenched her fists. Nicholas did not deserve the disdain her mother berated him with, and it was past time she found out *why* the woman insisted on viewing him with such contempt.

The warmth radiating from the hearth caressed her skin the moment she entered the room. She stopped a few feet from her mother and cleared her throat. The sound drew Mama's attention, and the viscountess smiled, eating away some of the animosity boiling inside Katherine's chest.

"Darling." Mama gestured to the empty chair next to her. "Come sit down. Tell me, how was your walk with Lord Emerson?"

Katherine bit her tongue and sat daintily in the chair, her posture perfectly straight. "He has no intention of calling off our engagement if that is your concern."

Mama took a sip of her tea before setting the cup and saucer on the small table between them. The glass made the faintest of clinks. "Of course not. I trust you reassured him that nothing occurred to harm your reputation?"

"I have half a mind to ruin it on purpose."

Mama stiffened. "Why in heaven's name would you do that?"

To spite her mother, admittedly, but Katherine realized that would be unfair to Lord Emerson. He was truly innocent in all of this, and she needed to proceed with caution. She had not yet decided what precisely she would do; a discussion with Nicholas, however, was at the utmost top of her list.

"Is Lord Emerson the only man who has ever called on me? For the purpose of courtship?" She would give Mama the opportunity to speak the truth. She would handle this with dignity.

"Where is this coming from?" asked Mama. "You had several callers during your first Season in Town. You know who they are as well as I do."

"I am not speaking of my time in Town. I mean here at Rusgrove." She hoped her pointed stare would encourage a confession. She certainly would not let it go.

Mama shifted in her chair. "Lord Emerson is the only one who has called on you here that matters."

"That is not your decision to make. Tell me who else has called."

"Katherine, you must understand. I only wished to protect—"

"I do not need protection from Nicholas!"

Mama's face twisted and tinted red. "You have no business calling that man by his given name. You will make the whole of Society believe you have a history with him, and not one that will be pleasing to your soon-to-be-husband. I forbid you from doing it anymore."

Katherine stood, her nails digging into her palms. "Forbid me all you like. Nicholas is my...friend. I will call him by his given name if I wish."

"You know not what your actions will do. This friendship with the marquess will ruin you. Lord Emerson could call off your engagement and our family name would be tarnished. Is that what you wish to achieve? You will live out life as a spinster."

No. As angry as she was with Mama, bringing dishonor to their family would not do. She loved her parents even if they did not always see eye to eye. Besides, any scandal she incurred would reflect on her brother, George. She had no desire for her actions to bring him shame.

"I want to know why you kept this from me," Katherine answered evenly. "Why do you hate Lord Keswick so much? What has he done to warrant so much disdain?"

Mama took a few slow, deep breaths. "I knew that day in the garden what he was. The way he put his hands on you with no regard to how it could affect your reputation. His father was the same, always taking what he pleased from unsuspecting young ladies without any intention of offering for them."

The day in the garden? Memories of Nicholas's arms, strong and warm, wrapped around her pushed their way into her thoughts. The moment seemed so long ago, and Katherine had given it little thought until recently. Thinking on it now made her blush, but at the time, the situation had felt harmless. Innocent. "You mean when we visited Uncle four years ago? Mama, I told you Nicholas caught me so that I would not wind up in the pond."

"He likely caused your fall to begin with," muttered Mama. "Despicable behavior. You were too young to know any better, and I'd wager the man was prepared to take full advantage of your naiveté."

"That is not true! He offered to escort Cecily and me. We were lost—"

"Which he seemed happy to exploit." Mama sighed and rubbed her temple as if the conversation were giving her a migraine. "After the first time he requested to call on you, I demanded your father send him away. Over a year I've kept that man at bay. Told him repeatedly he was unsuitable for you, yet he manages to wriggle his way into our lives despite my efforts."

"Over a *year*? Nicholas has been attempting to call on me since I came out?"

Mama's scowl was answer enough. Katherine's heart had leapt when George first told her Nicholas had been persistent, but an entire *year?* She could think of few reasons the man would put so much effort into obtaining her parents' permission to court her, and the notion filled her with a different sort of heat than the anger that had taken refuge within her.

Mama lifted her chin, her nostrils flaring. "I told him at Almac's during the opening of your first Season that his attention was unwanted. He came calling the very next day. Thick-headed man. I counted us fortunate that you had gone out with another gentleman to Hyde. No matter how many times your father and I turned down his petition, he persisted, but I refused to let him make a fool of you like his father..."

Mama swallowed, and the pained look in her eyes struck a cord of sympathy within Katherine. The woman disliked Nicholas, there would be no denying that, but was it the former marquess that Mama truly despised so greatly? The incident in the gardens four years ago had convinced her mother that Nicholas behaved no differently than the notorious man Katherine had heard about over the years. Was that the only reason Mama presumed his son was the same?

Nicholas may now bear the title of Lord Keswick, but unlike his father, he had never been anything but a gentleman.

"You are punishing Lord Keswick for the actions of his father," said Katherine gently. "That is hardly fair." She bit down on her lip. Part of her was afraid to ask for fear she already knew the answer, but she needed the truth. "Did you start the rumors revolving around Nicholas? Did you mark him a rake?"

Mama lifted her chin once again. "I did what was necessary to keep you and other young ladies safe from the man."

"You have judged him in the most erroneous way. He is a gentleman, and you would see that if you would only allow him a chance."

The viscountess picked up her saucer and teacup, but she never brought the china to her lips, instead fiddling with the cup's handle with a distant expression. When she finally finished what remained of the tea, the contemplative look had disappeared.

"Regardless of what or who you think Lord Keswick is, he is not your intended. Whatever relationship you believe you have with the marquess, it must end. I do not wish any harm to befall you, Katherine." Her gaze dropped to her lap, and she traced the patterns on the saucer with her finger. "You must sever ties with him and cease this foolishness before it is too late. Before he breaks your heart."

Mama's voice broke, and her eyes glistened with tears. Katherine had never seen her mother look so vulnerable, and it pained her. The viscountess had always been overprotective and strict. For the first time, Katherine understood why.

Mama had suffered a broken heart, and Katherine believed she knew the culprit.

A few slow steps brought her to Mama's side. The viscountess looked up, her lashes fluttering to hold in tears. Katherine placed a kiss on her mother's cheek. "I know you only wish to protect me, Mama. I love you for that, but you cannot be more wrong in this instance. Please reconsider your prejudices."

Her mother's brows furrowed, and her lower lip trembled, but she gave no response with words. Katherine left the parlor, her thoughts messier than when she had entered. The path forward remained largely unclear, but there was one thing she must do.

She needed to see Nicholas—speak to him. Tell him she knew about his attempts to court her. She needed him to know that she would not have accepted Lord Emerson's proposal so hastily had she been aware of his desire to come to know her. She would have given him that chance, and he deserved to know.

But most importantly, Nicholas deserved to know she loved him.

Chapter 27

Suffolk, 1815

Katherine

Katherine pressed her folded arms tighter against her stomach. The blanket covering her lower half kept her legs warm but the rest of her remained frigid as a block of ice. Their ride to Ravenhall Manor would be miserable. The weather seemed aware Christmastide was but a few weeks away and had chased the last bit of warmth into hiding. A thin layer of snow dressed the landscape in white, and frozen dew on the bare tree branches sparkled in the morning light.

"Shame we lack enough snow for a fight," said George with his wicked grin from the seat across from her.

Katherine narrowed her eyes. "I am not a child. Snowball fights are not for ladies, and you would do well to remember that."

"Just admit it. You would enjoy a good snowball fight as much as I."

She leaned forward. "I would, but only because I would win."

Satisfaction and triumph danced over George's expression. "Perhaps if it snows, we can talk Lord Emerson into joining us. I cannot have you marrying the man until I have thoroughly examined his snowball fighting skills." He tugged mindlessly at his gloves. "Unless, of course, you do not intend to marry him."

Katherine ignored the way her stomach twisted and pasted on a smile. There would be no fooling George, especially after how thoroughly she had to beg him to accompany her. She needed to speak with Nicholas, but Mama would never permit such a thing. So, she had been resigned to tell Mama that George was escorting her into town. She would owe her brother for playing along with the lie.

Her mind skimmed over all that she had learned. Why had Nicholas not informed her of his intentions?

In the two days that followed the revelation, her resolve had only hardened. She would speak to Nicholas, and if he even hinted at still wishing to court her she would call off her engagement. This she had not revealed to Mama, who had made herself rather scarce since the confrontation in the parlor.

The anxious energy twirling in her stomach ebbed the moment they turned onto the drive. Circular-shaped shrubs lined both sides of the dirt path. The road split halfway to the house, continuing to either side of a long pond teeming with lily pads and cattails glistening with frozen dew. Each path met again at the base of the manor where two sets of stone stairs descended to meet the carriageway.

White columns sculpted after the Greek fashion surrounded the front entry, holding a balcony for the master chambers on the first floor. They gave the building an aged but beautiful appearance, adding sharp contrast to the red brick walls.

The carriage pulled to a halt, and a shiver ran through her limbs when George opened the door. Her brother alighted first and then offered to hand Katherine down onto the snow-patched ground. Her breath escaped in cloudy puffs, and her teeth wished to chatter. She wondered if her lips had turned blue.

The thought brought with it a series of memories from the day of her return from the future. Warmth threaded through her as though she stood next to a roaring fire rather than in a frozen land of snowflakes and nipping air. She wanted to relive that moment, but outside the recess of her mind. She wanted to be in Nicholas's arms.

George leaned close as they moved toward the door, his breath rustling the hair at her ear. "Whatever you are up to in coming here, I hope it causes a great deal of mischief."

Katherine turned her head slightly to give him a pointed look. George's wide grin faded. "More than that, I hope it brings you happiness. Do not throw away love simply because the course is not easy."

Her mouth fell open. Perhaps George understood more than she gave him credit. Either way, she might just take all of his words to heart. Causing a bit of mischief had never sounded so appealing.

"I know that look," said George. "You, dear sister, are scheming something."

She feigned offense. "How dare you accuse me of scheming."

George shrugged. "Am I wrong?"

She suppressed a grin. George knew her too well. "You are not wrong, and I trust you will keep this visit to yourself?"

They stopped at the door, and George gave a dramatic bow. "Anything for my favorite sister."

She shook her head, grinning. George had grown up much over the last several years. A few more, and he would be facing a horde of young ladies vying for his attention. In a way she looked forward to watching him squirm.

With the utmost affection, of course.

"See to your scheme," said George. "I shan't say a word to anyone."

"Thank you," Katherine whispered as his hand met the door.

Her stomach felt like a ball of yarn, wound so tightly she feared her breakfast might not remain where it belonged. Mama had gone on morning calls, which meant she and George would likely have at most an hour before they needed to return. Mama would never believe Katherine needed more than that to shop given how she hated it.

The door opened to a wiry-haired butler, one much younger than Mr. Merriwether. He bowed. "Good afternoon, sir. Madam."

"We sent a card," said George. "Pardon the lack of notice, but is Lady Keswick at home for visits?"

Katherine bit her tongue to keep herself from asking after Lord Keswick. It was far less suspicious for them to visit the dowager marchioness, but she hoped Nicholas was home, too.

The man's lips lifted, and his brown eyes sparkled. "Indeed. Please allow me to show you to the drawing room."

Katherine and George followed him inside. The butler announced their arrival, and the decor stole Katherine's breath the moment they entered. The walls were adorned in a yellow paper mottled with white roses and vines. Pictures of the seaside town of Brighton hung on the wall opposite the window, catching the sunlight, and large white shells decorated every shelf and mantle. If she had closed her eyes, she might have heard the roar of the waves and smelled the salty sea, for never had she felt so near the ocean while so far away.

Lady Keswick waited for them, standing in front of a cream-colored settee. Her smile was warm despite the dark colors she donned, and despite seeing no sign of Nicholas, Katherine returned her smile. She wondered if she should offer condolences on the loss of machioness's husband, but based on what Mama had told her, the late marquess was far from honorable or kind.

Then again, Mama's opinion of Nicholas was inaccurate.

After an exchange of formalities, Katherine accepted Lady Keswick's offer for her to sit. George, however, turned the offer down. "Forgive me, my lady, but I wondered if Lord Keswick might be at home?"

Katherine shot George a look, but her brother's lips merely twitched.

"He is," answered Lady Keswick. "But I believe he went out riding a quarter hour ago. That said, I imagine he would wish to know of your visit." Her gaze flicked to Katherine. "If you are up for a ride yourself, I wonder if you would be willing to go look for him? The stablehands can point you in the right direction."

"I would be honored," said George with another bow. "I shall borrow a horse and return promptly."

"Thank you." Lady Keswick gave a curt nod, and George left the room. Katherine chewed her lip, uncertain whether she would need to thank her brother later or whop him.

A servant brought tea, and Lady Keswick and Katherine settled into light conversation. Lady Keswick placed her cup and saucer on the table and smoothed out the wrinkles of her black gown. The marchioness sat in the chair next to her, their backs facing the window. This close, Katherine could smell the soft hints of the floral perfume the woman used, which matched her personality, warm and inviting like the first signs of spring beckoning for one to enjoy time outdoors after months of frosty air.

"Tell me more about your interests," said Lady Keswick. "I fear I have not attended many social outings since you came out in Society to know your talents firsthand."

"Firsthand?"

The corners of her eyes crinkled. "I may receive few invitations, but my son does not. He has told me a great many things about you. I believe he mentions you more often than he realizes."

Katherine's cheeks burned, but this detail only added to the hope growing within her. Was it possible the marquess cared for her as much as she did him? Love had never been something she believed she would obtain, or even needed to, but the last week had changed her vision of the future. *Her* future.

Katherine twisted her fingers together in her lap. She wanted a future with the marquess.

"What sort of things has your son told you about me? Nothing too embarrassing, I hope? He does enjoy teasing me."

"Quite the opposite, Miss Garrick. My Nicholas admires you greatly. He has spoken of your kindness and intelligence. He claims you have a deep interest in mathematics."

"An unusual interest, I know," said Katherine hastily.

"There is nothing wrong with unusual." Lady Keswick's brows furrowed, and she leaned forward to place her hand over Katherine's. "Society will tell you to hide a talent that is not fitting to their ideals, but life is too short not to enjoy it. If you love numbers, then I see no reason to forgo studying the subject. Do not allow the opinions of others to steal away your happiness."

Withdrawing her hand, the marchioness's gaze shifted to the paintings decorating the wall, and sadness crept into her features. "I loved to paint when I was your age. My family ran out of places to hang the work, always proud to display anything I created. We lived in Brighton. I loved the sea."

She turned back to Katherine and tilted her head. "My husband despised it. No matter how many times I asked, he would not allow us to visit. I lost the desire to paint altogether after a while."

Katherine's heart ached for the woman. Perhaps her mother was not entirely wrong about the former Lord Keswick. The man sounded controlling at the very least.

"Surely he did not oppose you staying with your family for a week or so. Perhaps while he was in London?"

Lady Keswick shook her head. "Even if he would have allowed it, my family would not have accepted my visit." Her chin dropped, and a glimmer of tears glazed her eyes. "They disowned me after the wedding. I never spoke to my parents again. I have a brother, but he refuses to see me."

"Your family opposed your union with the marquess? Would they not have rejoiced that you made a strong connection with a peer?"

"They may have had my husband's reputation not been so mottled. My parents warned me, told me of the man's many indiscretions, but I was young...naïve . I believed he loved me—his actions spoke to the notion. It was not me he loved but my dowry."

A few tears slipped from her eyes, and she turned away, wiping them on the back of her glove. "Forgive me. We hardly know one another and here I am showering you with waterworks."

Katherine scooted to the edge of the cushion and took the marchioness's hands. "You needn't apologize. I am honored to be your confidant. I cannot imagine how difficult it must have been for you to endure this."

Lady Garrick squeezed Katherine's hands. "Thank you."

She had come to see Nicholas, but this visit with Lady Keswick had been what she needed in some strange way. His mother's experience explained so much of Nicholas's protectiveness of Katherine's reputation. Why he placed its importance so far above his own.

It only made her love him more.

Katherine glanced at the clock on the wall, and her stomach plummeted. "Forgive me, Lady Keswick. I must find my brother. We need to return home." She stood, and the marchioness did the same.

"I understand, Miss Garrick." Lady Keswick tilted her head, and her soft, sympathetic expression suggested she truly did understand. "I hope you will call again. It was wonderful having you visit."

Her voice choked on the last word, and Katherine's heart pinched. Without thought, she wrapped her arms around the woman. "I promise I will."

"Mother, I was wondering if you might—" The familiar voice cut off, and Katherine removed herself from Lady Keswick's arms, her heart beating madly. Nicholas stood at the drawing room door, handsome as ever in his olive waistcoat, even with his mouth agape.

She dipped into a curtsy. "Good afternoon, Lord Keswick."

Nicholas

NICHOLAS'S HEART GALLOPED FASTER THAN MAJESTY, THE BLACK stallion he'd just enjoyed a long ride on. The last thing he had expected upon entering the drawing room was to find Katherine Garrick in a deep embrace with his mother.

His traitorous heart leapt at the sight of her despite how out of his reach she remained. Katherine dropped into a curtsy, and upon straightening, her lips lifted into a smile. The joy that lit her angelic face as she met his gaze made his chest constrict unbearably.

"Is something amiss?" Nicholas glanced between the two women. Katherine may have been smiling but dried streaks of tears adorned his mother's cheeks.

"No, nothing," said his mother. "Miss Garrick and I had a wonderful afternoon."

Katherine beamed at her. "Please, call me Katherine."

"Only if you agree to call me Phoebe."

Heavens, what had he missed in his absence? He'd never regretted taking a ride so greatly. He had lost an opportunity to be near Katherine but also missed the conversation that had resulted in his mother's joyful demeanor. It was not often he saw her smile as she did now, with pure happiness.

Katherine glanced at the wall clock, and her expression twisted. "My apologies for leaving so abruptly, but my mother—"

"I understand," said Nicholas. "Your mother would not want you here."

"No, she would not."

Nicholas shifted on his feet. "But you came anyway."

He was uncertain what he meant by the statement. A question, perhaps, or desire to understand *why* she had gone against her mother's wishes. A hope he should extinguish, for it would only shatter his heart further.

"I did." She grinned, but it quickly faded to a look dripping with regret. "But I must be going now. Good afternoon, my lord. My lady."

Nicholas bowed when she walked past, her floral scent tickling his nose and begging him to follow. It took every ounce of his willpower to keep his feet firmly in place. He glanced at his mother, who tilted her head and gave him a stern look. Surly she did not think he should go after her?

Her brows raised.

She certainly thought so.

"Gads, Mother." Nicholas ran a hand through his hair. "She is *engaged.*"

"Are you giving up? You shall regret if you do, and I will have to be disappointed."

"You would prefer I ruin her like Father did you? Steal her away to Gretna? For that is the only way this could work. Her parents will never approve of me."

His mother's lips turned down, whatever joy that had been present in her expression before completely gone. Already he regretted his words and how they had chased away her happiness. "Forgive me."

She approached and placed a gentle hand on his arm. "You are not him, Nicholas. Your father may have convinced me to elope, but he did so under the guise of love. I was willing to accept the consequences because I believed he loved me. It was not until I learned the truth that I wholly regretted the decision. I was willing to leave my life behind when I thought I was spending the future with the man I loved. Some consequences are worth facing, especially when they involve *genuine* matters of the heart. Now go on. Go after her."

Blast it all.

He rounded on his heels and took long strides to catch up with Katherine. She had already descended the stairs to the carriageway by the time he exited the house, her brother, George, at her side.

Odd. Where had the man been the entire time?

"Miss Garrick!"

The siblings stopped and turned to look at him. She needed to return home, but he wanted a few more moments with her. It was foolish, he knew, given that she would soon wed, but the desire to be in her company overwhelmed logic, and his mother's encouragement did nothing to help.

"Ah, Keswick," said George. "I had gone to look for you but found no success in the endeavor. But here you are, catching us at the last moment. Fortune smiles upon us." His lips stretched in a cheshire grin.

Nicholas stopped in front of them. What should he say? He had no reason for chasing after Katherine beyond enjoying her presence. He certainly could not admit to that in front of her brother.

"The Morrisons' are holding their annual Christmastide ball tomorrow night," he blurted.

Katherine's lips pinched, drawing his gaze to them. "Yes."

"Will I see you there?"

"You shall if it is your intention to attend." Her cheeks turned a pale red, and she stared at the ground. "I hope it is."

She hoped he would attend? His heart gave another happy leap. Blasted organ. "It is my intention. Will you save a dance for me?"

"I would be honored, Lord Keswick."

George clapped. "Wonderful. Now that we have that settled"—he offered Katherine his arm—"we must be going." He gave Nicholas a curt nod and pulled his sister toward the carriage.

"I look forward to seeing you then," said Katherine over her shoulder.

"As do I."

They made it only a handful of steps before Nicholas called after her again. "Katherine?"

"Yes?" She met his gaze, and Nicholas could see the reluctance to leave in her haste to turn around, nearly tripping her brother in the process. It made feathers dance in his stomach, and although he wished for her to stay, he knew she must return. Lady Garrick would be furious were she to discover Katherine had been to Ravenhall. He did not know what circumstances had brought her to his estate, but he was glad for it. The happiness his mother displayed at having a visitor, and one not paying her a call to satisfy the expectations of society, filled him with gratitude.

"Thank you for visiting my mother," said Nicholas. "You've no idea what it meant to her...and to me."

"She is a wonderful woman. I am eager to know her better."

George tugged at her arm, and Katherine gave him an apologetic look. "I must go. Goodbye, Nicholas."

He bowed, his eyes never leaving her. "Until tomorrow."

"Until tomorrow." She gave him a firm nod. The way her expression brightened with her promise did things to him. He was a complete fool, but until Katherine Garrick said her vows, he might very well continue to be one.

Chapter 28

Suffolk, 1815

Katherine

Katherine accepted Papa's hand to assist her down from the carriage. Her slippers landed on the dirt drive, and cold seeped from the ground through the soles and into her toes. She tightened her navy-colored spencer around her. It did little to combat the chilly air, and she hoped the fires would be roaring within the Morrisons' estate. Regardless, a few dances would warm her frigid body, especially if a certain marquess asked her to stand up with him.

The carriage pulled away, and Katherine followed Mama up the marble stairs. Once inside, a footman took their coats and Papa's hat. Candles flickered throughout the hallway leading into the two rooms that had been cleared of furniture and rugs. Spots of melted wax speckled the walls and floorboards, sometimes mixing with the chalk designs decorating the space.

Men and women fluttered about the room and chatted near the refreshment tables. Katherine searched the many faces for a familiar head of blond hair and green eyes. When her gaze found Nicholas, he was already watching her. His lips lifted slightly, and he held her stare far longer than was appropriate.

I would meet your gaze with stilled breath and hold it until the lack of air finally forced my lungs to expand.

Nicholas's words, spoken only a week before, barreled across her mind. He'd said them during their lesson on flirting beneath stars veiled by the Los Angeles city lights. There was no charming smile, no quick turn of his head. Instead, he focused his attention on her continually until his shoulders shifted with a deep breath. Only then did his gaze finally drop away.

Flirting with genuine interest.

Her pulse quickened. She needed to speak to him directly. Nicholas had never chided her for impertinent questions, and although she had promised not to ask any more of him, this one was too important to ignore.

She glanced at him again to find his eyes trained on her. She smiled and gave a subtle wave that Mama could not see from her position beside Papa. Nicholas grinned back at her, but the joy in his expression faded quickly, and he turned away.

"Miss Garrick."

Katherine turned to find Lord Emerson next to her. She dipped into a curtsy, wishing it was a different man standing before her. The admission led to guilt, and she chided herself for the thought. Lord Emerson was a good man, and though she did not love him, he did not deserve disrespect.

"Good evening, my lord," said Katherine.

"You look lovely tonight," he said. "Might I have the first set?"

She forced a smile. "Of course. Thank you for the compliment."

For a compliment alone it was. No hint of mischief flickered in his soft eyes. No tease lined the words, not even in a subtle manner. Lord Emerson did not flirt with her now. In fact, he had only done so when she initiated it.

After their conversation a few days previous, she wondered if he would ever engage in banter with her again. Did he worry such interactions would open his heart, a notion the man was entirely against? If so, she had no hope of winning him over. Their marriage would be one of mutual respect and nothing more.

If they wed.

The music began. Katherine and Lord Emerson waited for their turn to participate, and though she tried to focus on her partner, her attention constantly sought Nicholas on the edge of the ballroom.

"You seem preoccupied tonight," said Lord Emerson when they came together again. "Is something wrong?"

"Not at all." Another forced smile filled her lips. The perpetual front made her cheeks hurt. Couples made their way down the line, but after a few minutes, Katherine stole another glance at where Nicholas had been standing.

He was gone.

She searched the room, her heart taking up a frantic pace when she found no trace of him.

"Miss Garrick," whispered Lord Emerson. A look of concern crossed his features, but he said nothing more. It was their turn to move.

Once they were standing still again, Katherine continued her perusal.

Her gaze wandered to the doors leading to the entry hall, catching on the familiar figure there. Nicholas walked through the door and disappeared from her view.

Did he intend to leave? A pang pierced her heart. She had little time left to speak with him before the final reading of the banns. She needed to know where his feelings rested in order to make a decision as scandalous as breaking off her engagement. Nicholas was taking what would likely be her last opportunity out the door with him.

The music continued for what must have been twenty minutes or more, trapping Katherine in a prison surrounded by joyous frivolity. When the first of the set completed, Lord Emerson approached her, his expression still holding worry.

"You look rather pale," he said, leaning closer to keep his voice low. "Are you unwell?"

"A bit of fresh air would do me good. Perhaps a glass of ratafia first?"

He offered his arm to escort her, but Katherine shook her head. "I should like to sit down before I faint."

The man nodded his understanding. "I shall return with refreshment then."

Katherine hated lying to him, but she had little choice at the moment. She could hardly tell the person meant to marry her that she needed to chase after another man.

Working her way through the participants of the last half of the set, Katherine moved toward the door with as much subtlety as possible, a difficult feat given the way her heart pounded and her mind demanded she break into a full run.

She passed through the open double doors into the entry hall. The area was empty but for a footman and a few servants carrying trays of lemon tarts. Katherine's heart dropped into her stomach. Why she had thought the marquess might still be standing here after so much time, she couldn't say. Hope in its most fragile form.

A footman bowed when she neared him, his expression perfectly stoic.

"Lord Keswick came out here a few minutes ago," said Katherine. "Has he called for his carriage?"

"No, ma'am. He took to the gardens." The footman pointed down the hallway.

Katherine gave one last look over her shoulder toward the sound of music and chatter and then followed the man's directive. The air hit her lungs with an icy blast the moment she stepped outside, causing her to inhale with a sharp gasp. She rubbed her gloved hands up and down her arms, keenly feeling the weather take advantage of any place her skin was bare.

She saw no sign of Nicholas in the barren landscape, but the tall hedges blocked much of her view. Holding her folded arms snugly against herself, she wandered the path stretching to the right of the house, peering over the dark stone walkway and searching the shadows. The full moon provided barely enough light for her to see, but she would not allow the darkness to deter her. If Nicholas were out here, she would find him.

Perhaps she ought to call out his name, but fear that she might have been followed prevented it. The last thing she wanted was to create a scandal. The man dealt with the harsh judgments of the *ton* enough as it was.

Rounding another hedge, Katherine happened upon a statue of Eros, his wings unfurled in a majestic display and his hands clenched around a bow. Beneath the weapon was Nicholas. He sat on a stone bench, hunched over with his elbows on his knees. She could not see his face, but the stream of moonlight from above revealed the slight movement of his shoulders, shifting in tandem with his ragged breaths.

Katherine's slippers allowed her to approach in silence, giving her the opportunity to observe him unabashed. His black suit hugged his form, tailored to match every muscular curve in his arms and legs. Strands of his hair draped over his forehead, and she longed to see the emerald eyes hiding behind his black gloves.

"Nicholas?" she whispered.

His head shot up, meeting her gaze long enough for her to glimpse the moonlight glimmering off of his damp cheeks before he turned away. He rubbed his hands over his face, his voice course with emotion.

"Katherine. What are you doing out here?"

"I came looking for you." She sat down beside him, smoothing out her satin ballgown beneath her. "Why did you leave? I owe you a dance, remember?"

His cravat bobbed with his swallow, his attention firmly on the leafless hedges across from them. "I remember." He wet his lips, dropping his gaze to his lap. "But I believe it best that I return home."

A sharp pain ripped through her heart. "Are you feeling ill?"

"Ill in a way." He finally turned to face her, giving Katherine a view of all the pain he tried to hide. It was etched into his furrowed brows and shimmered in his sad eyes. Nicholas smiled, but it was nothing like his usual grins of mischief, lacking in resolve and any sort of joy. "You needn't worry about me. I shall be fine."

She studied him, debating whether she dared ask the questions resting on the tip of her tongue. He cared for her, that much she knew. But how much? And why did he always insist on hiding his problems from her?

She lifted her hand to his arm, and his muscles tightened beneath her fingertips. "I know, Nicholas. I know you wanted to court me." His body went rigid with his sharp inhale, but she continued, "I wish I would have known sooner. Why did you never tell me?"

"Because without your parents' consent, it did not matter."

"Of course it matters! I might have helped you persuade them." She gripped the fabric of his sleeve when he turned away, and the action brought his attention back to her. "Do you not believe me capable of caring about your feelings? You truly think me so inconsiderate and vain as that?"

"No." He shook his head. "That is the last thing I think."

"Then answer me now. Why did you ask to court me? Why did you persist in your calls and requests even when you were denied?"

Nicholas opened his mouth to answer but his words never came. Someone called her name, their voice penetrating the cold air. *Mama.*

The marquess stood from the bench so suddenly Katherine started. He ran a hand through his hair, leaving his fingers woven in the disheveled locks at the back of his head. "I must go. They cannot find you alone with me."

He started down the path in the opposite direction of Mama's encroaching voice. Katherine followed him.

The moment Nicholas realized she padded after him, he halted and spun on his heels to face her. She nearly collided with him, and he lifted his hands to stabilize her. "Katherine, go back. You know my reputation. If anyone else is with you mother—"

"I do not care."

"But I do!" He closed his eyes, drawing in a deep breath that seemed to aid in calming him. "I will not let you be ruined because of me. Please."

The plea in his voice ate away her resolve...or most of it. "I will return if you answer my question."

Nicholas groaned, and she found amusement in his vexation. Her mother shouted again.

"The moments slip away too quickly to convey everything I wish. We are all forever chasing after time, and I fear mine has run out." Nicholas scooped up her hand, the warmth of his large ones engulfing her. Gently, he brushed his thumb over her wrist, lifting her glove to expose more of her skin. His lips met the spot just beneath her palm. Her pulse pounded against his soft touch as pleasant tingles crawled up her arm and into her shoulder, wracking her body with a hard shudder.

...until I was certain the touch would forever haunt you.

Nicholas lingered until the call of her name rang through the air, growing ever closer. His lips curled slightly, and before he completely pulled away, he kissed the spot again, as if he were hesitant to release her.

She wished he wouldn't; she needed more—more time, more of *him*—but once again the moment was stolen from them.

Nicholas lifted his hand to her cheek, tilting his head, a look of longing in his eyes she felt wholly. "Goodbye, Katherine."

The way he said it made her heart stall. It was as if he meant the salutation to be permanent. He turned, and in seconds the shadows swallowed him, the only trace of their interaction the prickle of her skin from his haunting kiss.

Nicholas

FOOLISH. COMPLETELY AND UTTERLY FOOLISH.

Nevermind that he had snuck to the gardens and *wept*. Wept like a child who hadn't gotten his way. But to have Katherine see him in such a state? He should have gone directly home as he'd intended upon leaving the ballroom, but something about the solitude of a garden had beckoned him. He'd only wanted to gather his thoughts for a moment, but he never would have chosen that bench had he thought anyone would follow him.

Nicholas barreled through the garden as fast as his legs would carry him. Deeper and deeper he ran until the stone path gave way to dirt. What the devil had he been thinking?

When Lady Garrick's shouts ceased, he allowed himself to slow. His breaths came in heavy gasps, though whether from the exertion or the proximity to Katherine, he couldn't say.

Once certain no one would find him, he leaned against a tree and closed his eyes.

Katherine knew. The attempts he had worked hard to hide now lay in the open; his heart had never felt so exposed.

And yet, she had not recoiled at the affection his actions surely spoke to, but rather demanded their expression. She wished to know how he felt, and her reaction to his kiss on her wrist suggested—

Gads. What a mess he had made. Katherine was engaged. Encouraging her attention to him was dishonorable, and every moment he spent with her proved him incapable of letting her go. He had to find a way—move to his townhouse in London, visit the Continent, *anything* to keep himself away from the woman. His mind wandered briefly to the pearls he had hidden away at his estate, but he gave them little consideration. He hadn't enjoyed his first trip to the future overly much, beyond the time with Katherine. Going again was ludicrous.

Perhaps his heart would heal in time, but not if the stitches he managed to sew were continually ripped open with every smile, word, and touch she offered him.

He heaved a sigh and pushed away from the tree. He needed to commit to a plan, and soon.

A rustle from behind drew his attention. From the shadows, something long swung toward him. With no time to duck, it smashed against Nicholas's head, and the impact toppled him to the ground. The area above his left ear felt warm and throbbed, but before he could lift his hand to investigate, another smack to his head made the world fade to a pinprick and the garden disappeared.

Chapter 29

Suffolk, 1815

Katherine

K atherine stared down at her plate. Her body may have been present at dinner, but her mind was elsewhere. A yawn escaped her. Last night had been long. After her brief discussion with Nicholas, she had watched and waited, hoping he would return to the ballroom and ask her to dance. But he never came, and while she never lacked for partners, her mind had focused on only one thing—Nicholas's soft, haunting kiss.

She rubbed a finger over the spot on her wrist. Her skin might never feel the same. Nicholas had kissed her there once before, but this...this one had been different. She'd felt everything he wished to say in that gesture. Nicholas Betham loved her.

Although she had never heard him say the words, nothing was more clear to her than the depth of his affection. He had fought hard for the opportunity to court her only to have his request rejected time and again. Many men would have taken things into their own hands, sought to ruin and force a marriage, perhaps even elope, but Nicholas had done none of those things. He had always guarded her reputation as though it were something precious, thus proving his character to be exactly as she thought—completely honorable and unworthy of the gossip surrounding his name.

And she was determined to make Mama see that. Once this dinner party ended, she intended to sit down with her mother and have a discussion about her engagement to Lord Emerson. She could not go through with marrying the man when her heart belonged to someone else. Cutting the ties would likely frustrate the earl, but as his heart possessed no attachment to her, she believed he would recover.

The same may not be said of her reputation, however, and that detail made her anxious. The cause deserved her bravery, and being with Nicholas was worth whatever repercussions she might suffer, but Mama and Papa would certainly not see things that way.

She glanced at Lord Emerson, who sat next to her. He had been rather quiet after her return from the gardens, not once questioning her absence, and she could not help but wonder what he was thinking. He had never been overly expressive, but still, she sensed something had changed.

He glanced up and caught her gaze on him. Katherine looked away, her cheeks warming.

"I heard something interesting about you last night," he said in a low voice.

"Oh?" She took a bite of her vegetables. What could he have heard? He did not sound displeased about whatever it was, but the man was hard to read.

"Yes. I was told you enjoy studying mathematics. Is that true?"

All attention at the table had turned toward her, but it was Mama's harsh stare that gained her focus. The woman's eyes seemed to hold a warning, one Katherine was eager to defy.

"I do enjoy the subject," she said, watching her mother's eyes widen. "I find it difficult to acquire new books on the matter or anyone willing to converse with me on the topic. Numbers have always interested me. I cannot see that changing anytime soon."

She dared a look at Lord Emerson. He studied her intently, but his expression, again, revealed nothing as to his thoughts about her confession. A countess who studied numbers in her free time? That might well make him question his engagement to her. Perhaps it had not been the most tactful way to reveal her oddities, but she could no longer hide who she was. Maggie had told her to be proud of her interests and talents, that the world would never change unless someone stood against expectation. Her declaration might not make a difference, but at least it gave her a sense of freedom. Let the judgments come.

Mama cleared her throat, turning toward Lady Aldridge, who sat next to Papa near the head of the table. "I must say, the Morrisons' outdid themselves with the ball this year."

"Exquisite, was it not? And, I heard there was more happening in the gardens last night than in the ballroom." The woman waggled her brows, ready to divulge whatever information she possessed the moment someone asked for it. Katherine tired of listening to gossip.

"Do tell us before you completely burst," said Mama, spearing another piece of meat, clearly satisfied to have steered the conversation away from her daughter.

"Rumor has it Lord Keswick spent most of the evening there."

Katherine stilled, her pulse taking on an uncomfortable pace. Mama swatted at the air. "Did you expect any of us to be surprised by this? That man is always sulking about, ready to take advantage of naïve young women."

Katherine clenched her fists and shot her mother a glare of warning. Mama squirmed in her chair.

"The young woman in question is hardly naïve ," said Lady Aldridge. "Overheard Miss Merell myself on my way to the refreshment tables. According to her, she and the marquess have quite the understanding. Perhaps he will offer for her. Finally reform enough to court someone of good breeding. None of his other interests have held any class."

Mama's forehead furrowed with a mixture of annoyance and offense. Nicholas's *other interests*, so far as Katherine knew, included only her. Lady Aldridge had unintentionally accused her family of lacking sophistication, the cause for Mama's frustration, but her mother could not reveal this offense without also bringing to light Nicholas's pursuit.

A grin tugged at Katherine's lips. She should not enjoy her mother's turmoil, but after everything the woman had kept from her, she took pleasure in Mama's discomfort.

"Miss Merell is not naïve ," said Papa. "Nor is she reliable. The talk in the card room was that another young woman was seen with Lord Keswick."

Mama clearly had not told Papa she had found their daughter in the garden; otherwise he would not have encouraged the conversation to continue. Had someone truly seen them? Mama's pale face suggested she had the same question.

"Did they say who, my lord?" asked Mama, hiding her panic with relative ease.

"Too dark," said Papa before taking another bite of his meal.

"Well, since we will never know their identity, perhaps we should cease making assumptions." Katherine sat her napkin down and met her mother's gaze. She did not care if the whole of England knew of her time with Nicholas, but she preferred not to fuel the gossip. Not until she could discuss the matter with Lord Emerson. It was hardly fair to him. "Perhaps the rumors are not true at all. Speculating when we have unreliable sources only creates chaos."

"You speak as though our chats cause damage," said Lady Aldridge. "We are merely passing the time by discussing the rumors that already exist."

Anger threaded through Katherine. She stood, and Mama gasped at the sudden movement. Manners or no, Katherine could not remain in the room. "You are adding to the fire. Do you not see the damage such talk can do? Spreading rumors when they may not be true makes you no better than a man who sets out to ruin a young woman's reputation. It makes you a hypocrite."

"*Katherine*," Mama warned with a hiss. "Mind yourself."

"I will the moment everyone in this room listens to me. I am tired of hearing Nicholas's character berated for things he did not do. If you must know, *I* was the one he met in the gardens last night."

Mama's mouth fell open, shock filling her expression. Lord Emerson stiffened next to her, but he said not a word. Katherine continued, "Lord Keswick is a gentleman—an honorable man—and your rumors have hurt him in ways you cannot begin to understand. He has suffered tremendously from the accusations, many of which I suspect were started by people in this very room."

"You met with a confirmed rake in the gardens?" asked Lady Aldridge, her tone a mixture of confusion and intrigue. "What reason did you have to follow Lord Keswick?"

"Lord Keswick is not a rake. He is my friend. We have both been through a great deal the last few weeks, and I wished to offer him my support. But that is beside the point. You have misjudged him severely, and I would ask that you discontinue gossiping about him. He does not deserve to be the center of your tittle-tattle."

Silence fell over the room. Perhaps those sitting within had never been so confounded. Their opinion of her had likely changed over the last few minutes, but Katherine found it difficult to care.

"Please excuse me." Katherine shuffled from the room. Her lungs demanded fresh air, and she would certainly not find any in the stuffy dining room. She rushed past Mr. Merriwether and his concerned brows, reaching the door before the man could offer her a coat. Once outside, the cold washed over her skin. The smell of moisture and dirt filled her nose, the scent soothing in ways she couldn't explain.

Hooves pounded against the drive. Two black stallions pulled a carriage closer to the estate. Katherine squinted, attempting to make out the details of the golden crest on the door. As they became clear with the conveyance's increased proximity, she knew at once to whom it belonged, and her heart leapt.

She lifted her skirts and took the stairs hastily, nearly tripping at the bottom. The carriage pulled to a stop, and a footman alighted. The young man opened the door and handed Lady Keswick to the ground.

"Phoebe. It is lovely to—" Katherine cut her words short the moment she laid eyes on the dowager marchioness's expression. Her pale face provided a stark contrast to the black gown and hat she wore, and the furrowed lines in her forehead made Katherine's pulse race. "Is something amiss, my lady?"

Phoebe shot forward and pulled Katherine into an embrace. The gesture startled her, but concern outweighed the surprise.

"Nicholas is missing."

The woman's whispered words sent ice flowing through Katherine's veins. Phoebe pulled away, her eyes glistening with tears. Katherine swallowed, but it did nothing to alleviate the lump that had settled in her throat. "What do you mean he is missing? When did you last see him?"

"Before the ball. When I did not find him at home this morning, I thought he might have gone somewhere on business before I awoke. But a few hours ago our carriage returned without him from the Morrisons'. No one has seen him since early last evening. Perhaps it is silly of me to assume the worse, but after—"

"It is not silly at all. You have every right to worry."

Phoebe nodded, gratitude mingled with the concern in her pinched face. "I was hoping you might have seen him last night. He intended to dance with you. He told me so."

He hadn't danced with her, and she regretted that most ardently.

"I spoke with him in the gardens." Katherine shifted on her feet. She had no desire for Lady Keswick to think poorly of her. "We were not...that is to say, nothing happened between us. Mostly nothing. Nicholas..."

Drat. She had no desire to offer the details about what *did* happen, either.

Phoebe took Katherine's hand and gave it a gentle squeeze. "You do not need to explain yourself to me. I know how my son feels about you, and I suspect it is similar to how you feel for him."

"Yes. It is. But you must know that he has never been anything but a gentleman. Nicholas is very protective of my reputation." More so than even she was after what she'd revealed moments ago in the dining room.

"We were nearly caught alone," she continued, lowering her voice. "Nicholas went deeper into the gardens to avoid scandal. I never saw him return to the ballroom after that."

Phoebe lifted a hand to cover her mouth, and her glove muffled her voice. "Something terrible has happened, I know it."

"We shall go to the Morrisons' and search for him," said Katherine, taking Phoebe's arm and guiding her to the carriage. "We shan't stop until we find him."

The footman opened the carriage door and waited to assist them. Phoebe shook her head, her emotions finally breaking her completely. Tears streamed down her cheeks, and her voice came out choked. "I have already gone to the Morrisons'. The servants searched the whole of the estate and found nothing."

Katherine took a slow breath, willing herself to remain calm. Lady Keswick needed her support, so she would shove her own fears aside. "Then we start in the village. Someone is sure to have seen him."

The dowager marchioness nodded and accepted the footman's outstretched hand. Before he could offer Katherine the same, the door to the estate burst open. Mama scurried down the stairs, her face fixed with a look of terror.

"Katherine, where are you going?" Mama stopped in front of them, her breathing faster than normal.

"Nicholas has gone missing," said Katherine. "I am leaving with Lady Keswick to find him."

"No." Mama grabbed her arm. "Katherine, if you leave here with her, the rumors will only double. Lady Aldridge already believes you and the marquess are far too acquainted with one another. What of Lord Emerson! What shall he think of all this?"

Katherine pulled her arm from her mother's grip. "I cannot control Lord Emerson's thoughts anymore than I can control yours. Whatever you believe of Nicholas, he is a good man. He is my friend, and I am going with his mother to find him."

"You are on dangerous ground, and I cannot allow you to throw everything away." Mama made no attempt to grab her again, but her voice pleaded. A deep sadness filled her tone, a hidden agony Katherine still did not understand. Mama tilted her head. "I can see it. That man has stolen your heart, but I beg of you to take it back before he shatters it completely."

"What does it matter when Lord Emerson has no desire for my heart, broken or whole?"

"Perhaps not yet, but with time—"

"Not ever, Mama. He has told me so himself."

Mama appeared taken aback by the statement, her brows furrowing. "He did?"

"Yes. Goodbye, Mama. I shall see you later tonight." Katherine accepted the footman's hand and climbed into the carriage. The door shut, but she could still see Mama standing a few feet away, her gaze cast to the ground with a look of heavy contemplation.

Lady Keswick knocked on the top of the carriage, and the horses pulled forward. The estate faded into the distance, and Phoebe's quiet sobs filled the space, a steady companion to the fear bubbling inside Katherine.

All would be well. They would find him.

Suffolk, 1815

Nicholas

Pounding, ever present, pulsed against the side of Nicholas's skull. His ribs had joined that injury hours ago and were now bruised from the beating he'd taken. He kept his eyes closed to avoid watching the world spin, but vertigo found him even in the darkness, making him tilt to find balance.

Not that he could fall over since he was bound to a chair, but his body seemed keen on adjusting despite this.

Voices, too muffled to fully understand, sounded from somewhere beyond the door in front of him. They were deep, one familiar and the other pressing on his mind like a lost memory. He'd only laid eyes on one of his captor's so far, thus leaving the second man's identity a mystery.

As the agitation in their tones grew, he knew they would return for him. Another punch to the jaw or stomach was to be expected given that he refused to hand over the information they wanted.

Nor would he ever.

Edwin had entrusted him with the pearls, and he would not divulge their location. That he had been abducted proved his decision to take possession of them had been wise. He had promised Luke that he would watch after his family, and by keeping the time travel beads, he removed any threat against Edwin and his daughter.

They were safe.

Footsteps—one, two, three. He pinched his eyes to combat the desire to open them. An eerie creak whined from the old hinges. More footsteps followed and then silence.

Surrendering, Nicholas pried open his eyes. The man before him grinned, revealing two rows of white teeth. He swiped a piece of his curly hair from his eyes and sneered. "Look who's awake. Are you ready to answer my question yet?"

"Beat me all you like, Doxly. I shall never tell you where they are."

"I enjoy bestowing regrets, and believe me, those words will be added to your list." Doxly laughed, and to Nicholas's surprise, retreated to the door. "We'll see how long your resolve lasts soon enough."

The door closed, leaving Nicholas to ponder his captor's scheme in the silence.

Katherine

KATHERINE'S SPENCER JACKET KEPT LITTLE OF THE ICY AIR FROM penetrating her skin and settling in her bones. With only a few days until Christmastide, the weather had taken a turn. Thick flakes of snow drifted from the wispy clouds, giving everything within view an almost hazy appearance.

The thin layer of snow crunched under her boots as she walked down the main street of Willowsway, the town near her father's estate. Nicholas's mother walked next to her, stiff and silent. They had begun their search with high hopes, but with every place they looked and each person they spoke to the feeling dwindled.

Katherine had never thought Nicholas was in the village. It made no sense for him to leave his carriage behind and travel home—or anywhere else for that matter—on foot with the weather being so dreary. But if Nicholas had not left on foot, did that mean he was still somewhere in the gardens at the Morrisons' estate?

The panic she had worked hard to suppress rose to the surface. She could think of only two logical explanations for Nicholas's disappearance. Either he was still hiding in the barren shrubs and leafless trees or he had left with someone else, perhaps not willingly.

The notion twisted her stomach. Phoebe had stated she had a horrible feeling something bad had happened to her son, and Katherine hated that she agreed.

The two of them entered the apothecary, the only shop in town they'd yet to search. The man behind the waist-high counter smiled and nodded when they approached. His dark gray hair fell over his blue eyes, soft as the falling snow outside his establishment.

"Good afternoon, Mr. Morton," said Phoebe.

"My lady, 'tis a cold day to be out. What can I do for you?"

"Nothing ails me at present, but Miss Garrick and I are searching for my son. Have you seen Lord Keswick today?"

"No, my lady. Have you tried the tailor's? Lord Keswick seems a fine dandy. Perhaps he is there?"

"We visited Mr. Ruckford already," said Katherine. She tapped her foot on the floor, her eyes wandering over the many vials and boxes lining the shelves. Was Nicholas a dandy? She had never paid much attention beyond noticing he dressed well, each waistcoat carefully cut to fit his handsome frame perfectly. "You are certain you haven't seen him?"

"Certain, miss. Wish I could say otherwise."

"We shall continue on then," said Phoebe. "Have a wonderful day, Mr. Morton."

The bell above the door chimed with their exit. Katherine stopped in front of the shop window and wrapped her arms around her midsection. Her limbs were growing numb. They could not stay out in the weather much longer, and if she were cold, she could only imagine how Nicholas must be feeling—assuming he was, in fact, still outside.

"What now?" Katherine asked through clattering teeth.

Phoebe's brows furrowed. "We take you home. You are freezing. You haven't even a coat."

"N-no. I shan't go home until we find him. Perhaps we ought to return to the Morrisons' and search the gardens again."

Phoebe tilted her head, dejection and sorrow filling her features. "The servants were quite thorough, Katherine."

"What of Windgate? Nicholas is well acquainted with the duke. Perhaps he went there?"

Lady Garrick shifted closer to place her hand on Katherine's shoulder. "I have already gone to see him. The duke has not seen Nicholas since the two of you returned last week." She bit her lip and sighed. "I do wonder if the people who abducted you before are responsible."

Katherine turned away, shifting her gaze to the couple walking on the opposite side of the street. There was a thin line between lying out of necessity and doing so for no reason. She and Nicholas had never been abducted, a fact his mother remained unaware of, but Katherine dared not tell her the truth. Not only might she think Katherine mad, but the confession would only add to the woman's concerns.

"Let us ask that couple if they have seen him." Katherine pointed to where the two people had stopped in front of the modiste's shop. "Mr. Ranson and Miss Isabel Hastings, I believe."

She stepped forward, but Phoebe caught her by the arm. "I shall speak with them. You must return to the carriage and bundle up in the blankets. I have no desire to see you strike a fever from being out in this weather, and if Nicholas were here, he would say the same thing."

Well, that was hardly fair.

"But you could catch a fever as easily as I. In fact, statistically speaking, those who have reached an age of seniority tend...to..."

Lady Keswick's grin halted the words. A blush creeped into Katherine's cheeks. "Not that I would include you in that group or believe you possess such a frail constitution."

"I cannot be offended when you speak the truth, Katherine. But please, return to the carriage. I shall be but a minute."

"Very well." Katherine heaved an overly dramatic sigh that made Phoebe chuckle. The woman crossed the street, and Katherine began a slow pace to the carriage that waited not far down the street. She kept her attention on Lady Keswick, straining her ears to hear the conversation, but the sound did not carry, muffled by the falling snow.

Mr. Ranson shook his head, and Katherine's stomach plummeted. Where would they search now? Nicholas was nowhere to be found in town, and early evening had already settled in, the small trickle of sunlight slipping through the clouds fading. She would try once more to convince Lady Keswick to return to the Morrisons'. Even if Nicholas were not there, perhaps they might find a clue as to where he had gone.

She brought her hands to her mouth and huffed a few breaths. The warmth seeped through her gloves but lasted only a few moments. The tips of her fingers tingled with the cold, and her nose burned with each brush of chilly air. No matter how much she wished to find Nicholas, she and Phoebe could not continue their search in perpetuity.

They needed to find him before nightfall completely—

A hard yank on her arm pulled Katherine around the corner of the haberdasher's and into a darkening alley. She screeched, but the sound cut off when a large hand covered her mouth. She writhed against a rather firm figure, and judging by the strength and height they possessed, she could only assume it was a man who pinned her.

He dragged her backwards until the alley opened at the opposite end. A black carriage awaited, one with no markings to indicate to whom it belonged. Katherine squirmed in her captor's hold, attempting another scream. It was also lost to falling snow.

Desperate, she bit hard into the man's palm. He wailed, and his hold loosened enough for her to break free. She darted back to the alley, the lingering taste of leather on her tongue, but made it only a few paces into the shadows before a set of strong arms wrapped around her waist and lifted her from the ground. She screamed but was given no opportunity to see if anyone heard before being thrown into the dark conveyance. She landed on the floor, her palms next to a pair of black boots.

The door slammed closed, and Katherine leaned against the seat, her eyes following the seam up the coffee-colored pantaloons across from her until she met Lord Doxly's smug expression.

"Thank you for joining me, Miss Garrick."

Suffolk, 1815

Nicholas

Nicholas attempted to pull his elbows toward him. The ropes pinning his wrists to the arm of the chair dug into his skin, each yank burning more than the last. Hours had passed since he'd seen Doxly. Perhaps Nicholas should enjoy the temporary reprieve from being punched, slapped, and mocked, but he could not ignore the foreboding that had settled in the pit of his stomach.

Doxly desired the pearls. Everyone knew of the man's gambling addiction. Debtor's prison awaited him unless he came into possession of something valuable like a set of pearls that allowed one to travel through time. How had the man learned of the beads' ability? Miss McCarthy had brought them from the future, and so far as Nicholas was aware, the only people in this era who knew about them were Edwin and Katherine...and apparently Mrs. Bielle.

His brows furrowed. The housekeeper remained a complete mystery to him, and she had not given up her secrets despite his interrogation. But he knew her well enough. The woman simply could not be involved in anything diabolic.

His mind wandered to his time in the future. Landon Atton had taken Luke and Maggie's pearls. The man now possessed the ability to traverse time. Could he somehow be involved? Doxly had an accomplice Nicholas had yet to see...

He groaned. Thinking only added to the throb near his ear. He had too many questions and too few answers. Regardless, Doxly was up to something and needed to be stopped.

He gave another hard yank, but the ropes bit into his wrists, holding firm to their assigned duty of keeping him trapped. Perhaps if he could find something sharp to rub against he might weaken the strands enough to escape.

He glanced around the room. The space was empty but for him and the chair, and he guessed it had once served as the bedchamber in a hunting lodge. The east wall sported a fireplace, but the inside had remained cold and flameless, leaving the room chilly. The only light came from the window behind him, and judging by the increased shadows, dusk approached. The thought of spending another long night in this room, freezing and sore, filled him with dread.

A soft, consistent clop met his ears, and Nicholas held his breath to listen. A carriage drew near. Hope surged through him, but it was quickly doused when Doxly's voice echoed from outside the window.

It took longer than usual for the creak of the front door to follow the man's arrival, but when it did, a scuffling sound accompanied it along with a muffled set of squeals.

"Bring her," said an unfamiliar deep voice. "This won't take long."

Her. The men had abducted a woman. Nicholas's stomach flopped as possibilities raced through his thoughts. He could have made guesses, but Doxly gave him no time to do so. The door to his room swung open.

Landon Atton entered first, his grin smug. Doxly followed, but it was the woman he held against him that stole every ounce of Nicholas's attention.

Katherine.

"I thought you might enjoy some company," said Landon, "and it didn't escape my notice the way you stared at her. She will make for excellent motivation, wouldn't you agree?"

Nicholas clenched his jaw. There was no good answer to that question. If he pretended Katherine meant nothing to him, Landon might shoot her here and now.

Landon waved Doxly forward. "I'll make this simple for you. Tell me where you've hidden the pearls, and no harm befalls her." He leaned close to whisper the rest. "And if Miss Garrick isn't enough incentive, I'm certain your mother will be. I've done my research. I know exactly where to find your estate—find your family."

When Nicholas took it upon himself to keep the pearls, he had not imagined someone would go to such lengths to obtain them. Landon Atton had traveled back in time to track them down. His drive spoke of desperate determination, a very dangerous thing.

"Release her," said Nicholas. "I will tell you where they are."

Landon *tsk*ed and shook his head. "You will tell me their location, Doxly will fetch them, and *then* I will release her. There's an order to things, and if you play nicely, the two of you will live to see Christmas morning."

The last thing Nicholas wanted to do was give the man what he wanted, thus failing Luke again, but he would not risk Katherine's safety. Her life was worth far more than time traveling pearls.

He swallowed the fury building inside him. "Very well. But if anything—"

"Miss Garrick will not be harmed." Landon held up his hand defensively. "You have my word."

"And your word is worth more than the dirt on the bottom of your shoes, is it?"

Landon chuckled and turned to face Doxly. "Take her to the guest room and lock her inside. You've got a set of pearls to track down."

Doxly tugged Katherine out of the room. She had not said a word since the two men brought her inside, and her terrified expression haunted Nicholas. Would she blame him for all of this?

She should as it was, indeed, his fault. He had taken the pearls and failed to keep them safe. But more specifically, he had fallen in love with Katherine, and his *tendre* for the woman had done nothing but put her in danger.

Landon pulled a pistol from the sheath at his waist and held it up to examine the piece. "Now, tell me where you've hidden the pearls. I would hate for Miss Garrick to become acquainted with this."

Nicholas closed his eyes. He was out of options. Landon Atton would get his hands on more pearls, but that was a sacrifice that must be made. He would not allow Katherine to suffer for one of his foolish mistakes.

So, he opened his mouth and told the man everything he wanted to know.

Katherine

A STRONG HAND GRIPPED KATHERINE'S UPPER ARM. DOXLY'S HOLD hurt, but she held in a scream. The idea of ripping out of his grasp and making a run for it had crossed her mind, but Mr. Atton had a pistol. Lord Doxly led her into another room and shoved her to the floor. A wicked grin crossed his face, stealing her ability to breathe. He took a step toward her, and she scooted backwards.

"Shame I need to leave," he said. "But once I get back, perhaps you and I can become better acquainted."

"I would rather kiss a pig."

The man's face darkened, but he said nothing in response. His glare held a promise, however, that sent a wave of shivers down her spine. Lord Doxly left the room and pulled the door shut with a bang. A hard click followed as he slipped a latch into place.

She released a heavy breath, and then the tears began. She'd held them in—kept her emotions in check long enough to find herself alone. Putting on a strong façade was not simply for her benefit. She hoped Nicholas would not give in to Mr. Atton's demands, perhaps lead him on some wild goose chase and buy them time. She doubted the man would let them go once he had what he wanted.

311

She wiped the moisture from her cheeks and perused the room. It held no furniture, not even a chair. The window in the back wall had been boarded shut, allowing a minimal amount of light from the setting sun to percolate through the cracks.

Katherine crawled to the wall and leaned her back against the cold, wooden planks. She would not cry more. Not now. Tears would not serve anything but the fear, and she would be strong and keep her emotions under control. Someone would find them. Nicholas's mother would have noticed her absence by now and called the constable. Someone had to have heard her scream.

She thought back to the carriage ride. Lord Doxly had gone on about his plan for what felt like hours, all too proud of himself and the scheme he'd concocted. Somehow the man had become involved with the same people after the pearls in the future. According to Lord Doxly, he would receive a rather handsome reward for his assistance, and given the man's rumored financial situation, he would likely go to great lengths to relieve himself of debt. The alternative, after all, was prison.

And then there was Mr. Atton. She had no doubt the pistol he carried would be put to use if needed, and that alone encouraged her to cooperate. He had put them in danger in the future, and she now understood the strange look she'd seen in his eyes—desperation.

What if Mr. Atton hurt Nicholas more than he already had? She had not missed the purple coloring on his right temple nor the dried blood on his lower lip. They had beaten him to get information, and when that failed, abducted her to pressure him into submission.

And it had worked.

Katherine pulled her knees to her chest and sucked in a deep breath. Her emotions lingered near the surface, ready to erupt with any break in her resolve. Fear pushed against the wall she created, attempting to break free—to break her.

The door swung open and crashed against the interior wall. Lord Doxly threw Nicholas to the floor and closed the door again.

He moaned, and Katherine rose to cross the room. Nicholas had managed a sitting position by the time she reached him. Without thinking, she threw her arms around his neck. His scent of citrus and leather washed over her, the familiarity of it calming her racing heart and mind as he enfolded her in a warm embrace. In the safety of his arms, her tears broke free, shaking her body with sobs. Bravery was an admirable quality, but she had no desire to be brave just now. Mama had taught her to hide weaknesses, to never let vulnerabilities show. How many times had she avoided socializing for fear of saying something she should not? How many times had she held back tears after making a mistake?

With Nicholas, she never worried about her imperfections and what he might think of her impertinence. She never wondered if he might think poorly of her because of something she said or asked. He had never sneered at her love of mathematics or chided her desire to study the subject.

It was as though the man created a space where she could be entirely herself and not feel ashamed of the person she was. Safety, comfort, and happiness existed in that space, and she never wished to leave it. She did not wish to be like her mother, and with Nicholas, she never had to be.

The marquess rested his head against hers, murmuring words of comfort in her ear. His fingers played with the strands of her hair that had come loose and draped over her back. She had half a mind to pull every last pin from her scalp and let him weave his fingers through it all.

The thought made her shudder, and Nicholas pulled away. The little light that climbed through the cracks between the boards on the window made his green eyes glow, illuminating the concern in them. He looked her over, his brows furrowed.

"No coat? You must be freezing." He shrugged off his own and swung it around her shoulders, just as he had not days ago when they returned to 1815.

"A little, but I admit it is warmer in here than it is outside. Your mother and I have been searching for you for hours."

"My mother?"

His expression twisted with more concern, and she hurried to alleviate it. "She is fine. Lord Doxly only took me."

Giving him that detail did not eliminate his worry as she had hoped. Nicholas turned away and ran a hand through his hair, a habit that she had come to recognize marked his worry. "This is all my fault. I am so sorry—"

Katherine grabbed his hand. "No. You cannot blame yourself for this. Luke asked you to look after his family. I presume you took the pearls from Edwin to keep them safe?"

He nodded but still refused to look at her.

"This is not your fault, Nicholas. You cannot control the things Lord Doxly or Mr. Atton does."

"Perhaps not, but..." His cravat, which hung loosely around his neck, bobbed with his swallow. "He only took you to force me into talking. If my feelings for you were not...I have put you in danger. For *that* the blame is my own. It is an irrevocable truth."

"Had I not gone searching for you, Lord Doxly would have never managed to take me. I chose to go with your mother. We searched the whole town over, and quite honestly I deserve to be given my due credit for this mess we've created. I believe the blame could be shared between us."

His fingers curled around hers, and he finally met her gaze. "And what percentage of the credit do you feel should be yours?"

Katherine looked heavenward and furrowed her brows in mock contemplation. "At least seventy percent."

"Seventy?" He reared back with a chuckle.

"Indeed. Had I not gone to His Grace's study, you would never know about the pearls' ability to traverse time and therefore would not currently be in possession of them."

"And had my heart not been so deeply engaged, I may not have followed you into that study at all. I would have returned you to the drawing room, and neither of us would have seen the future."

"I never objected to your escort. Surely that puts me at fault as well? I had every intention of finding the pearls before we even arrived at Windgate. I would have gone after them with or without you. Thus the argument could be made that I both instigated this entire situation and placed myself in danger of my own accord."

Nicholas shook his head, a full smile reaching his eyes. "You truly will not allow me to be the gentleman and claim responsibility?"

"I might, but it shall cost you."

"Cost me? And how great a payment am I to make?"

She had changed her mind. Bravery would be quite useful in this moment. Her heart pounded, but now was not the time to hold back or hide her impertinent nature. Nicholas was right—they were always chasing time—but she would not allow it to slip away again.

"Perhaps a trade would be better," she said. "I have no wish to drain your fortune."

"You have piqued my interest. Tell me what it is I am to offer in exchange for your surrender."

Her gaze dropped to her lap and then to the floor where their hands held one another's. Her courage slipped away, and the words came out hushed and unsure. "You must offer to kiss me."

Nicholas stiffened, and silence settled between them. Perhaps she had made a mistake in making such a request. Nicholas cared for her, but he had never taken advantage of their time alone.

She dared to look at him, thinking she would find him turned away, but he was staring at her. The shadows highlighted the deep wrinkle in his brow, a display of pain and confusion. What if she had been wrong? What if he merely saw her as a friend?

No. The spot on her wrist still prickled with his touch. Friends did not leave haunting gestures like that.

She turned to the window. Heat rushed to her cheeks, and she was grateful the shadows would likely conceal much of her embarrassment. "If my price is too steep, you needn't worry about accepting it. I will gladly keep my seventy percent should you not wish to kiss me."

"Not wish...surely you must know that is not at all true. Katherine, in a few days you are to wed Lord Emerson. Kissing you would be completely dishonorable...and it would be my final undoing to have something I desperately want only for it to be ripped away a heartbeat later."

Her vision blurred with moisture. She did not look at him, but the pain in his voice remedied her doubts. Nicholas loved her, but he would not kiss her—not because he did not wish to but because he valued honor, the very thing the *ton* believed he lacked.

"You are right," she said, choking on the words. "It was selfish of me to ask that of you. At present, I am promised to someone else. I simply wanted to know what it felt like to kiss someone I love in case I never have the opportunity to do so again."

Nicholas's hand tightened around her fingers. She looked up and found his emerald eyes glazed. They searched her face. Hope, fear, and longing all flickered in their green depths, each emotion fighting for victory.

He tilted his head, and his mouth opened and closed several times before any words finally came, soft and uncertain. "You...you love me?"

Suffolk, 1815

Nicholas

Nicholas held his breath. The world froze, time coming to a complete halt. Nothing else mattered until he had an answer. They were locked in a room, possibly awaiting death if Landon so chose, yet he feared more for the silence than his life. Did Katherine love him?

Her lashes fluttered, the only indication that time pressed forward. Then, slowly, her lips lifted into a soft smile. His chest tightened as if he were being strangled. The anticipation might kill him before Landon had a chance.

Katherine shifted closer to him and lifted higher on her knees, matching his height. She took his free hand and rubbed her thumb over one of the spots between his knuckles. "I love you, Nicholas Betham."

Whatever restraint he had left faded into oblivion. He slipped one hand from hers and brought it to her cheek. She closed her eyes and leaned into his palm. How many times had he imagined this moment, a dream he never believed would become reality? Katherine loved him. She *loved* him.

His lips descended on hers. Katherine offered no hesitation to return the gesture, and her enthusiasm only fueled his own. Years worth of longing passed from his lips to hers. All the emotion he'd kept hidden breached the surface in an explosion of desire. He forgot every reason for holding himself back, for surely no amount of logic could convince him this was wrong. Katherine belonged in his arms. She loved him, and he wished to show her just how deeply he felt the same. His entire world could revolve around her, and life would be a stretch of endless bliss—a dance neither of them ever wished to finish.

Nicholas tilted his head, deepening his kisses. Katherine gripped his waistcoat, pulling him closer, and his hand slid around her waist, sliding her closer. He held her tight, aware of every subtle movement, every breath. She smelled of flowers and sunshine, as she always did, but today it seemed stronger, intoxicatingly so.

He trailed kisses along her cheek and down her neck. Katherine permitted this for only a few seconds before placing her hands on either side of his jaw and guiding him back to her lips. If he had thought time irrelevant before, it paled in comparison to how lost to it he was now. Nothing existed but the two of them.

Nicholas slowed his display of affection to give them both a chance to fill their lungs. He rested his forehead to hers, and a smile pulled across his cheeks. Katherine mirrored his expression, the dim light catching the sparkle in her brown eyes.

"I love you, Nicholas," she whispered. "I love you, and I cannot imagine a life without you in it. The moment we escape from this place I intend to end my engagement. I cannot marry Lord Emerson."

Where he should have felt relief, panic overcame him. He loved Katherine, no amount of denial could change that, but he also knew what could never be. Memories flooded his mind. He could see the tears flowing over his mother's flushed cheeks and hear her sobs of despair. The pain she had worked to hide was scorched into his mind...and his heart.

No matter how much he wanted Katherine, he could not subject her to the sort of life his mother had lived, alone and melancholic, trapped in a prison from which she could never escape.

He held Katherine's face, the words causing him pain before they even left his mouth. "You must marry him."

Her expression pinched with confusion. "You still wish me to marry him? But—"

"I do not wish it. I never did, but subjecting you to a life with me and all that entails...I cannot do it."

"Subjecting me? Nicholas, I have just said that I love you. What better life could I have than spending it with someone I love...who loves me?" She tilted her head, a question twisting her features. He had not returned the spoken sentiment, had not allowed those words to leave his lips. He realized they would do more harm than good. Though he did not regret it, he never should have kissed Katherine, but her confession had taken him by surprise. It had overwhelmed his sense of logic.

But now, he saw everything with perfect clarity. Should he marry Katherine against her parents' wishes, she would end up like his mother. Society would cast her out, reject her, if she ended her engagement only to be with another man—one they deemed a known rake. The rumors alone would be devastating, would taint every ounce of her happiness.

Nicholas stroked his thumbs over her cheeks. "My mother married a man of whom her parents did not approve. They despised my father, something I never held against them. But it hurt her deeply. I know how much you love your family, Katherine. I cannot allow you to give them up for me. You will regret doing so; you will come to resent me. That is to say nothing of how the rest of Society will treat you."

She shook her head with earnest. "I could never resent you."

"Even if that were true, we still lack your father's consent."

"I will reach my majority in less than a year. Or we could elope—"

"No." Nicholas dropped his hands and turned away. If there was one thing he refused to do, it was steal a young woman away to Gretna Green like his father had. He would not become like the man he so greatly despised. He would not ruin Katherine's reputation for his own selfishness.

His attention returned to her, his resolve firm. "You know not what you suggest."

"I know that I want to marry you. I want to be with *you.*"

He needed her to understand. This was greater than their feelings for one another, and he could not wed Katherine knowing the consequences as well as he did. "You would lose your family. They do not approve of me, and the mostly probable scenario is that you will be disowned. I know how much that weighs on a person; I saw how it affected my mother. For years, she would sit alone and cry, never offered an ounce of comfort from anyone. It destroyed her, Katherine. As a child I saw only a woman who disliked being out in Society, who preferred to keep to herself. It was not until I grew that I understood the entirety of what happened. When I saw the loneliness in her eyes, the daydreaming and the tears, I finally understood what marriage to my father had done. It was more than his abuse and indifference. She lost everything, and it pained me greatly to watch her fall further and further into a sea of melancholia, to lose herself and her beautiful spirit. I cannot bear to watch the same happen to you. Please do not ask it of me."

A soft sniffle escaped her, and Nicholas wrapped her in his arms, pulling her against his chest. He rested his chin on the top of her head, whispering into her golden hair. "I wish things were different. My inability to convince your parents is the greatest failure of my life—right next to allowing Landon Atton to get his hands on more time traveling pearls."

"You told him?" Her voice tickled the skin exposed at his neck.

"Yes. I would never allow any harm to come to you so long as I have means to prevent it."

She remained quiet for several minutes, tucked against his chest. Her quiet sobs eventually faded, but Katherine made no effort to move. Nicholas savored the moments, each a precious gift he would never be allowed again.

"What if we talk to my parents," Katherine whispered. "We could change their minds. We could—"

"I have tried for years. I cannot imagine another plea will do any good." Nicholas tightened his arms around her. "Doing anything that may jeopardize your engagement is out of the question. Lord Emerson is a good man; you will be well cared for under his protection."

"And you are satisfied with allowing him to be my protector? Satisfied that I should marry a man who claims he will never love me?"

A sharp pain ripped through his heart. Surely she did not speak in earnest?

"You cannot know that," said Nicholas.

"But I do." Katherine looked up at him. Darkness had overtaken the room, and he could barely see the furrowed lines in her forehead. Her hand slid from his chest to his cheek. "He told me so himself. His heart was broken once, and he has no intention of making it a participant in our marriage."

Nicholas's gut twisted. Could he do this? Sentence the woman he loved to a marriage where she would not be treasured as she should?

He inhaled a steady breath, hoping it would keep his tone even. "He will change his mind; I am certain of it. No man who comes to know you as I have could keep his heart locked away. Time will heal his broken heart. You will come to forget about me. Move on. Find happiness."

The words were meant to reassure himself as much as her, but they lacked the fervor required to be convincing.

"Is that what will happen?" she asked. "You will forget about me?"

Hot tears pricked at his eyes. Nicholas placed a kiss on the top of her head, his voice cracking. "No. I could never forget you."

Hoofbeats rattled through the still air. Muffled voices sounded from outside the window, the familiar tone filling Nicholas with dread. Katherine seemed to recognize Doxly's voice as well, tightening her hold on his waistcoat.

He squeezed Katherine against him. "I will not let him harm you. Promise me you'll do as I say." She glanced up at him, and though he could not see her face, Nicholas sensed her opposition to his request.

The front door creaked and the sound of footsteps followed. Nicholas took Katherine by her shoulders and pulled her away. "Promise me, Katherine. Please."

"I promise," she whispered.

The latch screeched, and the door swung open. Atton entered and hung a small lantern on a nail in the wall before looking down on them with smug grins. Doxly, who had followed him inside, held out a small leather sack and gave it a shake. Soft thuds echoed from inside it, like a dozen pebbles bouncing off the ground.

"Wise choice telling me the truth." Landon lifted his pistol. "But as I said before, I don't keep loose ends."

Nicholas pulled Katherine against him. "You're a fool for believing you shall get away with this."

"Not a fool. I'm a man who has the power of time travel at his fingertips." He shifted his aim to Katherine. "Should I take care of her first?"

"You promised to let her go."

Not that he'd once believed Atton would keep his word. The man had no honor. Perhaps if he could push Katherine aside quickly enough, he could take the man by surprise. He just needed to—

"Ah!" Atton pointed the pistol at Nicholas when he shifted. "You first then. Can't have you making a mess of my plans, now can I? So long."

Nicholas closed his eyes. Emerson should have been Katherine's protector. At least the earl would have kept her safe, unlike him. He had failed in so many ways, and now he and Katherine would pay the price.

Chapter 33

Suffolk, 1815

Katherine

A soft click reverberated around the room, but there was no pain, no screams. Katherine opened her eyes. Mr. Atton glared down at his pistol and rushed to examine it.

An instinctual impulse overtook her. A foolish one.

Katherine ripped from Nicholas's arms and lunged forward. She slammed her fist into Mr. Atton's knee before he could take note of her approach, and his leg buckled. He caught himself before falling to the ground and grabbed a fistful of her hair, eliciting a scream as he yanked her to her feet. "Stupid girl. I should—"

He released her with a yelp. Katherine fell to the floor and glanced up to see Nicholas throwing a punch at Mr. Atton's already bloody nose.

The man stumbled backwards with a wail, but before Nicholas could strike again, held up his pistol. A shot fired, and a ping echoed around the room.

"A fine aim you have," said Nicholas, rushing forward again.

Paralyzed, Katherine could do nothing but watch their flailing arms and shifting forms, but so far as she could tell, Nicholas was unharmed. Mr. Atton had missed.

Nicholas grabbed for the pistol, and in his attempt to keep it from him, Mr. Atton lost his hold. The gun fell to the floor and skidded to the open door. Katherine crawled over the wood planks. Her fingertips brushed metal, but only for a second before a larger hand pried the pistol from her grasp.

Lord Doxly grinned down at her. "Afraid not, my dear."

He started to reload, and Katherine grabbed for the gun, but Lord Doxly twisted out of her reach with each attempt until he finally tired of the effort. He slapped her cheek, and the force sent her crashing into the wall. Her skin burned, making her eyes swell with tears.

"That's enough!" shouted Lord Doxly. He pointed the pistol in Mr. Atton and Nicholas's direction. The two men ceased fighting and stared at him. Lord Doxly waved the gun, directing his words at Nicholas. "You, against the wall."

Nicholas stood firm, his breathing heavy. Lord Doxly rotated to aim the gun at Katherine. She gasped and pressed herself tighter against the wall.

"Now, or I shall shoot her," Lord Doxly said with a growl.

Nicholas met Katherine's gaze and heaved a sigh before making his way to the wall. He stopped at her side, and Mr. Atton swiped the gun from Lord Doxly's hand, cutting off any protest the man made with a glare.

No, no, no! They had been so close. She tucked into Nicholas's chest. This was her fault. They were going to die because she had wanted to see the future. Nicholas would have never been involved with the pearls had it not been for her.

Nicholas's arms tightened around her shoulders. He whispered into her ear, but the words were lost. Fear gripped her like night shrouded the world with shadows—without mercy.

"Now, if we're done with this nonsense." Mr. Atton wiped his jaw and the splotch of blood there. "I have places to be."

"Like in gaol?"

The question came from a few feet away, just inside the doorframe. Katherine lifted her head, and her mouth dropped.

"Edwin?" Shock filled Nicholas's voice, mirroring Katherine's confusion.

Mr. Atton pivoted to aim the pistol at the duke. "Who are you?"

"The Duke of Avendesh," muttered Doxly, pointing at Nicholas. "They are close acquaintances."

"And how did you find us?" asked Mr. Atton.

"When Lady Keswick informed me of Keswick's disappearance, I went to check on the pearls myself. Followed a suspicious character back here." He turned to Nicholas and frowned. "Why you believed our old treehouse was a good place to hide them, I shall never understand."

"Who would have thought to look there?" said Nicholas defensively. "It isn't as though I have children running about my estate."

"I clearly thought to look there, and you put them in the most obvious location—our old treasure box."

"Enough." Mr. Atton tapped his foot impatiently against the floor.

"Who else knows you are here?"

The duke pursed his lips and hummed for a moment. "By now? Everyone in the village, I should think. I sent several footmen to inform the constable, Keswick's mother, and Lady Aldridge."

"Lady Aldridge?" Nicholas scowled. "Why the devil would you inform her?"

"Because she shall inform everyone else." The duke's lips lifted into a wide grin. "What do you think, sir? With so many people aware of your crimes, there will be nowhere you can hide. You now have three people to dispose of, all with noble bloodlines. The entire country will be searching for you. Whatever hopes you had of escaping have been thoroughly slashed."

Except Mr. Atton did have the perfect escape—the pearls.

Katherine's brows furrowed. Actually, Lord Doxly was currently in possession of them. She had watched him tuck the tiny pouch into the pocket of his greatcoat. She could not help but wonder how much he knew. Mr. Atton likely had not told him how the pearls worked, which made them worth no more than regular pearls for the nobleman.

Mr. Atton's gaze darted between them, and the pistol shook in his hand. "I won't be going to prison. I've got what I came for." His expression twisted, and he glanced at Lord Doxly. Katherine could not douse her smile. Realization could be an amusing thing.

"Hand over the bag," Mr. Atton demanded, his focus on Lord Doxly.

The Englishman's jaw clenched. Lord Doxly was no doubt considering his options. Without knowledge of what those pearls were capable of, he had no reason to believe escape would be simple.

"You risk being shot on sight if you run," said Nicholas, seeming to sense the man's hesitation. "Hand the bag to His Grace. Do not be more of a fool than you already have."

"I shall not go to gaol," muttered Lord Doxly before reaching into his coat pocket and withdrawing the bag. He tossed it on the floor, and Nicholas reached down to retrieve it.

"No!" Mr. Atton lifted his gun.

Katherine's body sprinted into motion. She would not allow Nicholas to suffer for her decisions. She would not lose him.

Her hands met Nicholas's side, and she gave him a hard shove. He toppled over, hitting the floor with a thud, the small pouch dangling from his fingers. A spark of light filled the room, and the sound of the gun set her pulse racing.

Fire raged down her arm, starting from the curve of her shoulder and moving to her fingertips. Something warm trickled across her skin, and she looked to the place for confirmation of what she already suspected—Nicholas's wool coat, dampened with blood.

The room spun. Katherine reached for the wall, but her legs gave out before she found it. She hit the floor, and muffled shouts and voices pounded in her ears. Like the night, darkness overtook her vision, turning everything into shadows.

Nicholas

"NO!" NICHOLAS CROUCHED NEXT TO KATHERINE, HIS HEART BEATING SO frantically he feared it might fail. What had she been thinking! Had she not shoved him, he would have taken the brunt of the bullet.

Somewhere in the background, Edwin fought Atton for the pistol. More bodies had entered the room, but Nicholas was too distracted to take measure of who. He looked over Katherine, only finding blood on her upper arm. The small pool saturating his coat offered some relief given how little there was, but until she opened her eyes, until he knew she would be well...

A hand fell on Nicholas's shoulder, startling him.

"Forgive me." Edwin looked down at him, his chest heaving and a look of sympathy gracing his features. "She will be fine, but we should take her home and call for Doctor Thistlewaite."

Nicholas nodded and then peered around Edwin. A man with broad shoulders and curly brown hair had shackled Doxly's hands behind his back.

"What about Atton?" asked Nicholas.

Edwin shook his head. "The other man ran off after Miss Garrick was shot. I tried to stop him, but with both him and Doxly trying to escape and I having but two hands...well, I could only do so much." He gave a wry smile and pointed to the bag Nicholas held. "The pearls are safe at least."

"What should we do with them? I still believe I should keep them. You have a daughter—"

"We can discuss that later. You have other things to concern yourself with right now."

Nicholas returned his attention to Katherine. Her chest rose and fell with steady breaths, and beyond the pale color in her face and the blood staining his coat, she appeared fine.

"Swooned at the sight of blood," said Edwin. "Ironic for a woman who threw herself into the bullet."

"It was foolish. Katherine has always been so logical. Her actions make no sense." Then again, being held at gunpoint was bound to make anyone irrational.

Edwin chuckled. "Love, my friend, makes us all do illogical things. Even the most sensible of us." He patted Nicholas's shoulder and then walked to the door. "Bring her outside. You and I shall take her home. I am certain Lady Garrick is in another fit of nerves."

Once Edwin had left the room, Nicholas scooped Katherine into his arms. He held her tight against him and placed a kiss atop her head. She loved him, and he loved her. Why could that not be enough?

He wished he could cast aside the memories of his mother, depressed and sullen, but they persisted. He could not subject Katherine to a life where she was ostracized by both her family and Society. Overcoming one was perhaps manageable, but both would lead her to resent him despite her insistence otherwise.

He would rather bear the pain of never having her than to lose her in that way, to trap her in a marriage she did not want.

Nicholas rose from the floor, Katherine in his arms. He would hold her close, savor his last moments with the woman he loved. And tomorrow, he would leave for London. He would let her go.

Chapter 34

Suffolk, 1815

Nicholas

Nicholas crossed his arms and returned the glare that pinned him in place. Three footmen stood at the opposite side of the room, glancing from him to Lady Garrick with some measure of fear. Whether they would be more afraid of attempting to toss him out or of the woman with the peacock feathers adorning her head, Nicholas could not say, but should they choose to follow the viscountess's instructions, they would have a fight on their hands.

He refused to go anywhere.

"I shall not ask you again, Lord Keswick. We have no desire for your presence here."

"Desire or no, I will not leave until I know Katherine is well. Drag me out if you must, but I shan't go without throwing a few punches."

Lady Garrick clenched her fists. "You would threaten my staff? How dare—"

"Might I suggest we all remain calm," said Edwin. He threw Nicholas a chiding look, which did nothing to temper his irritation.

The matron's shoulders slumped, but she retained her scowl. "I am well within my rights to ask that man to vacate the premises."

Edwin held up his hand and shook his head. "No one is questioning that, my lady. I assure you, the moment Doctor Thistlewaite has updated us on Miss Garrick's well being, we shall leave. Understand we only wish to stay out of concern."

"Concern." Lady Garrick scoffed. "Perhaps for you it is concern, but he—"

She had barely raised a finger to point at him before Nicholas interrupted. "You think me not concerned? Surely by now you must know that I care for your daughter. What more can I possibly do to prove it to you?"

"I do not desire proof. I want you to stay away from her." Her voice dropped to a murmur, but Nicholas could still hear. "If you truly cared, you would not risk her reputation on a regular basis."

He had no argument against that. He had risked Katherine's reputation on numerous occasions, and the more times they were involved in *incidents* together, the more the gossips of the *ton* would talk.

"I more than care for her. I lo—"

"Shush!" Lady Garrick lifted her chin, and those stern eyes penetrated Nicholas to his bones. "If you insist on staying, then the least you could do is be silent. I will hear no more of this."

Lord Garrick entered the drawing room, his eyes heavy with

exhaustion and drunkenness. He collapsed onto the sofa near the window and spread his legs out over the rug. Lady Garrick rushed to his side and plopped onto the cushion, startling him. She began an in depth recount of the day's events.

Edwin shuffled to Nicholas's side and leaned close to whisper. "You must stow your irritation, Keswick. The woman is too distressed to be sensible, no matter how well rehearsed your pleas."

"She despises me. The distress is irrelevant."

Edwin nodded slowly, his expression drawn into a tight grimace. "I cannot deny that."

"How very helpful you are."

"I am not saying you should give up, but perhaps now is not the time for declarations of affection."

Nicholas grabbed Edwin's arm and turned him so that their backs faced the viscount and his wife. "My declarations do not matter. I will never offer for Katherine without their permission. I shan't do it, Edwin. My father coerced my mother into eloping with him, and she has spent her life completely miserable. I know what happens to ladies who are involved in such disgraceful acts. How can I embroil Katherine into something like that? I cannot. The fact that she is engaged only amplifies the repercussions. This entire situation is impossible."

"Impossible, you say, but from where I am standing, that is not so. She has not married Lord Emerson. True, breaking off the engagement will be frowned upon by Society, but as your reputation is already scarred, I see not why it matters."

Nicholas held in a growl. How could the duke not understand? The matter was not as simple as he believed. "My reputation may as well sink to the bottom of the sea, but Katherine's remains unblemished. Should I drag her down with me? Is that what you want?"

Edwin glanced heavenward and peered over his shoulder at Lord and Lady Garrick before responding. "I want you to cease being so dramatic. Gads, man, you love the woman, do you not? It is a rare thing to find someone our hearts are compatible with, to find someone who forgives our faults and fully accepts us as we are while simultaneously seeing the potential of what we can become. Such connections are a gift—a treasure deserving of pursuit and worth more than even the wealthiest can pay. Squander this opportunity if you must, but know that if you do, I shall not offer my sympathy. Fight for her, Nicholas; otherwise, you do not deserve her."

Fight for her? Had he not done enough of that already? Perhaps Edwin was right. Katherine had wished to marry Nicholas even after he explained all the reasons why they could not be together. She was willing to pay the toll their relationship might have on her life, but did she truly understand the consequences?

Katherine had said she cared not how society viewed her or about what she stood to lose. Was love enough to overcome such things? His mother hadn't any support from his father. The man had left her to wither away in solitude while he continued as he always had. Their marriage had not been built on love; not the real thing, at least. Could that one difference mean a life with Katherine where they were both happy despite the consequences?

Luke had given up everything to be with Miss McCarthy. His friend had never been happier. Perhaps Nicholas had been wrong all along to assume he could not achieve the same thing—that Katherine could never care for him enough to overcome the obstacles that their marriage would surely bring.

Hope burst in his chest like a broken dam. Perhaps love *was* enough.

The door adjoining the drawing room and a small parlor swung open, pulling Nicholas from his thoughts. Doctor Thistlewaite entered and immediately moved toward Lord and Lady Garrick. The matron stood, placing her hand over her heart with a panicked expression in her eyes.

Katherine's wound had not been severe, merely a slight graze over her upper arm, but that had not calmed Lady Garrick's nerves in the slightest. Nicholas would not hold her at fault for the concern. How could he, when his pulse had yet to calm, either.

He attempted to focus on the quiet exchange between the doctor and viscountess, but the effort was discarded the moment his gaze settled on the woman standing in the doorframe. Katherine's eyes searched the room until they landed on him. She exhaled a sigh of relief, and without delay, sprinted toward him.

Katherine

NICHOLAS MET KATHERINE HALFWAY ACROSS THE ROOM AND SCOOPED her into his arms. She sank into him, so overcome with relief she felt she might collapse. Her injury still ached, but he was careful to avoid touching the bandages, one of his hands splayed across her back and the other holding her head against his chest. She breathed in deeply, allowing his familiar scent to soothe the tension building in her body.

Mama's scolding, or rather commands, met her ears, but she ignored them. She would not forfeit this moment—not when so much uncertainty lay before her. Nevermind that her mother, the duke, and the doctor were all watching her and Nicholas embrace in a most compromising way. Let them make of it what they would. With any luck, Papa would awaken and demand Nicholas marry her.

Earlier, Katherine had heard her mother demand for Nicholas to leave, but he had refused. It gave Katherine hope. She knew the marquess loved her, though he had not said the words. She could feel it in the way he had kissed her, with all the longing and desire she felt herself.

"What the devil were you thinking?" Nicholas whispered, his breath tickling the top of her head. "You could have been killed."

"Mr. Atton has a terrible aim."

He laughed, but it was choked with emotion. "We are fortunate that is true. Promise me you will never do anything like that again."

"I shan't make a promise I cannot keep. I care for you far too much to do so, and it seems we are often getting ourselves into trouble."

His arms tightened around her, and he rested his chin atop her head. "Promise me even if it is a lie. It shall make me feel better, nonetheless."

Katherine pressed her cheek into the ruffles of his loose cravat, dropping her voice to a whisper. "I promise I will love you for the rest of my life."

The marquess's exhale was wrought with lament. His body trembled, and Katherine felt his tears working their way through her hair. More than anything, she wanted him to know how much she loved him. Nicholas worried how his reputation would affect her, but losing him would hurt far more than any consequence a marriage to the man could do. If only she could make him understand.

But Nicholas had pleaded with her not to ask this of him, and she could not ignore the request. She would not cause him more pain, and if that meant tossing away her wants, so be it.

Mama cleared her throat, reminding Katherine they were not alone in the room. It was surprising, indeed, that her mother had allowed the interaction to go on as long as it had.

Nicholas pulled away, glancing behind Katherine, his cheeks glistening in the light cast over his face by the fire in the hearth. His expression filled with hesitation, but when his attention returned to Katherine, his tight features softened. He lifted his hand to cup her cheek, his eyes wandering her face for a few moments before he leaned forward and left a gentle kiss on her forehead.

"I am glad you are well," he said. "I must go, but..." He pulled away, just enough to meet her eyes. "I leave the decision to you. My heart will always be yours, no matter what you decide."

Shock stole her words. Nicholas slipped past her, and her heart felt as though he'd ripped it out and taken it with him. Other than the crackling fire, his footsteps to the door were the only sound in the room. The duke paced toward her and dipped into a bow, his expression a grimace.

"I wish you a full recovery, Miss Garrick."

"Thank you, Your Grace."

He nodded and followed Nicholas out of the drawing room. She swallowed down the sobs reaching for the surface. Should she run after him? Declare that she had already made her choice?

She glanced at Mama, who was staring after the two men with furrowed brows. Did she understand? Could she not see the genuine affection Nicholas displayed? Papa certainly could not, as his eyes were closed and loud snores were escaping his nose.

Footsteps sounded from the hallway. Katherine held her breath, her heart pounding with hope, but it was not Nicholas who appeared at the door. George stepped inside first, followed by Lord Emerson. Relief washed over both of them when they spotted her.

George crossed the room and pulled her into a tight embrace. "Oh, Katherine. We've been searching everywhere for you. What happened?"

She shook her head, not wanting to relive the ordeal again. George seemed to understand, squeezing her tighter.

"We passed the constable on our way back, " said Lord Emerson. "He is hauling Doxly to London. They are still searching for the other man."

Mama placed a hand to her forehead. "I will sleep much easier once he is caught."

"As will we all," said Lord Emerson. His eyes darted to Katherine, and she did not miss the slight pinch in his expression. "Might I have a private word with Miss Garrick?"

Mama bit her lip, worry evident in her brow. "Of course, my lord." She crossed the room to the sofa and roused Papa from his slumber. Papa grumbled, but followed her encouragement to leave the room. George pulled the door closed behind them.

Katherine turned to face Lord Emerson. He had clearly been worried about her...again. Had the man had enough of her misadventures and decided he had no wish to take her as his wife? It hardly mattered anymore, because whether Lord Emerson still intended to marry her or not, she could not live a life without love.

She had made her decision. It was time to end her engagement.

Chapter 35

Suffolk, 1815

Nicholas

Nicholas paced the long, maroon-colored rug in the hallway outside his bedchamber. He had lost count of how many times he traversed the space, talking himself in and out of his next request. Inside his room, his valet worked to pack his things for Town, and the man would be none too pleased when Nicholas asked him to cease the activity and put the clothes back into the wardrobe.

Again.

Nicholas had ordered his trunks to be packed that morning only to have them emptied again an hour later. His valet, Henry, had given him quite the annoyed look when he ordered them packed a second time.

He had given Katherine a choice. At first, he had been confident that she would follow him out and end his suffering right then and there. But reality had caught up with him, sobering his enthusiasm. If she did decide to marry him, she had an engagement to end first. Katherine was too kind to declare her feelings with the man intending to marry her present.

And then the fear had set in. What if Katherine chose not to end her engagement? That was the reason he had his things packed—so he was prepared to run.

Nicholas scoffed. As if that would save his heart. Still, he could not bear to be anywhere in the vicinity during the wedding. *If* there was a wedding.

He continued his pacing. Having decided he would rather be confident in Katherine's affection for him, he intended to instruct his things to be unpacked. It had not even been a day since he offered her a choice, and a little patience would serve him well. She would come. He believed she would.

"The devil take it," Nicholas muttered, raking a hand through his hair. He would go mad waiting.

He drew in a deep breath and pushed open the door to his bedchamber. Henry lifted his head, his hands gripping one of Nicholas's navy waistcoats, and paused. The man grimaced and swallowed thickly. "My lord?"

Guilt pricked at Nicholas's chest. "Henry, I...I am going to owe you quite the bonus, aren't I?"

Henry sighed, but his lips twitched. "Indeed. I shall be sure to remind you of it." He dropped the waistcoat to the bed and tapped a finger to his temple. "And don't get any ideas about me forgetting. Just because I am wrinkled does not mean my memory is lacking."

"I would never dream of making the assumption," said Nicholas with a chuckle. "I do offer my apologies for my indecisiveness."

Henry began pulling clothing from the trunk on Nicholas's bed, his smile growing. "I may be willing to accept your apology. Rumor has it a young lady is the cause of this disheveled state of yours. If you were to, say, bring home a mistress for the estate, I imagine many of the staff would overlook the extra work you've caused them today. They are all looking forward to a new generation of Bethams, I think. A house is far more lively with children about."

Nicholas lifted a brow, but he could not stop the grin from erupting over his face. "Children? Let's not get ahead of ourselves, Henry. I have not yet officially offered for the young lady in question. She may not have me."

"She would be a fool not to do so, my lord."

"And why is that? Because I possess a title and wealth?"

Henry looked him up and down and shook his head. "Because you are a good man."

Warmth spread over Nicholas's skin. "Thank you, Henry."

The valet moved the trunk to the floor and crossed his arms. "I believe a change is in order, and perhaps a fresh shave?"

Nicholas tilted his head. "Change and shave? It is the afternoon. What do I need to do either of those things for?"

"Because I shan't have you blaming me should the lady deny your offer. Come, my lord. Let's see how impressive we can make you."

Laughter escaped Nicholas, but he did as his valet asked. A distraction of this sort was precisely what he needed.

After nearly an hour, Henry declared him ready.

A knock sounded at his chamber door, and Nicholas crossed the room to open it. His butler bowed and offered him a tight smile. "Forgive the intrusion, my lord. Lady Garrick has paid a call."

"Lady Garrick?"

"Yes. She is waiting in the drawing room. The woman was rather insistent. She seems to believe an audience with you is of great importance."

Nicholas groaned. The woman had likely come to chide him for what had happened yesterday. The embrace he and Katherine shared was nothing short of inappropriate, and he had been surprised Lady Garrick had allowed him anywhere near her daughter in the first place.

Then again, her expression during his departure had reflected more befuddlement than anger. But Nicholas hadn't the time to analyze what that meant, and now he would face her one last time.

Nicholas entered the drawing room. Lady Garrick curtsied, and for once, no disdain lined her features as she did so. "Good afternoon, Lord Keswick. I hope you will forgive me for not giving you proper warning of my arrival, but the matter is urgent."

Nicholas's stomach swooped. "Katherine...is she well? Has something happened?"

The gentle lift of the woman's lips only served to confuse him further. "She is recovering well." She gestured to the settee next to her. "Might we sit?"

He blinked. "Sit? Yes, of course." He crossed the room to join her in the sitting area, uncertain what to think of her lack of hostility and vague comments. The viscountess had never spoken to him with anything less than venom. He tapped a finger against his leg. "Shall I call for tea?"

Lady Garrick shook her head. "I thank you, but I believe we shall wish to leave straight away after our discussion."

Leave? What the devil was the woman on about?

Lady Garrick smoothed out her skirts and sighed. "Before I ask anything of you, I must apologize."

Nicholas opened his mouth to say something but quickly snapped it closed again. What did she wish to apologize for? Until he knew, he could hardly say a word. He had always been on shaky ground around the viscountess, and though he had planned to speak with her today, he needed to proceed with caution.

"In fact," she continued, "one apology may not suffice. You see, I have come to realize a great many things in the last twenty-four hours—misdeeds and ill judgments. Some for which I do not expect forgiveness, but I must confess them all the same. I have treated you poorly—no, horrendously, and for no reason but my own insecurity and need for vengeance."

Well, he had not expected *that*. "I never understood why you despised me so much. I know that day in the gardens with Katherine...but I never meant to jeopardize her reputation. And my father was—"

"A rake and a complete scoundrel, yes. No one knows that better than me, save for perhaps your mother. All this time I have punished you and her for his actions, but I was wrong to treat you with such contempt. The two of you are victims of his atrocities the same as I am."

"You? I'm afraid I do not understand."

Lady Garrick turned toward the window, and a deep line formed on her forehead. "I once thought myself in love. A handsome gentleman began courting me after the opening at Almack's my second Season. He called on me every day for weeks after that. I adored him...admired him. He was always the perfect gentleman, and considering his personality in conjunction with his title, I thought myself the luckiest woman in all the world.

"He visited my family's estate after the Season ended. We took a walk in the gardens—he held my hand like always. I thought he would offer for me that day, that we would marry and live happily. Instead, he informed me that he had proposed to someone else. He mocked my reaction, my tears. Said I was naïve and foolish, that his interest had been in my dowry alone—an interest that faded the moment he found someone with a larger one."

Nicholas leaned forward, resting his elbows on his knees and pressing his mouth against his clasped hands. He had always known his father was the worst sort of man, one who paraded as a gentleman for the sole purpose of getting whatever he desired. He had hurt many in one way or another.

"My father abandoned you for my mother," said Nicholas. "I understand how that must have upset you, but my mother would never intentionally—"

"I know." Lady Garrick placed her hand on his arm, her voice cracking. "I've always known your mother innocent in all of this, but I suppose that knowledge became buried under my anger and resentment. I imagine your father treated her the same way he treated me, deceived her into believing he was an honorable man."

Nicholas's eyes burned. "You do not know how fortunate you were to escape him. My mother has suffered since the day they wed."

"And I did not offer her my support as I should have. I blamed her. She did not deserve it, just as you have not deserved my treatment of you. When I saw you that day in the gardens with Katherine, it was as though I were reliving that dreadful moment all over again, and I feared my daughter would be hurt as I was. You look so much like him."

Nicholas winced, and Lady Garrick patted his arm. "You are nothing like him beyond appearance. I am so sorry it has taken me all this time to realize that. Yesterday in the drawing room, my mistakes became clear. Your emotion was not an act. You love my daughter."

"I do love her. Completely. But she is engaged—"

"Not at present." Lady Garrick chuckled when his face contorted with surprise. "Katherine spoke with Lord Emerson last evening and called off their engagement. The man took it well. Disappointed, perhaps, but he promised to take responsibility for the dissolvement. Katherine's reputation will suffer somewhat, of course, but I believe the damage will be minimal so long as you agree to wait a few weeks to announce your engagement. And with our support—"

"My engagement? I...you are giving me permission to..." His heart thudded so hard it hurt. This must all be a dream. He would soon wake and be tormented with disappointment.

But as the moments ticked on and Lady Garrick continued to explain her ideas for the announcement, Nicholas realized the truth of the matter. His dream had become reality.

Lady Garrick stood, her expression lit with a happiness he had never seen the woman display. "Come. We must return before dinner. You will stay, won't you?"

He stared up at her, afraid movement might break the spell she was under. "I truly have your blessing?"

"You have my blessing and Lord Garrick's as well, or you shall once you have spoken to him officially. But that does not mean anything until Katherine accepts. However, if you would like my opinion, I do not believe you have anything to fear in that regard. Now, let us be off."

Lady Garrick headed for the door. Nicholas stood and took a moment to fill his lungs. He would be proposing with her parents' blessing in a matter of minutes.

A smile crept over his lips.

It was time to tell Katherine Garrick he loved her.

Katherine

KATHERINE PULLED THE BLACK GREATCOAT IN HER LAP CLOSER TO her nose and breathed in deeply. Nicholas's scent lingered in the fabric, the smell filling her mind with memories of being in his arms. He had given her his coat in the hunting lodge, and though Cecily had offered to have it washed and returned to the marquess, Katherine had declined. She wished to return it to the man herself.

She played with the folds of the fabric, twisting pieces between her fingers, but ceased when they found a little resistance. Something thicker than paper but pliable rested within one of the pockets. Katherine rotated the coat until she found the opening and pulled an envelope from inside. The outside was free of writing or any sort of address and had never been sealed.

She removed the contents from within and gasped. The envelope had contained a portrait, but not the normal sort painted by professional hands. No, this was a moment in time, captured by Maggie during their journey to Los Angeles.

Her lips lifted, and she traced the outline of Nicholas's face. He was looking at her in the picture and she at him. They both wore smiles, and for the first time, Katherine could see the emotion in her own eyes. Just as she had observed the love between Luke and Maggie, she saw in this captured moment the affection between herself and Nicholas. Though her feelings for the marquess had been new and young at the time this picture was taken, they were there, clearer than she had realized.

How had she ever thought Nicholas's flirtatious remarks were anything but genuine?

She pressed the picture to her heart. That Nicholas had been carrying the portrait around with him only made it more meaningful.

It was time to return his coat.

Draping the bundle of fabric over her arm, Katherine left her bedchamber and descended the stairs with haste. At the door, Mr. Merriwether offered her a thick spencer, and with the amount of excitement flowing through her, she struggled to convince her arms to enter the sleeves with any sort of grace.

"Katherine?" Mama entered the entry hall from the drawing room, her head tilted. "Where are you going?"

At one time, she would have cowered under Mama's inquisitive tone. She would have taken the forthcoming chide and obeyed when Mama told her she was not permitted to see the marquess. But Katherine no longer believed her mother's judgment was sound, at least not in regards to Nicholas. She would never trust rumors or allow someone to formulate an opinion for her ever again.

"I am going to see him." She did not need to speak Nicholas's name. Mama would know precisely who she meant.

Katherine waited for the rebuttal, for the demands and the threats to take away her pin money, as if she had ever cared for it before. None of them came, however, and when Mama's lips lifted into a smile, her eyes filling with a mischievous light, Katherine could only claim confusion.

Mama's reaction was as strange now as it had been last night. She hadn't appeared surprised when Katherine announced the end of her engagement last evening. She hadn't said a single word.

"Very well." Mama clasped her hands in front of her, a smile still playing on her lips. "But I must ask that you speak with your soon-to-be husband before you leave."

"What?" Katherine's gaze flicked to the drawing room door. Surely Lord Emerson had not returned? Had he changed his mind about allowing their engagement to dissolve? He had been quite understanding last evening. Indeed, he spoke as though he had suspected Katherine's heart had been stolen. She'd apologized profusely, but the man had bestowed on her an endearing grin and bid her farewell without a hint of contempt.

"You owe him that much," said Mama. "Please speak to him."

"Mama, I will not marry Lord Emerson."

Her mother chuckled. "Yes, dear. I know."

Mama gestured toward the drawing room, and with a bit of trepidation, Katherine followed her lead. She preceded her mother into the room, keeping her gaze on the woman over her shoulder, for it was far better than placing it upon the man she had rejected. Mama smiled brightly and closed the door without following her inside.

Katherine drew a breath and perused the room, searching for Lord Emerson, but it was not her once intended she found. Staring at her from in front of the glowing hearth was Nicholas.

Her breath caught. His emerald green waistcoat matched his eyes. They sparkled with reflected firelight and added to the handsome smile lifting his lips. Everything about Nicholas Betham was perfectly poised, from his confident stance to his neatly parted dark blond hair. Indeed, he had never looked so handsome as he did now.

He crossed the room, and Katherine held her breath until he stopped in front of her.

"Nicholas, I...what are you doing here?"

"You called off your engagement."

How did he know that? "Yes. In fact, I was on my way to see you." She held out his coat, and his gaze fell to it. "To return this."

Nicholas took her free hand and rubbed his thumb over her knuckles, sending shivers up her spine. "Only to return this?"

"No."

"Then why?"

Katherine swallowed. She had practiced her speech late into the night. She needed to ensure Nicholas had overcome his misplaced beliefs that she would resent their marriage. She would not, no matter what trials came their way.

"To convince you to marry me," she whispered.

"Convince?" He chuckled and took a step closer. "Miss Garrick, you have intrigued me since I offered you my mathematics book in the gardens. I adore the way your mind works, the way you see others with a lens of practicality and genuine worth. When in your presence, I feel as though someone sees me for who I truly am and not as the rake Society has painted me.

"Every moment we spend together serves to increase my growing affection, and I wish to spend whatever time I have left in this world with you. You made me a promise to love me for the rest of your life. I know of only one way to hold you to that promise. Will you accept me, poor reputation and all, and do me the great honor of becoming my wife?"

Her eyes filled with moisture, but she blinked the tears away and lifted her chin. "Is that a genuine offer or are you merely flirting with me, Nicholas Betham?"

His smile reached his eyes. "My pupil has become a master. I believe she knows the answer to that question."

"In that case"—Katherine dropped the coat next to her on the floor and wrapped her arms around his neck—"my answer is yes. I will marry you, Lord Keswick, and I swear to uphold my promise."

His lips fell on hers. Nicholas withheld nothing, kissing her deeply and ensuring she knew just how much he cared for her. His arms enfolded her, pressing against her back to bring her closer to him. Time pressed on, but her future was in her grasp. Her future was with the marquess.

With ragged breath, Nicholas leaned away from her but kept a tight hold about her waist. "I love you, Katherine." His strong arms lifted her into the air and spun her in a circle before settling her feet back on the floor. "I love you. I love you. I love you."

"It is not a competition. You do not have to catch up with me."

Nicholas tucked a strand of her hair behind her ear. "Indeed, I must. I spent years waiting to say them, and I cannot contain them any longer, for surely I will burst should I try. So I shall say them, repeatedly, until you grow tired of hearing them."

"Then I suppose you will be saying them forever."

"Oddly enough, I look forward to the redundancy."

He tilted his head and leaned forward for another kiss, but the drawing room door swung open before he could land the gesture.

A wide grin filled Mama's face. "Good news, I presume?"

Katherine shrugged. "Nicholas is merely flirting with me."

Her future husband chuckled. "I will *always* flirt with you." He dropped his chin next to her ear and whispered. "And I will always love you."

He would, she knew, for she felt those words penetrating deep into her soul, and no matter how Society would paint their portrait, that would never change.

Epilogue

Suffolk, 1816

Nicholas

Nicholas shifted on his aching feet, attempting not to grimace. Surely they must be nearly finished for today? The air outside the walls of Ravenhall was cold, and although he wore a heavy wool coat, taking a place by the glowing hearth in the drawing room sounded far more pleasant than remaining out of doors.

"Stop moving, Nicholas." His mother peeked around her canvas and scowled. "Do you want your face to look like a pig or some such?"

"Not particularly, but I am tired—"

"Hush. Give me a few more minutes, then we can conclude for today."

Katherine giggled from the chair in front of him. "You mustn't say that, Phoebe; otherwise, your son will take it as permission to ignore his ledgers this afternoon."

"Can a man recently married not ignore his ledgers for a few days?" asked Nicholas. "They shan't be going anywhere."

Katherine tilted her head slightly to look up at him. "And neither is your wife. We leave for London in a week. You must have everything in order before then. Once you have, I am all yours."

Nicholas hummed, narrowing his eyes. "You drive a hard bargain, Lady Keswick. What better motivation can I have to do something than you as a reward?"

Her lips lifted into a bright smile, and warmth spread through his chest. Even on the darkest days, Katherine was the sunshine his life needed. Many rumors had spread after their announced engagement, but his wife had faced them all with grace and patience. Nicholas had even overheard Lady Garrick defending him on a number of occasions. Perhaps such efforts would make little difference in regards to how he was seen by the *ton*, but he found himself caring less about Society's opinion.

He knew who he was and who he was not. His wife knew him. Loved him. And for Nicholas, that was more than enough.

"There," announced his mother. "I believe that will do for now. Would the two of you like to see the progress I've made?"

Nicholas offered Katherine his hand and assisted her from the chair. He clasped her tightly, guiding her to his mother's side. His gaze wandered over the painted canvas, a portrait of him and the woman he loved. Katherine sighed and rested her head against his shoulder.

"You have done a wonderful job, Phoebe. I do adore your artwork."

Nicholas's mother chuckled and began cleaning her brushes. "Is it my work you adore or the man who's image I have captured?"

"Both," said Katherine with a firm nod. "Most assuredly both."

Nicholas wrapped his arm around her shoulder and gave it a gentle squeeze. "Katherine is right, Mother. Both the art and I are perfect for adoration."

His mother *tsk*ed, but amusement lit her eyes. He had never seen her so happy as he had the last few weeks. His mother had taken news of his engagement with unbridled excitement, and she and Katherine had spent many afternoons together leading up to the wedding. The sight of them sitting in the drawing room, laughing and enjoying one another's company, filled his heart in ways he had never thought possible.

"I should go inside," said Katherine. "It is time to dress for dinner, and I have no desire to make our guests wait on me."

"You take your role as marchioness quite seriously, my lady." Nicholas tweaked her nose, and Katherine wrinkled it in response.

"A good hostess always takes her guests' comfort into consideration."

Nicholas led Katherine by the hand toward the house, whistling until they were out of earshot of his mother. "I suppose I cannot talk this good hostess into spending some time with her husband before dinner, then?"

She gave him a look that answered without words, making him laugh. "Can you blame me for asking?" His wife put on a façade of annoyance, but he knew better. She enjoyed his flirting.

"Edwin is our friend," said Katherine. "Making him wait for either of us would be rude."

Nicholas heaved a dramatic sigh. "Oh, very well. I shan't be rude. I did promise Luke to watch after his family, and if my wife insists that includes arriving to dinner on time, then I shall oblige."

"Indeed. Besides, I need proper time to conduct my observations."

"Observations?"

The smile that spread over her lips matched the mischief in her brown eyes. Gads, did she know how they drew him in? Likely not, for she continued. "Finding Edwin a wife will be far easier if I know him better."

Nicholas laughed. "Find him a wife? That is quite the undertaking. The man proclaims he shall never marry again, and though at one time I believed this attitude folly, I now understand. To lose the person one loves most would strip away any appeal of new attachment."

"It would be difficult, I admit, but I believe it is possible for him to find love again. I think it is what Luke would have wanted for his brother, and I am determined to help in any way I can. I owe him. He did encourage you to court me, after all. Both Halford men did."

"You realize I did not listen to either of them, do you not? I ignored their advice."

"It is not their fault you are stubborn."

Nicholas grabbed her around the waist and lifted her in the air. Katherine squealed, clutching his coat. He held her against him, a treasure he had worked hard to obtain, and leaned forward to touch the tip of his nose to hers. "Stubborn, am I?"

"A little, but no more than I am." Katherine placed a soft kiss on his lips. "But I am grateful you were too stubborn to give up."

Nicholas set her down but kept his arms about her. "Perhaps the only time that particular quality of mine has proven useful."

She tilted her head and lifted a hand to sweep a strand of hair away from his forehead. Her gentle touch made him shudder harder than the cold air ever did.

"Did you and Edwin decide on a plan for the pearls?" she asked, her voice lowered to a whisper. "Mr. Atton could come for them again."

"We have hidden them, and the two of us are the only ones who know where. I do not wish for you to carry that knowledge. It will be safer for you to remain ignorant on the matter. Just know that all sixteen beads are safe where no one shall find them."

Katherine's brows furrowed. "Sixteen?"

"Indeed," said Nicholas slowly, studying the way her lips curled into a frown. "What is it?"

She shook her head, a crease of worry lining her face. "There were twenty pearls. Mr. Atton stole three from Luke and Maggie. There should have been seventeen left."

Nicholas's stomach twisted. One of the pearls was missing? But how?

Katherine nibbled at her lip. "Are you certain—"

"I am. I counted three times. Perhaps Doxly stole one from the pouch before handing it over?"

"But they never found one on his person after his arrest."

That was true.

Katherine slid her hands up his chest and clasped them around his neck. "Perhaps it is still at the duke's estate. Maybe one fell out of the glass jar?"

Her tone suggested Katherine did not believe that anymore than he did. Pearls did not simply abandon ship and hide in studies where few people entered. No, his gut told him someone had taken it. The question was who?

"Something to discuss with Edwin tonight after dinner," said Nicholas. "You needn't worry over it. The two of us will find the missing pearl and all will be well."

One of Katherine's brows lifted. "You are my husband. Your concerns are now my concerns, remember?"

"Ah, yes. In that case, I am terribly concerned you do not spend enough time with me."

Katherine pinched her perfect lips, but her smile fought its way through them. "We cannot be late for dinner."

His wife left a great deal up for interpretation with that response.

He swooped his arm under her knees and hoisted her against him. Katherine clung to his coat as he moved toward the house, her words so mingled with laughter she could barely get them out. "What are you doing?"

"I be kidnappin' this here beautiful mathematician," said Nicholas, attempting his best pirate accent, which had failed miserably judging by Katherine's increased laughter.

"You are a terrible tease, Lord Keswick."

"Aye, but I am *your* tease, and that, my dearest Katherine, is all that matters."

THE END

Thanks for reading!

I hope you enjoyed Nicholas and Katherine's story. Please consider leaving a review on your preferred retailer's website. Reviews help authors develop their craft and gain promotional marketing, and we love hearing from you!

What trouble will the time pearls cause next? Edwin and Diana are about to find out.

Courting A Modern Lady

Widower Edwin Halford has lived a tranquil existence seeing to his estate and raising his daughter. Now that his late brother has left him the title Duke of Avendesh and all the responsibilities it entails, Edwin struggles to navigate his new duties.

A meager income has kept Diana Rodriguez from following in her parents' footsteps helping children in need. While attending the wedding of her best friend and the man who crossed time to be with her, Diana seizes the opportunity to befriend Juliana, the spirited seven-year-old niece of the former duke, who has participated in her own time-traveling escapades.

Diana's child-tending skills are put to the test when the wedding is crashed by time pearl thieves, and she and Juliana are transported to 1816. With the pearl missing, Diana has no choice but to stay with the girl and her father until the cursed heirloom can be recovered.

As Edwin comes to know Diana, his heart opens to the possibility of love, and he finds the modern lady's zeal for life buoying him out of troubled waters. But the final effort to retrieve the pearls and destroy them proves dangerous for all involved and places more than Edwin and Diana's hearts on the line.

Stay up to date on all my booksish things!
Follow me on:

Instagram: brookejlosee

Facebook: https://www.facebook.com/brookejlosee

MY BOOKS

Romantic Comedy:

I HEART NEW YORK
You Wish | If The Suit Fits

Historical Romance:

THE TIME PEARLS
In Time With The Duke | The Future With The Marquess | Courting A
Modern Lady

Fantasy Romance:

CHRONICLES OF VIRGÁM
The Matchmaker Prince | The Prisoner of Magic | The Witch of
Selvenor | The Warlock of Dunivear | Origins of Virgám | The Seer of
Verascene | Shadows of Aknar | Path to Irrilám | The Sorcerer of Kantinar

CHILDREN OF MAGIC
Blood & Magic | Love & Magic | Revenge & Magic | War & Magic

AUTHOR NOTES

As my second historical romance, I find I'm continually learning so much about the Regency era. The customs, as you likely know, are vastly different from today, and I find them fascinating. This book required a great deal of research, and while I did my best to impart accuracy, for the sake of the story, there were times when I needed to lean into the fiction a little more. I hope, dear reader, you will forgive me for that and were able to enjoy the story despite its flaws.

One of the things I learned about was how suicide was handled during this time. This was not a topic I added to this series lightly, and I would like to explain my reasoning for choosing to make it part of the plot line. In Regency era, a title could not be simply given up or handed over. By law, it could only be inherited when the previous title holder passed away. With Luke having gone to the future, this left me with a bit of a predicament to passing the title on to Edwin, who would not have been allowed to claim the title until Luke was officially declared deceased. With no body having been found, this could have taken years during that time, so in the interest of moving the plots forward, I had Luke leave a suicide note behind instead.

Now, suicide was highly frowned upon by the crown and church during this time. Unless the person was proven to be mad, their title and any land they owned would have been confiscated by the crown. Nicholas, along with Luke's brother, were able to navigate this by claiming Luke had descended into a depressive state, ie madness. In truth, the title in all probability would not have been permitted to remain in the family despite these circumstances, but I was more eager to give Edwin a happy story in the next and final book in this series, *Courting A Modern Lady*. I hope you look forward to it as much as I do.

ACKNOWLEDGEMENTS

This book was quite a struggle for me, and I have so many people to thank for helping me get through it.

To my critique partner, Justena White, to whom this book is dedicated. I would not have made it without you! Thank you for always picking me up after a hard day and encouraging me to keep going. I can never thank you enough.

To my family who are always patient (mostly) and allow me to write and stare at the computer. They put up with a lot, and I'm so grateful for their encouragement and support.

To my alpha and beta readers: Beba Andric, Leigh Walker, and Teah Weight. Thank you for all your help getting this story ready to go!

To Jacque Stevens who helped me nail down the themes and sort out so many issues. Your guidance is the absolute best and I would be completely lost without it.

To my readers who continue to follow and support me on the author journey, I thank you from the bottom of my heart. Your words lift me up and keep me going, even when it feels like all my words are garbage.

To my Heavenly Father, who gifted me the inspiration to begin writing in the first place and knew it was what I needed in my life. I've grown so much the last few years, and I know that it is by thy love I was led to begin this journey at all.

ABOUT THE AUTHOR

Brooke Losee lives with her husband and three children in central Utah where she enjoys fishing, exploring, and gathering as many rocks as her pockets can hold. Brooke obtained a BS in Geology at Southern Utah University but has always had a passion for all things books.

Brooke began her journey to authorhood in 2020 with the notion of publishing one novel. That book turned into a series of seven, and the Pandora's box of ideas was unleashed. Her works range from fantasy to historical, all featuring a sweet and clean romance.

To follow her writing journey and keep informed about upcoming stories visit http://www.brookejlosee.com.

Made in the USA
Monee, IL
18 September 2023

42958828R00217